Jade

Hotel

STUFF

BroWN

Copyright © 2022 by Jade Brown

First paperback edition April 2022

Book Design by Vlad "Fevo" Fedorov

ISBN 978-0-578-28795-9

HOTEL STUFF

For JOIE.

Notes

Hotel Stuff is based on a dream that I had when I was sixteen. I wasn't sure how to introduce it to a page, but so glad that I could get it out.

Chapter 1

:)

A bonfire on a cliff.

Who thought of that?

"Your skin when the sunlight hits it...I wish I could remember what I wanted to say!" He giggled. I was face to neck with a freckled collarbone. Striking. I try not to look at anyone who is beyond a foot radius.

"My skin tends to change colors," was my response.

"It went from *free* after-school chocolate milk to *expensive* frozen hot chocolate. Have you ever had frozen hot chocolate, *Basieee?*" My name ends with one *L*, not *eee*.

"I have."

"Darnit! That would've been a nice second date idea."

The arch overlooked the Hudson, and I was staring off as a cheap escape from this wall-talk. I wasn't sure what shimmered more, the bank beneath my nostrils, or Wesley's hairless chest. It all smelled too good, as if the guppies wanted to sprout up and kiss me into a fairytale. I assumed Wesley was the antagonist reverting my direction from adolescence. He sparkled in technicolor next to the azure sunset. My eyes from time to time pretended he wasn't there.

We were hanging, like most of us do on the days we're not moaning over lesson plans and dodgy substitutes. I don't hang like them, and it was my first time hanging *with* them. The bonfire reminded me of belated passion as if that was so easily acquired. A grubby group danced outside the stone barricade to someone's free online mixtape; the song was pretty bad, but the dancing was reprehensible. The broken up pines gave me the impression they wanted us to go, like now.

Precisely twenty-four minutes before this moment,

"I tnk you shud know wesley is currently hookin up oposit the trail," the saddest part is, Milo Hunter thinks I can understand him right now. Milo excused his high-self into my daze, acknowledging me for the first time ever. This was before Wesley decided to pay attention to me on the date that *he* invited me to.

If it weren't for Milo Hunter, I probably wouldn't be here. Milo Hunter is the junior at Villeton High School that everyone assumes is a senior, teachers even allow him to heat up ramen in their lounge. A lacrosse player with spider limbs that impede underclassmen girls, and Wesley Conner. Milo never figured that Wesley would be one of his many fans fumbling knock-kneed into his crotch. To Milo's reassurance, Wesley was only using him as a tetherball to get to me.
Me.

"You," his carnation-colored hair hid beneath a crocheted lime beanie. Wesley towered over my locker, and it was my first time seeing him without the etching of Milo's fans.

"I?"

"You're my date, right?" Wesley was sparkling in everything post British punk—an icon. His usual attire was taut jeans, studded belts, and suggestive tees. "You're coming with me to the bonfire! You just can't say no."

I should've known how scarce charm was. My parents were short at setting any examples. Blistering high school sweethearts that took high school wherever they went. I was high school. Conceived and emotionally exiled right from the beginning, it made it easier for them to accept my existence. Now they synchronize when caroling the story of my birth.

"Want to get away?" Wesley nudged my elbow, and it was then I remembered I was at a social event.

"Away?" I smiled at him, or at least I think I was smiling —salvaging a past one.

"Mhmmm," Wesley play-dough'd my cheeks.

"I don't know."

"Come!" He snagged my palm, dragging me away from everyone else.

We ended up opposite the trail, more than likely in the exact place Milo warned me about. I was hoping to encounter some lipgloss stains sewn into a gibber somewhere. But no, instead the sun was coming in and made an x-ray over my lackluster fit. Some trees tooted and whooshed around us, while wildlife creaked about. I get it nature, you want to see the show.

Amongst Wesley's undaunted possessions, his appeal was his strong suit. I wasn't sure where to start, but he def did. I quickly found myself pressed against a boulder, having my lips suctioned with his tongue. Wesley wasn't a good kisser, he was one of those kissers that made-out with nothing but force, and it's often disguised as passion. Villeton peeps must love this, and because I am nothing but a Villeton High School dweeb, I must succumb.

"May I take off your clothes?" How polite, how fast. We were only forty feet from everyone else crammed between everything I might lose and the only night I fought for my gains.

"I don't want the group to see," also contemplating my virginity, and if Wesley Conner is the person who I want to eternally link it to.

"Hehe, no one can see us, Basie!"

Do I like Wesley? No, I like salt covered cucumber. My mom once told me that being antisocial will be the bane of my teenage years. My mom also got pregnant at seventeen, and her best friend is now my pet rabbit, Purple. To like someone is a strenuous task with not enough prosperity, growing pains are stifling by themselves, I can do without mouth-breathing boys. I was a bowl of hot popcorn and a season finale away from bailing on tonight, but my mom convinced me otherwise.

I don't go to these things. I'm not chained to social stigmas, however, I am wearing thongs.

If this was going to be the way I lose my virginity, then this isn't any different than how I've always drawn it out. Cliffside. Moderate drugs. Drinks, and a skinny white boy with blush hair. The ambiance wasn't as dark as I'd hoped, but I get what I get. The smell? Peppery mint and Kool-Aid sitting out for way too long, projected from a quarter back's intestines. I always knew that love looked like this, maybe a little more meaty and swollen with imagination.

I guess this was the time to do it.

"Where's my paper?" Of course someone decided to appear. I couldn't see who it was past Wesley's malnourished shoulders.

"Hmmmmm?" Wesley's hand was in my crotch—IN. I couldn't like, see this person, but I knew they were staring down *there*. Yeah, this was a congregative act.

"My rolling paper, you had it last," they had a high pitched raspy voice.

"But...I don't smoke!"

Grunting sounds. "Dammit, all Milo has is MDMA. Now I'm going to have to slerb some from off of him," not sure the last time anyone *had* to do MDMA. Also, who brings MDMA to a bonfire? "Have you two seen him?"

"Nope," Wesley and I simultaneously shook our heads.

"If you see him, text me!" They rustled away like a defeated homework assignment.

Wesley returned.

Cranking his hand from under my skirt and back to his face slurps. He swiftly squatted down, pulling my undergarments off in the process, jaw slipping.

I had shaved two nights before, so I knew I didn't have the smoothest of 'em, but he didn't have to stare at it. I had a rough time indulging in hypothetical blogs initiating self repulsion. How pretty can it really be when it's masked by cotton and blood for a week? How luscious can it taste while simmering in latex and thigh gaps? It's there, and I'm offering it up without wrangling with my conscience.

I wasn't sure if I wanted to whimper or groan, sex noises are all too convoluted. I wandered into the noctilucent clouds, they catered to my getaway. The last glimpse of sun begged the edge of the cliff to stay sturdy; I was grateful in its suggestion. The crowd of Villetoners all muddled together, and obstructed any chances I had with dusk. It was alright, I had to teach myself to be in with this crowd, and Wesley was a step towards the premature stages of teenage mockery.

"If you think too much about it, it won't be as fun," that wasn't Wesley's voice. Perfect, the gathering continues.

"When did you get here?!" Wesley pushed himself backward and onto the dirt, forcing his beanie off. I quickly plucked my thong back between my cheeks and wiggled my jean skirt down.

"I've been here," the dude's voice was so tender, but I still couldn't see exactly who was talking. They were a silhouette outlined with amber rays.

"You were watching this whole time?" Wesley jumped up, his body springing towards nightfall.

The closer the guy came, the more pronounced his footsteps were. The more pronounced he was.

His hair was a forbidden and unseen brown that tickled his shoulders. The darkness of his mane and brows set off the faded pinkness in his ivory skin, that panted in the cool evening. He was tall, but not Wesley tall, a cozy tall. He didn't look at me like he thought I was attractive, he looked at me as though he could care less. And, for some reason, he wanted me to know that.

He was hot.

"I was in my car, they're about to start the fire."

"Yay! I'm only here for the s'mores anyway!" Wesley galloped up and down before jolting towards the crew. Yup—he is mosdef only here for the s'mores.

The guy stared off at Wesley and then immediately went back into visually pulling me apart. I was holding my breath as he analyzed my awkwardness.

There was something about being in his presence that made me submissively drown. In my town, there aren't people that look like this; there are hardly people. Popularity is measured by the number of intentional rips in your blue jeans, and whether or not your messy bun can bob right. Girls who go on dates with guys like Wesley Conner because he's all we have—or so I thought.

"Do you like pictures?" He asked and sharply inhaled, so much I could see his chest expanding through his flannel.

"I hate them."

"Elly!" Someone in a car called out to the guy.

Elly.

"I didn't know you were going to be here!" They continued.

Elly.

"Yeah, my little sister invited me. Now I'm hanging with," he glanced down at me. "Basil, right?"

So this is Elly Hayes.

Chapter 2

;)

It was one of those stories that took a really long time to tell, but the ear never fled from coherence.

I heard it from a girl who was telling Miss Lowe during lunch period. The girl was inadvertently slipping the fable to me, and I felt included. I wasn't sure how in tune Miss Lowe was when it came to Villeton tales, but this one had to be the most outlandish. I was only a freshman at the time, I had yet to know the mythical lengths some students would go to receive societal admittance.

"He attached a lock to a bridge with the initials E.H and belly-flopped forward," the student was overcome with gossip.

"I heard he was on a motorcycle," Miss Lowe responded. She knew too much.

The story would distort itself, depending on whose teeth it hid behind:

"His seat belt was strapped around his neck. In fact, he had both seat belts strapped around his neck."

"It was raining that night, he hopped on a bobsled and skirted through mud into the river."

"Okay, hear me out—an American black bear was chasing him..."

All the stories started folding into each other. I knew very little regarding Elly Hayes, except that he was Declan Hayes' older brother. People loved Declan. Like, LOVED. Students prayed to be Declan—her looks, her coy persona, her unmatchable stride. We all couldn't get enough of her, which is why we turned her into a shrine. People thought about Elly, but people never stopped thinking about Declan. I never knew who the popularity stuck to first. They were perfection, they were gold, bespoke commodities.

They were
White.

"Do you want some ketamine?" he poked my arm as we sat thigh by thigh on a log. Elly Hayes poked my arm.

"No thanks," I wasn't even sure what that was.

It had been a solid forty-five minutes of Wesley ditching me for fifth grade treats, and Elly sitting next to me because everyone else wanted to sit far enough to visually vex him. His hair smelt like vinegar, and I was happy to know that he washed his hair with things other than water. The darker it became, the more his cerulean eyes would glow. I couldn't tell if me borrowing his air was bothering him, or if he preferred the meditative silence.

Being surrounded by darkness always brought me back to playing Dead Man as a kid. Running through and around houses, trying to escape the Dead Man's possession. There were no streetlights—only me, my cousin, and her friends relying on late night sitcoms that shot from the inside of family homes. This was all before we aged and decided to hate each other. As I cringe at those times, I also privately pray for something comparable.

Wesley was on his fourth s'more, speaking into the neck of someone else across the seated circle. Elly sniffed some stuff out of a clear baggy and took a video of anything that fell from his snuff. Once he had finished recording, he watched the video back and played it in slow motion—it almost looked like a buffering blizzard at midnight.

"So sorry I'm late," she wore nothing but a cheer skirt and a Villeton sweatshirt. I could feel my skin convulse at the shock of her.

"Declan!" Wesley chanted, flying into Declan's rear.

"They ran out of beer," Elly muttered.

Declan dug a pair of denim shorts out of her duffle bag and slid them up, zipping off her skirt. Her crop top revealed her light pack and the denim shorts emphasized her tapered waist. Her skin was ferociously dewy, and her hair gallivanted to her waist—forever in movement. Her face had a natural grim like Elly's, but when she smiled, it could make thunder sound harmonious.

"Crap! I wish you would've texted me to let me know."

"Where the hell are my rolling papers?" The light gritty voice from earlier barked from an anonymous corner.

"I don't know!" She looked over at me with a playful nature, reaching her hand out. "Hi, I'm Declan."

I took it. "I'm Basil."

I know a name is only a part, but they are a part of many things that I like to fall under. Names are valueless, but they hold so much worth. To know that I'm so minute under the stars with people whose names are only hearsay to others encourages me to decimate my identity. Who I am isn't charted by them, but even as someone who strays from social clans, I'm thankful that Declan Hayes knows my name.

The fire had started riling up, and the crowd became imitations. Everyone was hunched next to the person they'd probably spend the night with, and I was sitting beside a brother and a sister. The blaze made me want to shave my hair off, but instead, I decided to release my kinks from the single braid that kept them slapping people; maybe they should slap people. I could hear the conversation between the Hayes siblings simmer down as I did this.

"So Basil, are you dating Wesley?" Declan had a really soft voice, almost inaudible, but it was magnetic.

"No, we're not."

"That's not what he's been telling everyone," Elly remarked. How does Elly know that? He graduated like two years ago.

"This is our first date."

"What a lame first date," he smirked and shifted his hair back. One of his front teeth slightly sat on top of the other, almost like a person crossing their legs. Why did this make me want him more?

"Ignore him, please. Are you in my economics class?" Declan questioned.

"No, I'm only a junior."

"Really? I could've sworn we had physics together last year," we were in the same physics class, and I want to cry because she remembered.

"We did! Do you remember Mr. Bernie?"

"*Uck*, he asked me out y'know?"

"He asked me out too!" We both laughed at predators until Elly disrupted us with a growl. I muttered. "I'm sorry, it must be boring hearing us talk about Villeton."

He turned his nose up at me, his eyes slanted down with an unusual stare. "I could listen to you narrate my nightmares. Declan though, not as much."

Before I could reimagine the scenario without Declan, two guys in front of us started smacking each other's backs, but it wasn't an ordinary back pat, it was embedded with intentional aggression. Their convo got louder and everyone else's boiled down to nothing.

I could see one guy, who had on a tee with Brigitte Bardot snarling on it, folding over to reach for a stick. The other dude tripped back, and with the strength of a zebra, kicked Brigitte right in the bottom lip. We all remained seated because it presented itself as stupid. I couldn't make out what they were saying to each other under their drunken slander, not until one guy so clearly shouted,

"NIGGGEEER!" From the base of his tonsils.

It was dark, but I could sense everyone's gravitational pull lunging to me—the only black person in sight. They all ignored the now hazardous fight and awaited the chink in my neutrality. It was as if everyone had realized that there was a black person there. There was actually another black person, but they were so used to him, he just became *that black guy*. I should've known my hair would rat me out the moment someone decided to use racial defamations.

"That word was cool like ten years ago," someone tossed a cigarette bud at them. Ten years ago I was six, not sure if that was the peak of segregation.

Elly stood from the log and walked over to the fire pit. He plucked a noticeable stick from the heap, and levitated it above the spark, waiting for the entire branch to catch the flame. He had taken the attention off me, finally—because now the suicidal Hayes might also be a pyromaniac. People were clutching their dates and their cool. I was apprehensively awaiting the fire to take hold of Elly's shirt, but before it could, he swung it towards the brawling bros.

"Stop," Elly abrasively whispered.

The Brigitte shirt kid somersaulted upward, slapping his chest to make sure he was abiding by the *stop, drop, and roll* sequence. The other guy was so mentally gone at this point, that his opponent decided to lend him a hand from off the ground. The second he was up he realized, yes—he *was* almost on fire. I don't know who started to dry cry first, but they each collapsed in a wail. That was when I knew I had to be the one to dump water onto the flames.

My bottle hurled all over the campsite. Feeling accomplished, I turned and noticed Elly giving me a look that wasn't very interpretive. My eyebrows crinkled up before he shrugged away. I looked at Declan, who was probably flabbergasted by the reality of people still saying the N-word. She ran her delicate fingers through her hair and swallowed her face with her palms. I wanted to ask her if she was alright, knowing her brother, and knowing that there wasn't anything she could do about it. I wanted to, but my mental compass was navigating me to Elly.

"So, you're not Wesley's girlfriend?" What. I was two feet behind him, he had gone off to stand closer to the border. He was stock-still amid the glittery stars and subdued traces of smoke. With all the scents that strewed through the woods, I could pick Elly's out instantaneously. The gravel beneath my feet told on me as I progressed behind him.

"No. I told you we just met," I said.

"And, you don't like him?" He faced me. The rim around his eye socket was red and irritated, but I could tell by his dry eyes that he wasn't crying.

"I don't like anyone," yet.

Elly's vision found my hand, and he bumped his pinky into my thumb. I extended my fingers to see if he'd take hold of it, but he refrained. Instead, he lifted his eyes up and over the river. I knew that if Elly could drink the water, he probably would. He was sinking so deep into the tyrant ripples, I was witnessing him become them. He couldn't be human, or maybe, he couldn't be a Villetoner. People from Villeton don't see me. I'm a black hole beyond a crevice of shattered eggshells.

"Do you like sex?" And there goes the suspense.

"I wouldn't know," I answered. A slim simper marked his lips, shooting his eyes at me.

"I think sex is the closest thing there is to the moment right before death. Right before people die, they receive an overbearing sense of self," he handed me a full smile. "I feel so selfish around you."

Chapter 3

;*
;

Baked goods have a scent right before they reach perfection. It's not only letting me know that the ingredients are aligning, but that I'm minutes away from becoming a part of that sensation. I may be an extension of the creation, but I adore the responsibility. I'm only half as good as the most notable patisserie, but I like ruining myself if it's for a pleasurable good.

"Take this," my mom doesn't usually stuff my face with drugs, but she has her exceptions.

"Can you crush the pill for me?"

"Basilene," that's not my name. "You are too old for that."

I snatched the overflowing glass of water from her, resting the tablet between my front teeth before gulping it down.

I could swear it was stuck at the tip of my throat pipe, but another swallow, and a lot of panic, eased it further down. My mom sat at the edge of my bed with wholesome satisfaction.

"Good job! See—you didn't die!" She giggled. Her tiny head shook with her.

"How long till I stop spinning, and how long till I can walk past dad without fear?"

"At least twenty minutes. Please stay clear of him for now. I don't need to hear his mouth about you drinking," there were two things my mom detested: one of them being my reluctance to any form of garden work, and the second was hearing my dad's mouth.

"GAWWWD."

"Sooo, tell me more about what happened. Did you two kiss?" My mom knows the kind of person I am, but she loves to persuade herself into thinking otherwise.

"Of course we kissed," and it left me having to remind her. "And I wasn't the only person he was kissing that night."

My mom squeaked. "That jerk!"

"It's okay, I wasn't that into him from the start."

"Basilene, like I tell you, high school is all about the experience, but if you aren't actively creating an experience for yourself, you'll graduate with nothing."

"I'll graduate with a diploma."

"I'm jussayin', there's nothing wrong with making a few friends."

It was really too early for this. The sun had just got back from its one-night stand, and my room splashed in the half-woken glimmer. She stood up and slid into her slippers, removing the satin bonnet from her head. Her hair used to be a short clay-like color, but now it's growing into a light fro, showing her dark roots. My mom is too young to have a full head of grey hair, but ever since she quit her office job for her online business, she's been experimenting with "daring" shades.

My parents pride themselves on being approachable, my mom more than my dad. My dad's ultimate motive is to be crude and elusive—it comes from him being a young parent, and no one believing he could do it successfully. By default, he's extremely approachable due to his looks, the old white women in our town can't resist his tall broad stature, brown ombre dreads, and walnut skin. It's gross.

People favor my mom cause she's tiny and occasionally smart-mouthed. The older I get, the more I can see the resemblance between my mother and me. I veered from our twinage for years, until I decided—y'know, my mom is kind of cute. We both have the same dense dimples that sink whenever our mouths move. We both have those hazel doe eyes, that took me years to get used to, and we both have hairlines that come down a little further than I'd like; I just have a lot more hair than her.

"I'll be back later to check how you're feeling, text me if you need anything," she kissed my forehead before abandoning me completely.

Is this how Sundays should be?

Also, was it criminal for me to want to think of Elly?

Maybe I shouldn't think of him right now. I mean, my mom left the room like two minutes ago.

Okay.

That assignment for Englishelly.

Crap.

I feel like I believe in Elly. I believe in him the way theorists negotiate their present ideologies for a flicker of something more palatable. It could be harmful. A little maniacal, but so totally pedestrian. It's not like me to crush on anyone, I'm way too much of a narcissist to make up reasons to be interested in anyone else besides myself. I'm a narcissist in the same way Cher is probably a narcissist for erasing her last name. But Elly, where did you come from?

My bed felt like a whiskey furnace, and I was slipping into inebriation. My breath has never been so rotten, but aching from a zesty spark. My stomach wanted to house whatever it was that defied the gargling acids. The sky wept through my blinds, creeping up on my hangover—ridiculing my underage drinking. Where was the medicinal magic from this capsule? I was def turning into a stereotype of a high school Villetoner. Becoming everything I hated through a montage of regrets.

We got drunk last night. We all got super drunk. I wish I could recall the moment I convinced myself that I am no longer the stoosh junior I worked so hard to become, the one that is too cool for friends and too complicated to assimilate to the status quo. I remember the second I realized I was actually hanging out with the Hayes siblings, it sent me jogging through denouements, and me seriously roleplaying with myself. Drinking could fix that, I said—probably even out loud.

"Do you like to play pretend?"
Elly had this lazy way of speaking, which was then accompanied
by an alcoholic lubricant.
"I wish I could give you the answer you want," I
hiccuped. His gaze slouched and lingered into my cognition.
"As beautiful as you are, you aspire imagery."

That sentence hung to me more than my need to puke all morning. It was almost as if Elly wanted to synthesize romance because he was so used to being the beholder. I was also fine with plunging for his hidden charisma. I know it was buried somewhere in there, but he wanted to play hard to get. Which I get. I couldn't see the faded division between Declan and Elly. She always came across as desirable, and Elly seems to chaff desire.

I wanted to get out of bed, but like, I also really didn't. I still had on the thongs from the night before, tracing between my lips. I shivered my hand down and retracted the wedgie from climbing to my cervix. It felt nice, it felt like I could breathe once again, but now I was just horny. I fiddled the tip of my clit, enough to test whether or not I was really in the mood. I was. I waved my palm over and suctioned everything in—creating tension.

"Elly," my teeth stroked the tip of my bottom lip. Saying his name out loud felt like hot fudge winning me over. All over again. "I want you, Elly."

I never materialized Elly as being concrete. He was more like an awaited illusion, but even a little less evolved. At the very least, I pinned him as being obtrusive, but he was nowhere near. He was so slick with his identity, but also extremely alluring. Like, woah. Being surrounded by the senior's prime cut was lovely in all that it was, but being exposed to Elly aroused me. Not in a sexual way, but def in a sexual way.

"Yes!"

I tossed the blanket above my head and descended into my mattress. My shoulders locked up, jittering with myself—creeping up my happy trail. My head tossed back into my fluff of pillows. I edged a finger inside and slowly removed it, all the love-bits sprouted onto my sheets. This was a typical Sunday morning for me, but this time I had someone to hone in on, and that was Elly.

I embraced my coils and welcomed my hair to spike out to form a halo. My skin was damp and plump, my toes shot to the edge of the sheets. I was going to erupt, gracefully too. My depiction of Elly fondled my thoughts, and I wanted nothing more than to play with my imagination. I may be a virgin, but for Elly, for Elly I would...

"Basileeene!" My mom whistled through the second floor. I quickly propelled the blankets towards the ceiling, readjusting my almost-off undies.

"Yeah?!" I presented myself crosslegged with a smile. The smell of morning vag secreted throughout the room. Please don't notice.

"How are the meds working out?" She wiggled through the doorway; playing waitress while her petite frame struggled to balance the entrees. She placed a loving kiss on my forehead, now inviting the sweet aroma of fried eggs into my space.

"Well, besides growing an extra pair of legs, I think the side effects are pretty mild," I removed the dishes from her arms and shoved some junk onto the floor to make room on my nightstand. She haaaates that.

"You're going to need the extra stability when I tell you this news," she over-exaggerated a pout. "Your dad knows."

"What?!"

"Yup, he mentioned it while he was cooking breakfast."

"How did he find out?"

"Apparently he saw you come in last night," she sipped some non-apparent tea. "With a boy."

If my brown skin could change colors, I'd be invisible. Before I could truly tumble down my apologetic spiral, my phone started to ring. It was a Sunday, which meant the caller had to be my grandmother.

I frog leapt off of the bed and dashed for my shrieking device. My clothes were scattered throughout my fuchsia carpeting, and I started to ask myself why I ever thought fuchsia was a good color. I hoisted my skirt off the ground, and retrieved my phone from its back pocket. At this point the call had ended, but when I checked the caller ID, it was a number I couldn't recognize.

"Hey," a symphonic male voice answered the other end.

"Who is this?" I shrugged towards my mother, and she returned it with a facepalm.

They laughed, but not like, an annoying laugh. "You called me. Who is *this*?"

"This is Basil," silence.

"Good," it knocked me into daylight the minute I figured out who the caller was.

"Can I help you with something?" My mom rose from my bed and tiptoed toward the mic. I could hear Elly smiling, he was smiling so hard.

"You can help me with a lot."

Chapter 4

:0

I tried to guard the speaker from my mom, but she was already on the sloppiest mission to find out who was on the opposite end.

I wasn't sure if it was the pool of saliva gathering on my bottom lip, but she knew that I was majorly geeking out right now. Boy-geeking left my shuddering presentation unequipped for smooth. I wanted to talk, maybe even ask how he got my number, but before I could regather language he was cunning my linguist.

"I'm so rude. Good morning, Basil."

"Good morning," I rudely blocked my mother's free pass to my conversation.

"You left me last night," his voice came closer to the receiver. "How could you?"

I made a gesture to my mom that the door was wide open, specifically beseeching her grand exit. She hip bumped me before stylishly parting.

"I don't really remember anything," so, Elly wasn't the one who brought me home.

"You don't remember we fucked?" I damn near dropped my phone onto my toe. There it goes—the hard *F*. I could feel the speaker gliding across the top of his mouth. "I'm kidding. You wouldn't kiss me."

Intoxicated Basil rejected a kiss from Elly, and more than likely allowed Wesley to piggyback me into my room, where my dad was probs chilling by the dining table with my good bread knife. That Basil is no longer in charge of my social eliteness. If I had a better hold on my alcohol, I'd be able to send a breakup text to my v-card with the name *Elly Effin Hayes* in capital letters.

Phone calls are the biggest tease ever invented. I'm sure in sunlight Elly's complexion chugged daytime. Damn. For a slight second, I told myself this wasn't happening, and that I was only picking apart a gutty mirage.

"Basil, are you there?" He lightly nibbled on his lip.

"Yeah."

"Can I ask you something, but I don't want you to be upset. I really don't."

The bare wall in my room, the only wall I spared the compilation of self-help quotes with, streamed unfavorable occurrences from the previous night. Elly looking great amongst the grainy highlands that enclosed his somber smear. His sister, Declan, sitting beside us, happy because ugly never crossed paths with her. My giddy sight triggering bravery, telling them I would do anything to behold the world in front of them, to view me other than how I've rendered myself for sixteen years.

"Sure," I mumbled.

"What would you say if I asked you to be the star of my film?" This was already journeying somewhere I wasn't expecting.

"I'm not an actress."

"You didn't let me finish," I could see Elly's face materialize in a group of clouds beyond my window. I should run towards them. "This may sound forward, but when I first saw you, I knew I needed you. Your faceyoureyesyourskinhair," swallow. "I need you, Basil."

I tripped up. "So, you're in school for film or something?"

"I'd like to be a director someday."

Instead of running, I started twirling. My soles reveling and gliding, swooning and spinning for Elly. The music churned through his inflection, curling and dripping past the paint on my walls onto the God awful carpet. The light tucked itself away from my pleasures—peddling me into hypocrisy.

A film. The closest I've ever gotten to acting was being an extra in my cousin's music video, this was back when the family figured she'd be a star. Even then, I couldn't allow myself to act as if I really wanted to be there because I didn't. This is why I chose baking over the limelight. I don't think I was meant to be seen this way or to be the headliner at that. The only thing that kept me from straight-up declining was having the opportunity of being beside Elly again.

It could be okay to be seen, a little bit of redirection never killed anyone I guess, maybe landed them with some felonies or whatever, but that's what comes with chance. Elly had conviction in his voice, and if I timed my answer right, I could get even closer to him than I was last night. The warmth that expanded throughout my chest was more than a crush, it was temptation taking the wheel.

But wait, I'm still on the phone.

"Uh-huh," I actually haven't moved at all, I wasn't even standing. The back of my cellphone started to burn the hair off my thigh.

Ouch. "What's your attachment to clothing?"

"What?"

"Do you like being naked?"

no.

"I don't really understand what yo-" I lassoed my sentence.

Swallow. "Tell me you do," he pauses. "There are strands of nudity."

Of course there are.

"That changes things."

"Is that a no?" He asked. The question spilled between my toes and echoed through the line.

I hung up, and the second I couldn't measure his pulse through a wifi connection, I wanted to call him back so bad. My fingers uncontrollably bustled around my locked screen. I really wanted to pull my hair out, but eff that—it took me way too long to grow. The conversation swooned me back in; reeling and projecting itself among the thoughts I couldn't calculate. Comprehending Elly was all sorts of disorders.

"Don't call him back," I am now talking to myself. I am now talking to myself.

Bzzzzzzzzz.

I didn't have to call him back.
"Yea-ye-yeah. Yeah?" He called me.
"So?"
"Why me?"

Villeton High School always appeared dim, even more so on Monday mornings—it was simply the deemed ambiance of the institution. Villeton was the school for the students who couldn't afford to go to Mallory Prep, or kids whose parents thought public school would get the job done, like my parents. Villeton wasn't an ugly building by any means, it used to be an elaborate and respectable church. Now they use the chapel to store all the theatre equipment, which is too over budget. I don't hate my school, but I also really wish it would cover its shame.

I only checked my phone three times this morning, and that's about three times less than I checked it last night. I wanted Elly to shoot me a sign that I wasn't the first bullet point off his list of potentials. Does it even matter? I couldn't be caught posing nude for a college sophomore's experimental flick. I have dignity, maybe not too much of it, but dignity that will lay out all the plausible reasons as to why this would be a very rep-wrecking idea.

But Elly. I don't know what there was in our short meetings, but I couldn't get over that vinegar smell that arose from his hair—acidic it was, but so gratifying.

It's just some clothes, right? It would probably only last a few minutes, if that, and that would be more time I could roam away with him into a closet somewhere. Now, that's just lust talking—and a whole lot of it too. Elly! I would let him do whatever he wanted if that meant flashing some side-boobage for two secs—tops. No one has to know about it, no one but a class of students at the University of *WhotheHellKnows*.

My hormones are okay with this, my parents definitely won't be.

All the locker doors popped out of their crevices and greeted me. It was semi nasty being back after the weekend I had, never said I wasn't into it though. The way Villeton High felt on my skin this morning was close to being tranquil. I'm sure the other students standing beside me were holding onto my inability to decipher my placement. I share almost identical feelings with the inside of an abandoned locker; wishing that someone would just dial me into soundness.

"Yo, where you going?" I knew that voice. It was the same high pitched raspy tone from the bonfire. The one on the scavenger hunt for rolling paper. "Basil! Are you hard of hearing?"

Lane Vincent. The smartest senior Villeton barely has. "What class you got next?"

Why was she talking to me? "English."

"Can you get out of it?" Her head tilted, sending her blonde bangs cascading to the side, a glimmer ricocheting from her broad-brimmed glasses. "We're waiting for you."

I'm kinda scared of Lane Vincent. She stood with her arms crossed under her vegan leather jacket, tapping her worn-out canvas shoes. She was a tall girl, with nothing but menace on her bones. A few Villetoners passed by us waiting for someone to throw a blow since that's what usually happened in standoffs like these. I've personally never had to scrap with anyone in my life, but I've seen Lane take a few people down with her signature Lane-Pain.

I know that Lane is also best friends with Wesley Conner and Declan Hayes, and the three of them were prominent pieces in the Villeton mockup, but what does their throuple have to do with me?

And then Elly returned to my reasoning.

"Let me just grab something out of my locker."

So, where is Monday? Catching up with their homies while smoking on the edge of a breakthrough. Having that breakthrough, then forgetting that the rest of the week is made up of days that don't give a damn. It's almost like it was all meant to happen this way, that things are aligned for a purpose or something like that.

A stray of smoke snaked around my vision as Lane and I walked through the parking lot. I turned to see her budding donut-shaped clouds from her lips. Smoking was a separate functioning organ to Lane, whereas if I were to join her, I'd be coughing into Tuesday morning—getting over a panic attack. Lane knew just the way to curve her lip to allow the smoke to seep upward—this was a skill I found most potheads to have. I prolly wouldn't consider Lane a pothead, she was too in-tune with her hobbies.

"Take a bum," she offered me the blazed-out spliff. I declined. "Don't smoke?"

"I do. Occasionally."

"There's no better occasion than now," she caw-cawed. Her laugh freed itself from underneath her drugged exhales. Such a bad laugh. "Before he gets here I gotta ask, are you dating Wesley?"

I winced, and who is getting here? "No."

"Weird. So, you're just hooking up?"

She did see him finger frolicking through my undergarments the other night. These aren't the introductions I should be having. "No."

"Dude, I bopped you two doing stuff."

How do I misguide this conversation, and why is everyone obsessed with giving me and Wesley a label? I can bring up my pet rabbit, who I haven't seen all weekend because I was delving into popularity. I can let my hair down again, the last time I did that it swooned the room and caused a fight. I could lie for like, the first time ever—or second, or fourth. I don't like to lie because the shrouded truth gives me hives. Um, what kind of lie should I tell? If I'm gonna lie, I better make it worth it. Like, I can almost walk through walls.

What the hell does *almost* mean in that context?

"You're here!" Wesley leaped across the empty lot, slinging his body around mine. His checkered green skinnies swung across my belly. "Your dad is so nice, by the way!" So it was Wesley who brought me home the other night.

"You met my father?" I knocked on Wesley's back to get him to let me out. I could see someone right behind him, pushing their body weight against a dusty green jeep, while patiently awaiting their chance to get to me.

"Basil," he said my name. "Can you give me an answer?"

"Elly," I was so right. "I'll do it."

He looked hella good in the sun.

Chapter 5

:D

"Basie looks so cute when she's sleeping."

"Why are you in her face like that?"

"Come see Laney-Lane, she also drools from the corner of her mouth. Ohmygaw! Look at those precious poutiful lips!"

My body was configured to the silk leopard sheets that wreathed me. These looked like items my mother would own, but my mother would never draw out her wallet for a silk bedspread. My eyes were still puffy from robbed sleep, and my mind wanted to declare the setting as my room, or somewhere not too far from it. These sheets were *nice*, and they almost canceled out the view I had of Wesley leaning over me. His hair was free from his usual mint beanie, and all of the pinks made a scenery out of his freckles.

I slumped up enough to examine the quarters. Lane was rolled out on an elongated bean bag chair, picking gunk out of her nails with her teeth. The bed I sat on was huge, almost double the size of mine, but the room itself was five times bigger. Obscure and gruesome posters were slapped around the bright orange walls. A fully naked mannequin dressed in neon signatures took up one corner of the room, and the other corner was decked out in some high-tech computer software.

The windows were large doors that lead to a lush balcony. It was starting to get dark outside, so I couldn't see the balcony in its entirety, but it was decorated in nothing but glass figurines and table sets. The ceilings were high and embellished with floral patterns that introduced the main doorway. The closet entrance was left open, revealing a deep walk-in that was in no way kept tidy.

This for sure is not *my* room.

"Welcome home, my beautiful Basie!"

I love a good rumor, and I think one of my favorites was a rumor I could never accurately detect. Wesley Conner wasn't mesmerizing in his own right—he was wealthy. The Conners came from a long line of inherited wealth, wealth that can only be acquired through nepotism, but I didn't want to be the person to bring it up. No one at school knows what Wesley's parents do, but they do know that they don't have to do a lot of it, and Wesley was a product of exactly that.

"When did I fall asleep?"

"On the ride here. Dude you slept for like four hours, I wanted to wake you up but Elly was so against it," Lane removed her glasses and wiped them on the bean bag's exterior.

Elly is here too? That means Elly def caught sight of my drool train that was now at my clavicle. He's seen me at my worst. I can't be the heart of his film now, that being if he hasn't already removed me from the cast and crew. I should've signed a contract specifically highlighting my need to drool when I sleep because I keep too much in when I'm awake.

It was my first hangover, and the first time my parents couldn't lure me out of bed with homemade nachos. I stayed up late last night creating a *Fallin' For You* playlist on my phone, that consists of exactly twenty-seven songs because I never thought I'd need to know romance as a genre. My conversation with Elly was the only track I was missing, but I tried to make a voice recording that ended up only being embarrassing—I can't imitate a voice like that.

Wesley's bedroom door began to swivel and shake, eventually impelling the door forward. An elderly woman who was half my size waltzed in, and in her hand, she held a tray full of warm treats. The woman had a lovable face and wrinkles that could store money.

"I saw your friend downstairs scavenging through the cupboards for food. I told him I had some treats in the oven if he didn't mind waiting," the woman sat the scones on the ottoman at the edge of Wesley's bed. Her articulation was quick and refined as if she was trying hard to veil her birthplace. "I hope you enjoy!"

"Thank you my Fen-Fen!"

"Thank you again, Fen," Elly sleekly moved past Fen and into the room with a box of *Grain-Os*. "Have any good dreams?"

Not enough.

"Yeah, I'm sorry if I was asleep for too long. I couldn't get to sleep last night."

"You don't have to apologize. I enjoyed carrying you inside, you're also lighter than you look," so I look heavy. "Are you hungry, Basil?"

Shards of Grain-O crumbs coated Elly's lips. He dug out a handful and waved them beneath my nose. Yes—I'm hungry now.

i'm hungry.

I plucked a single *O* from his cupped palm and placed it at the back of my tongue, anticipating its flavorful breakdown. Yum. I stole another one and swallowed it whole—jacking a couple more. Pieces flew from my crunch and garnished my lips; we match now.

Mmmmm.

He moved onto the bed, next to me. I knew why the two of us were together, but Lane and Wesley were complete questions. I always identified them as being Declan's friends more than Elly's, but when I really tear it apart, I can't hark back on a time when I've heard of Elly Hayes having any friends at all. He was always described as a meteor; falling through Villeton's astronomy, crumbling into almost nothing, and then decaying onto the people that came after him.

I could recite the mythologies that came from Villeton's halls covering everything there was to know about the notorious trio. But with Elly, everything was too extraordinary to digest. One day I would hear that he was found sunbathing naked on a teacher's car, the next I would hear that he was running a plant shop out of the janitor's closet—which probably doesn't get much sunlight anyway. I could never know Elly for myself, not until now.

"How drippy would it be if a big-time production company picked up this movie," Lane blushed, stuffing weed into a cigarette sleeve with a pencil. They do know about the film. "Imagine all the septiccurrency I could sell."

"Money!" Wesley giggled.

"When I say 'we', I'm referring to the people that actually need it. Poor ass people, like me! How much is the prize again?" Lane barked.

"Ten thousand," Elly announced. "But that amount will only grow with the traffic it'll pick up."

"Are you two going to be in the movie too?" I asked. They all exchanged wordless dialogue.

"Lane and Wesley are going to be the producers," Elly answered.

"I'd like to think of myself as a creative director slash visual effects connoisseur," Lane lit her cigarette thingy.

It wasn't like all of them hadn't already seen my bits, it was also the idea of me being at the center of something. A film. Where I'm nude for like...I still don't know how long. There were so many shades to me that were being uncovered simultaneously, and I was adapting to my newest vignette. Hesitations stripped me bare and vulnerable, but each second my eyes trekked to find the consolation in Elly's stare, I'm somehow okay with all of this. Also, money is kinda cool.

"If this film wins the Brunhart Festival, it could change me," Elly leaned up, munching on a couple more cups of the cereal before sealing it away. "This character is everything I believe you to be, Basil. Do you understand?"

"How can I live up to your beliefs of who I am?"

"You already have," I couldn't even look at him when he said that. I was not PREPARED.

"What is this film about?"

Lane casted her leather jacket off as she budded from her station. "Well, Black Beauty. I'm glad you asked."

Tartula, the protagonist of the story. Sixteen-year-old young femme unearthly teen with multicultural vroom-vroom skin. Tartula has the backside of all nymphs combined, and absurdly nappy waist length hair - the kind of long hair that is so long she must place it into a bun before wiping her ass. Feral. Tartula has the face of a fetus and is often questioned about her age, she could very well be mistaken for a child or a grown ass woman. But she is not a woman, she is a nature deity.

A camera follows Tartula around the world of Wheatermite, a grassland with little moonlight and nighttime. The exposition of Tartula's story is shown through indistinct montages, with implied sexuality. Very little tit scenes. Tartula's body becomes a galore but with copious bounty. The camera zooms in at these moments, Tartula shies away, whimper-whimper. Tartula places her eroticism up for debate, it is now, and has always been, between her and Wheatermite.

The story is left with Tartula knee down, hips open and mouth gaped. She speaks subduedly as the camera zooms in from a high angle, transitions to dutch and ends at the rear.

Tartula is heard mewling before everything fades to black.

"Uhm," my back constricted. "This sounds like something straight out of Goblin's Guild."

Goblin's Guild is the reason my dad forgets he has a child to raise. Every afternoon I come home from school, he's in the middle of attacking an eight-foot virtual barbarian with his party that is made up of twelve-year-old boys. He says he doesn't know anyone's age, but it doesn't really matter when their M.O is to kickass.

"Do you play?" Elly...no.

"Not at all, but my dad loves it."

"What's his screen name?"

"Darksky-king?" I'm totally guessing.

"DarkSkyLord is your father? He's in my party."

"I love that you two are bonding, but bondage don't pay bills!" Lane called out.

"But it can!" Wesley shouted.

"Sorry. I'm a little confused about the plot," *little* is an understatement.

I grabbed a scone from off the platter, it looked like it had some fresh blueberry filling inside—my fav. I took a quick bite and now I'm confident I lost a tooth. The berries inside had a gristly texture, and the dough itself was undercooked. I'm not sure who Fen-Fen was to Wesley, but she definitely needed some cooking lessons, or needed to retire from cooking altogether. Her recipe was missing heavy cream which is a must for dry pastries. I didn't want to come across as rude, not at my first gathering, so I had to *accidentally* drop the rest on the floor.

Lane squealed. "Talk about butter fingers, Black Beauty!"

"I'll eat it," Elly lifted the pastry from the ground, molding it into his mouth with one slug.

"To explain to you the premise a little more, the story is a coming of age tale modeled after the greats," Lane was evidently proud of this.

Elly bumped me with his shoulder, he was proud of this too. "It is the moment of peak pubescence; the thrill of uncovering yourself to a mucky disposition. Have you experienced that before? You are a virgin, right?"

I'm not the kind of virgin that eats cold pizza—I've done stuff. Nothing that I felt the need to tell my parents about, but enough to solidify me as an actual teen. The guy wasn't very tall or affable, but he was grounded. I'd sneak out some nights and bike down to his four story house that hugged the Hudson. My parents had no idea, but his parents had *all* the ideas. In fact, his mom invited me over to her shuffleboard team brunch. We did enough, just not the big *unf*.

"Mhm," I answered. Wesley and Lane tried not to look my way but subsequently ended up looking my way.

"You got this. Sex is all an act anyway. Plus, I got so many ideas," Lane plopped on the bean chair once again.

"I have ideas too—for wardrobe!" Wesley added. He skipped around the room as if he was trying to leave his sparkle on it. His feet looked ginormous underneath his ankle-sucking jeans.

"I hope you don't think you're in charge of wardrobe, you can barely dress yourself," Lane scoffed.

"People love the way I dress! I get compliments all the time!"

"I need you to take all the compliments you've ever received, and subtract them by the ones that come from Fen."

"Uhm," I chirped. They each spoke over one another, canceling my input.

"Pink-tails would look so cute on Basie!"

"Tartula would never have pink-tails, you sleeb!" Lane erupted.

Elly scooted closer than he was, pulling my perception. He analyzed me so intensely, he's done it before, but this time nothing was holding him back; not the night, not a heap of strangers, or the bickering tunes coming from Wesley and Lane. His eyes were such a sympathetic blue, the color of sorry. I prolly was reading too much into them anyway. His peculiarity soothed me so freaking much.

"Did I say thank you?" What was I thanking him for? Being contagious. He purred behind my lobe.

"Not yet," he was so close, I second guessed my breath.

"Thank you."

Elly needled his arm around me. It wasn't like when high school boys did it, he did it with so much self assurance. His hand rested in the middle of my back, jostling me further into his torso. My chin pressed up against his heart, and the *thump-thumps* attempted to drive me away—they could never. Elly had a heartbeat that tried hard to match his intonations. His head hung forward, and he picked me, making wishes with the gazes that budded from my eyelashes.

"I should be thanking you," it was like his words coasted along a melody as they came out.

"Elly," I gulped. Lane and Wesley returned zero attention to us. We were so alone.

Sweet.

"Call me, Elias."

I closed my eyes and pictured the name, but for some reason, I couldn't articulate it. It was as if the name dissed my dialect. Strange. I've def sketched out his entire name many days in my mind, putting it into a vault where someday I'd be able to stick it to a face. Not only was I now given that, I was bubbling in it. I wanted to gift Elly the utterance of his own name, but there was weight.

Too. Much. Weight.

Chapter 6

:S

When I was nine, I asked my parents for a bundt pan to make monkey bread. I had just conquered my first creme brûlée with the unnecessary supervision from my mom, she still dallies around whenever I'm taking on a new treat. My initial request was for a kitchen torch, but I had to settle for an appliance that was less hazardous. When I was thirteen, I baked a four-tier cake following a recipe I found in *Bake like a Beast* with my fav cousin, Taz—who was only there as the taste tester. It was easy to follow the recipe, but it was my errors that made it my own. It was then when it registered to my parents that my baking was more than a pastime, it could be the only thing I'm truly good at.

Home Ec wasn't required. All the students that took the class were on the coast to failing, and home ec was easy enough to receive a passing grade that would help drop kick the delinquents out of Villeton. All anyone had to do was bring in a steno pad, take some notes on how to prep choco-chip cookies, and come in the next day to watch Miss Lowe sweating behind a brick oven.

"I can't add whatever student I want to my roster, Basil," Miss Lowe always wore bandanas as headbands and yoga pants with platform slides. At some point in her lifetime, Miss Lowe had to be vegan.

"I can help you out, I can be like, an assistant or something," she liked when I said that. The idea of someone besides her doing the cooking hadn't presented itself since she got the job. "You love my baking!"

"I do! Alright, let me talk to some people, but I can't make any promises."

The next day I was added to her attendance sheet as the instructor's assistant.

Why do I make these mistakes?

It was all wonderful for the first month, maybe I can even say it was revitalizing, all up until recently.

"Her and Elly are a thing."

"WHO?"

"Shhh, not so loud. The black girl over there."

"She's dating Elly Hayes?"

"I know right?"

"Hold up, isn't he dead?"

I picked the wrong day to get a head start on washing my bakeware.

The slippery dialogue head butted me the entire day. Students swirling through my peripheral, inciting soliloquies to my underdeveloped relationship. Thumbtacking titles to a ruthless void. Ruthless being me; the void being anything connecting Elly to standards. I found it at the bottom of the dutch oven pan during home ec. Anywhere but here.

When I passed Lane in the hallway earlier on, she delivered a moist high five that predictably molded into a pound. Lane was hard to miss, not cause she hovers over most of the underclassmen, but because she was someone to know. So, as our hands met in questionable solidarity, it sent a stampede of allegations.

Basil Francis is now popular.

"How's the caramel coming along?" Miss Lowe gave me one of those, teacher friendly back smacks.

I wish it wasn't inflamed with interrogations. "Great! I asked Maude to get started on the egg mixture," I peeked over at Maude, who was clearly menstruating.

Miss Lowe slanted by my ear. "Please go help her."

If there was anything I knew about Maude, was her love for hightop trainers and jogging suits. That's all. She turned her nose up at anyone who proceeded in verbal communication with her but loved communicating with every single follower she had on social media. Woah, I know more than I thought.

"Do you think she's pretty or like, what? Be honest."

"Elly's girlfriend? She's O-K."

"Yeah, she's not ugly, but I think Pavia is way prettier."

"Yeah, and even Pavia looks like shit to Elly."

When will this stop?

"Maude," I groaned. Her legs were perched up on the counter, the bottom of her dirt engraved sneakers waved at me.

"Ugh," she remarked. All I said was her name.

"Did you start blending the eggs yet?"

Her blinding orange phone case was greased up with fingerprints and cheap nail polish. She blended the screen in with her makeup, the blue light serving as contour, "I'm not doing anything."

Being the teacher's assistant comes with trials in many forms. My greatest trial was encouraging other Villetoners that baking could be fun, and they often dismissed me because I was proud to be the teacher's pet. I don't necessarily see myself as a pet because I'm not being led by Miss Lowe—my assistance is to her benefit. But, people don't care to see that, and students like Maude would rather not see me at all.

"It's because Maude hooked up with Elly."

"She's so mad."

I wanted to tell Maude that my interactions with Elly were nothing more than a university thesis. I'm def fibbing; there is a knotted and undeniable yearn that surges through both me and him. I can also explain to Maude that that knot restricts the longer I'm isolated from him. His skin tested the sounds of my pores whenever he demurely slid past me.

Does she know how that feels?

"We didn't just hook up, we dated," a flood of text messages flew beneath the bags under her eyes. Maude quickly rammed her phone into the saucer that was meant for the misplaced eggs.

No one was sure who Elly was tied to. Villetoners played telephone with all his relationships, some even adding themselves to the mix for enthrallment. At the time, Elly's appearance was a multitude of everyone's fantasies. I never knew him for myself, but Elly was what they wanted. He was described as a giving lover and also no one's lover. I'm not sure where Maude landed in the mix—if she was ever in the mix at all.

"Elly's girlfriend is pussy."

I am pussy.

"He feels so comfortable right now, doesn't he?" Maude's high ponytail became a car wiper, sweeping across her pomegranate face.

"What are you getting at?" I had a bit of an idea. Maude pounced up from her seat and dug into my proximity.

"It's all for show. His interest doesn't hold for long."

"I'm going to guess you're talking about Elly. We're only friends."

"That's what he calls you, right?" He hasn't called me anything. "Before he broke up with me, he called me his friend too."

If I didn't get back to the first batch in the oven, the flan would overheat and unwelcome all potential moisture. The eggs will lose the elasticity in the gelatin and harden almost like bad cheesecake. The caramel coating will burn, darken, turn tart, and indigestible. No one would want to eat it then. Wasteful food gone to waste for a wasted conversation.

"Is this all because you don't want to cook?"

Maude raked her fingers through her scrunchie, tugging it out. The band caught hold of some of her faux blonde strands, attempting to persuade her otherwise. She yanked it out one last time. A clump of frizzled dead ends fled from her grip and froggied across the classroom. She came closer to me.

"Are they going to fight?"

"Over Elly?"

"We can hear you!" Maude cried. "Everyone can hear all of it!"

"Ignore them," I reached for her hand, but instead she swallowed it into her pocket.

"Don't touch me, you freak," does she know what I agreed to? Did Elly ask her first?

Maude had this glint in her eye, almost as if the idea of Elly ever wanting me would be inconceivable. I believed that glint because I ask myself the same. What could I do for a nineteen-year-old's student film besides be exactly what he tells me to be? Maude made those differences dice into me and now I was that. Every second of my childhood was brought back to me, with a cherry whose stem read *freak*.

"How am I a freak?"

"You're friends with them. They're all freaks and weirdos. Why do you think everyone keeps talking about you? They're trying to figure out what's wrong with you too."

I brought my tone to a whisper, trying to borrow some privacy. "You dated that weirdo, Maude."

"How do you think I know?"

The room door blasted open, and the shortest girl I ever seen came tripping in. She was really short, like, fifth grade short. "Basil!"

"Yeah?" Is she the gnome fairy coming to protect Tartula?

"Come outside, now!"

I jogged to the front of the building where I met a mound of dirt I never knew before. Out on the front lawn of Villeton was a deep and crisp penmanship, surrounded by few students that knew they shouldn't be there. My immediate reaction was, I didn't do this. I looked over at the tip of the *B*, and there he was, sitting with his legs rounded into his chest.

I've never had a crush before, on food—many times, but never a thing I could hold. Watching my classmates around me become overzealous from their two second crushes made my inclination of ever having one plummet. But when a crush inflates into a tangible object, there is nothing that compares.

As he noticed me, he stood up—letting everyone know he was the one to blame and the first to admit. His face was eager and ready, I've never seen it harboring so much color. I didn't know I could do something so spectacular.

"Basil Elaine Francis,"

"Will you be my girlfriend?"

Maude had accompanied me outside, and knew there was no way I could chalk out an excuse for this. This was more than a small handshake before first period—this was significant. The intimate flock hung on my aphonic speech. I instead propelled a gleam.

"My middle name is Eugenia."

Chapter 7

:O

"Come with me," he held his hand out. Funny how our palms almost look identical.

We haven't had a terrible movie night. We haven't apprehensively walked through a crowd of people. We haven't forwarded each other pictures of kids falling. We haven't confessed to each other that we might like one other, before the bigger confession of, we actually *do* like each other. We haven't sat across a table, playing out what could possibly happen through impatient toes. We never held hands—we've barely touched. We never kissed.

But boyfriend.

I have a boyfriend.

"What do you have to get from the mall?" Before I fled into Elly's car, I placed the rest of my baking responsibilities on a platter, handing them to Miss Lowe. Poor thing.

"Costumes," his eyes trickled. "What size are you?"

"Small," I answered. His lips clenched, devouring a chuckle. "What?"

"Nothing, I don't want to offend."

"Please tell me, Elly."

"You have a very big," his thoughts shifted; the glee filled tension subsided. "Nothing."

It was an early afternoon on a weekday, so no one was gonna be at the mall besides school cutters and pregnant women. The storefronts barfed white lighting onto its inactive workers. Totally tattle-telling. The scent of butter drenched pretzels overturned the natural aromas of formaldehyde. Chic.

Elly sauntered into a women's negligee shop. The accent lighting made it more posh than it was. My mom couldn't stand this place. She'd always complain about their unordinary color distribution and poor inventory. I wish I had such distress. Elly covertly sneaked around, not even like he was trying to be inconspicuous, he was inherently coy. One associate really liked that, she steered in, almost motor-boating his attention.

"Do you need help?" She was like, my mom's age.

"No," Elly pushed his attention onto an aqua bikini set, the color transmitted to his pupils.

"We usually don't let men shop in here," she snorted. "But since the shop is empty, it should be okay."

The waves in Elly's hair overflowed onto his left shoulder, allowing a small ooze of light to splatter across my dimples. The saleswoman's attention finally found me, but her bemused glare told me she didn't want to. She checked back at Elly, then back over to me, and finally back at Elly. Elly eventually decided to swamp his lengthy arm around my torso.

"I'm here with her," he winked. "This is my girlfriend."

She unwillingly nodded. "Oh, alright."

"Do you have clothing in her size? She's a small."

"Uhm, yeah. We have smalls," I could hear the crackling noises from her feet echo in her Mary Jane's.

The table she lead us to wasn't too far from the display we were already standing by. The colors were a gaudy compilation of pastels and unicorn spit. I knew I was younger than Elly, but she didn't have to insult me like this—so playfully too. She wagged by our side before frolicking off to another corner, where I could vividly make out her shadow.

"These colors aren't right," Elly picked up a pair of mermaid sequent thongs.

"What did you have in mind?"

"I prefer you in nude," don't they all. "Colors."

He dug his palm into his pants pocket and pulled out a pair of lace brown hipsters. The scheme was so similar to my pigment, it was almost revolting. Like, who has been watching me? I loosened the loop he had around my neck, trying to discover the surface that held articles of my flesh. No where to be found. Elly's clench clung to my revealed bicep.

"This way," he mouthed, and *that way* was the dressing room.

The garment had a sheer piece of plastic securing the spot where my vag was supposed to go. The tag was still on them, and a bit of me felt relief knowing Elly wasn't a mega panty hoarder. The glossy tag that held the store's brand twinkled behind a disparaging bulb. The only thing the reflection of my body fought more with was the bitterness that stiffened the organza curtains.

I wasn't one of those people that got fully naked in a dressing room to try on a pair of panties. I had a tank top on that did more favors than it anticipated, and it also gave me a bit of shape alongside the netted trousers. I could hear Elly shuffle 'about on the opposite side of the room, I was surprised he even got this far. My thighs called for my concerns, mauled at them in fact.

"I'm sure it looks fine," Elly's laughter flew down from the ceiling.

"Everything looks fine if no one ever sees it," I huffed. The burn from fresh gust tapped my backside.

Elly's face casted toward me—entering the room. His lower lip fleeting from the top of his sullen grin. "Everyone should see this."

I should tell him to get out, but instead, I pressed against the reflection that outlined my hesitations; Elly pressed against all of us. His look broke the silence that carried itself so well in his eyes. They howled and bowed. Choose one. He swaddled his grip around me and effortlessly spun me to face myself. I wanted to tell him that it was all too soon, I wasn't used to seeing myself so exposed.

I don't hate my body, but no one has ever witnessed it like this before—including me. Even when I was messing around with that guy who had the shuffleboard mom, I was never unfazed enough to be fully naked. It was either my breast were shunned by a blanket, or my wide ass was smothered by a basketball tee.

Even though the tank top sealed my lower belly blubber, Elly considered all of me. I could see him breaking me up into sections, trying to figure out what he can do with each part. I was a task to Elly, but I was also a mine full of extravagancies. He had me, and he knew what to do, but somewhere, his overconfidence forbade him.

"Your face is nothing to be ashamed of," his palm dug across the skin beneath my bellybutton.

"It's not my face that's the problem."

"I don't see any problems."

I felt like, "I don't know if I can do this, Elly."

"You can."

I felt like asphyxia.

Elly moved further back, removing his fingerprints—though they still showed so well. His head coiled from left to right, settling at a point of focus that was never stagnant. It was too hard to notice him, to be within a vicinity that mishandled my reverie. Crap.

I could feel my hair tie working downwards, relinquishing my strands. My hair was now the room. Elly placed the knot into his pocket, the same where he removed the hipsters.

"Elly."

"You're the perfect Tartula. You're a star, bAsil."

"I am?"

"More than any I've ever wished on."

"Excuse me!" Her profile towered over at the peak of the changing room; the same woman from earlier. "Only one person at a time, please!"

It was sleeve demanding temperature. Much more bitter without Elly near me. He stood by the ice cream hut, right behind a guy who wasn't too much older than him. I chilled at a bird stained table, dismantling him from afar. Elly and the man talked for a little bit while waiting for their orders, the guy had on a beaten-up crewneck and cracked up at Elly's playfully prudent manner. The cashier called out to Elly, and he rose our milkshakes to the sky before excusing himself from the colorless dialogue.

"Smack smack, eat eat," Elly's nostrils twisted in enjoyment before taking his first sip.

The vanilla was clumpy. "What?"

"My dad's abbreviation for *eet smakelijk*," he scooted closer. "It's Dutch. It's like saying, *bon appétit*."

"Are you dutch?"

"Sure," sip. "How was school today?"

Should I tell Elly about Maude? Maybe I won't. The proper thing to do would be to ignore the bad and celebrate everything good. Like, my new relationship. My very first boyfriend ever. Who is also one of the most popular boys in town, not for all the right reasons, but damn—reasons that are so right to me.

"Uhm, something really weird happened in Home Ec today," go for it, Basil.

"Like what?"

"This girl Maude was like, mad I was dating you. Even though we started dating this afternoon, she assumed we had been dating for a while."

Sip. Elly puckered his lips out, but not for a kiss, in a thought sketching way. "That's very peculiar. Maybe this girl Maude wants to secretly be friends with you."

"No," I slightly stuttered. "Maude—the one you dated."

"Mmmmm-aU-D."

"She's blonde, always has her hair in a ponytail. I've actually never seen her without a ponytail till today."

Elly shook his head, which I assumed welcomed his new friend over. The guy had also gotten a vanilla milkshake and complained about how all the ice cream seeped to the bottom and made it lumpy. Also, brain freeze.

I couldn't stop thinking about Maude, and how she was not a fraction of pixelations. My mind envisioned her too well for her not to be authentic. The spoiled scorn staking out in her iris, her eyes when she looked at me were agitated with criticism. The distrust that dehydrated her sass the moment she saw him outside. The moment she recognized our differences.

The deteriorating sweatshirt guy pardoned himself to a table of freshmen near us. There were rules against that, I'm sure.

"She was there when you asked me to be your girlfriend. Did you see her? She was standing beside me."

"When you're around I only see you, Basil."

"No," my speech wasn't sturdy. "You have to know who she is because she almost slapped the color out of my skin."

Elly targeted the point of his straw at me, a moderate contrast against the blood colored plastic and his alabaster. "She touched you?"

"No, but she wanted to. She was so angry," he rested his cup.

"People see you," he replied. His focus wavering.

"She wasn't only angry, she was rotting," I continued.

"They see you, and they braid themselves into your metaphysics."

"She insulted you."

"bAsil."

"She warned me."

CLaNk!

The teenagers next to us scattered from their table, yelping with shock. A gooky layer of vanilla mazed its way through the cracks of the pecan wood. They all immediately questioned the apparentness of the balding guy. He was embarrassed, but he wasn't going to let any high school students know. He aligned his finger into the crevice of the accident and scooped up a now soupy vanilla texture.

"I'll fix this!" He roared. Specks of cream shot from his broken boast.

Sip.

Elly placed his drink under our table, his head never revolved towards the fiasco. To him nothing existed, "I'll fix this, Basil."

But me.

Chapter 8

:T

I'm home. Two stories, a half renovated basement, and a bunny rabbit named Purple to confide in. She's as cranky and vicious as I can be, but way more adorable. I fibbed for a good chunk of my life, telling myself that I am *all that* and it has taken me nowhere. Maybe ditching football events for failed attempts at online challenges. It wasn't like anyone has ever asked me to go with them. It wasn't like I'd rather be anywhere besides with my parents at home.

Well. That is what I used to say.

I could hear Elly's jeep from my front porch; It sounded like a missed opportunity. Before I exited his car, he touched the end of my shoulder with the panty's bag and whispered my name. The motor overturned our solitude. The windows dusted up, and a strain was placed between my lips and his. He resisted, and we ended up gawking with cheeky eyes right before my hand hit the door handle.

"We can't kiss," he stated. I was on the opposite end of the car by then, reading his lips through a rolled up window.

I know that if I tell my parents about Elly, they won't believe me—they won't even believe Elly is a real name. I can bake his characteristics into my fav soufflé and they'd impale my cravings. I'm not sure how to insist on a project that I'm not coherently sold on, but Elly makes me bold. For those same reasons, he is plaque on my teeth that is too savory to brush off.

"Home!" I crept in; trying to smother the jollity screening against my face. We didn't kiss, so now it's my time to put on a false smile.

"Where have ya been?" My dad's voice is similar to a Brooklyn sidewalk in ninety-degree weather.

"School?" For the most part.

"You don't got a job yet?"

"When are you ever working?" Because he does nothing but play Golbin's Guild, which I now know he is playing with my future hubby.

"Basil! Are you home?" My mom whistled from the top of the steps.

"No, she left," my dad grunted.

"Jerr, I see her right there," my mom was in one of my t-shirts, holding my bunny closer than I assumed she's ever held me.

I spent years of my life thinking my parents were going to get a divorce. This stemmed from overhearing one of my classmates in the second grade gloat about their parents getting a divorce. Ever since then it made sense. Divorce? Yeah, that's something my parents are going to do. It wasn't until seventh grade I learned that my parents weren't circling around arguments, that's just the way they communicate.

My dad is basic. Give him a computer game, his favorite éclairs baked by me, a less than two hour movie to wrap up the night, and he's set for life. My mom deals with him well, and she and I laugh about it more than we should. Their tradeoffs are extended time alone and very little time together, and my dad also accepting that my mom will never leave him for Don Cheadle.

"You're home earlier than usual. Did your boyfriend drive ya?"

How does he know? I barely know. I should've assumed that the word would get around Villeton and back at my place in zero speed. It was also naive of me to not prepare a, *I have a boyfriend* speech because that could've saved the disdain.

"What boyfriend?"

"The white kid who looks like shrooms."

"Honey," my mom made her way down the steps, freaking finally. "A person can't *look* like shrooms."

"Liv, he looks like everything ya see when you're buggin' out on shrooms."

Elly was def supernatural, but for my dad to describe him as being nearly trippy is almost *too* befitting.

"I was going to tell you both today. He just drove me home, that's why I'm so early," also, I cut like half the day to go to the mall with him.

My dad emerged from his computer desk, which is a thing he never does unless it's to go to his other computer desk upstairs. His fists were rolled and inflamed. He flounced in my direction, his feet nearly levitating from the ground.
So, this was it.
This was adolescence.

I repented my sins under my breath, and I always promised myself that the moment before I die, I will rap my favorite Lil Foun-Tain verse.

"Kickin'. Drip-drip tickin'. Workin' like I'm slurpin' on yo' best friend's vixen," my pitch was shaky, but I'm sure it would do Lil Foun-Tain proud.

"Why are you rapping Lil Foun-Tain?" My dad paused, my mom was equally fazed.

"Because I knew the day you'd find out I had a boyfriend you'd kill me, and I told myself that that verse would be my closing line."

My mom and dad exchanged a, *but this is your daughter* look. "I'm not going to kill you."

My mom became nothing but laughter, and my dad had no other choice but to join her. Both of them piled onto each other, my mom resting into my dad's hold and him trying to shelter her from the floor. They couldn't stop themselves, and eventually started choking for oxygen. My mom had tears streaming down her cheeks—it wasn't that funny. I'm glad to know that my death was their personal standup routine.

"Basil, I'm happy for you," my dad tapped the top of my head. "I'm glad you're dating that guy."

"What?"

"When he brought ya home the other night, I took a look at his car. *Wooooo*, an orange Porsche. Of course I like the kid, I even offered him an élcair."

Wesley.

"Dad—no, that's not my boyfriend. That's my friend Wesley," my friend.

"So, why was he bringing ya home if he's not your boyfriend? What is your relationship to this young man?"

My dad's tone flip-flopped and my mom was quick to catch it. "She told you, Jerr. That was her friend who wanted to make sure she got home safe."

I want to go to my room now.

"Who the hell is outside of my house?" My dad wasn't wrong, there was a shadow lurking in the front yard.

My mom preemptively wriggled forward, and I wasn't too far behind her. A misty figure crowded the entrance of our home; a person was hiding and I was betting on that person to be Elly. I wanted them to be. My mom moved in, and I held my breath trying to mask my enthusiasm because this time, my parents will meet my *actual* boyfriend.

How should I introduce him? This is Elly, my boyfriend. This is Elly, who I was telling you about. Elly Hayes. Boyfriend. Oh! Hey Elly, these are my parents. Elly, why'd you leave me here for so long? Meet Elly, whose full first name I can't say, but his last name is a breeze—hey Hayes! Film? What film? You're hysterical, Elly! Anyway, this is my boyfriend, mom and dad.

"Hello," she chewed on a chocolate cake pop. The scraps spilled from her mouth and onto her golden Villeton sweatshirt. "Is Basil home?"

"Hi Declan," it wasn't Elly. "What are you doing here?"

My mom's face was almost a sequel to my reaction when I first saw Declan. The stunted glare and crisp joints, those were nothing but mild symptoms when around the Hayes siblings. I should've warned her, but I was too preoccupied prancing with the daydreams that cemented Elly and I together.

"Elly picked me up from Wes' place, you live pretty close to him. He also said you forgot this," she passed me a closed brown paper bag.

I took a quick peep inside and saw the underwear scrunched in the corner. Please don't ask what this is. "Oh, thank you."

"I don't know what's inside, but I guess it's important," that would be hard to explain.

"Who is Elly?" My mom asked. About time.

"Declan's older brother," it began cramming through my organs, kicking itself out. "Who is my boyfriend."

"Your boyfriend?" Declan crisscrossed her astonishment with my mother's. "I didn't know you two had started dating."

"Me either," my mother mildly ejected the surprise, lifting Purple back to her side. I just told her. "How about you and Basil's boyfriend come in for dinner. Her father can cook us something."

"I'm not cooking dinner!" My dad's echo steamed out through the front door. He's never this polite. "Where is this boyfriend anyway? He can't come out of the car to meet his girlfriend's parents?" My dad intimidated Declan and it showed on her face.

"Uhm, our mom is cooking dinner now, so we should probably get going soon. Thank you for the invite though."

Declan stood at the foot of the door with her wide eyes roaming about. From the front door, she could see the circular hallway that expanded to our domed ceiling. This was the selling point, as my dad always liked to remind me. We had photos of family members that took up the gardenia walls in the hallway, but mainly humiliating toddler photos of me. It was the first illustration of who our tiny family was to anyone who walked through the front door, and the last thing they saw before they left.

"It's a shame you can't stay, Declan. We'd really-really love to have you. I was listening to a podcast this morning and they talked about cauliflower pizza, and I was hoping Jerrell could make some."

"I'm not cooking!"

My mom continued. "Oh! And maybe Basil can make dessert. She's an exceptional baker. Last night she made this del-" I clutched her arm before she could go on.

"I prefer *Pastry Chef.*"

Declan wavered beneath the coned front light. She almost appeared dented, "I didn't know that about you, Basil."

I nodded. "I try very hard to seem untalented," I don't.

"I'd really love to stay, and I know my brother would too, but we really have to get home now," Declan spoke into the hall, as I stood on one side of her sentence and my mom and dad stood on the other.

It was easy for Declan to look like a toddler, in the same way it was easy for Wesley to act like one. She stood with an eclipsed outlook into my world, and was one of the first Villetoners to do so. I was so busy contriving how I could insert myself into her group's tableau, that I hadn't stopped to unbox my own fragments.

Chapter 9

: 9

11pm sugar rushes are the best, but 1am is even better. My parents are dreaming of paperwork and fax machines that no one uses anymore. My dad is drawing up his gaming to real-work ratio, and my mom is skimming through tax information. The house is inkling for a tang of my honey baklava, and I have the stove preheated to 350. I should turn down right about now. This season is so much more enjoyable when something is in the oven.

All I have is a bag full of trail mix and enough will to separate chocolate covered espresso beans for the next five minutes. I mix my sugar, honey, and water in a shallow pan over a crying fire. Every ingredient dissipates into the other, the smell already professes its love for me. I smile and coat the trail mix blend with a dash of brown sugar and cinnamon. The platter greets me until I abandon it for a pot full of unmelted butter.

It took me a few tries to finally source the phyllo dough, but after shoving several pounds of leftover hot wings to the side, there it was. It had defrosted perfectly; nothing in my life goes to waste. I unravel the roll and wash my hands over the thin material. I dip my fingertips in our jar full of flour and begin to sprinkle them across the phyllo. This is unnecessary but makes me feel like I belong to this mess I call a meal.

I smother the first layer with my paint bristle. I repeat for the next nine layers before I trickle my trail along the top. The cranberry gives the adjacent nuts a glimpse of radiance. I never knew fruit as being so visually decadent, especially when they're almost dying. Before I take a mental picture, I draw another layer of phyllo to seal the crackling collage.

My cousin told me I was boring once and I believed that for a really long time. My cousin Taz lost her father two summers ago to a long battle with brain cancer. And like, I was sad about it, but he was the kind of guy who would nip the spoon whenever he would take a bite of lemon meringue—making that *ting* noise. I would grouch to my mom about how infuriating it was, and she would tell me how I needed to be kinder—but like, he was married into the family.

I added some more mix on top of my now plump dish. I can smell something in the oven burning, and I scowled at my father knowing he never took anything out of the oven—doesn't he know I'm the ruler of all midnight snacks?

My parents both grew up in the real New York City. My mom was from Queens and my dad was from Brooklyn. My dad said the first thing he noticed about my mother was her bad attitude, and it's one of the minor traits I inherited from her. My mom is the nicest person I know, and I know most people say that about their parents, but she is *too* nice. She always tells me that I'm going to grow out of my snarkiness, but I'd have to want to change to initiate it.

Thirty more layers to go.

Like my father with my mother, Elly must've seen something in me that made him want to ask me to be Tartula; I have the *je ne sais quoi* that probably fascinates him. He located me opposite Wesley's glare—now I'm his. Well, I'm my own, but I don't mind that submissive exterior that emerges whenever he's around. He doesn't find me boring at all, someone boring wouldn't release their body to a screen.

During my freshman year at Villeton, I remember seeing Elly in the hallway but not knowing who he was—I just thought it was a cute kid. His back aligned with the vinyl floor tiles and his legs were perpendicular to the lockers. I don't know what he was doing in the freshman hall because at the time he was a senior, but I did know something, he clashed against every high school dream. It was the first and only time I had seen him until the more recent bonfire, and even then I was cheated oxygen.

He looked like algae pulled out from the depths of the ocean. His hair was even longer then, unkept and wringing out malevolent thoughts. He played with a small toy, something that rang when it jiggled. It was evident that this was someone I shouldn't get too close to, but wanted nothing more. I'll never forget what he had on. A soaking wet maroon crewneck and navy cargo pants that were oddly dry. I wanted to wait and see what would happen when the bell rang, but I instead walked in the opposite direction.

I turned around once to see if he acknowledged me at all.

He did.

Twenty more layers.

How am I going to tell Elly his film scares me? That my pubescence is brimming with syrups, cocoa and fondant. I don't bake at 350, I poach until I'm reasonably tender. I've gone far enough to get a grip on how things are, but I'm not sure when it's okay to make things stop. I should keep going because I've made it this far. Like, I've made Turkish cuisine.

Ten more layers.

I'm friendless not because I'm moody or harsh, but because I can't stick. Maybe that's what watered my pastry venture; the quality of meshed ingredients that become irresistible when combined—it makes me look like a fool. I don't go with anything, I only conduct the process.

Not until I met Elly was I the finishing touch. He drizzled me all over his scrumptious clan.

Now I'm the secret component.

Time to bake.

Chapter 10

:P

Me then Declan then Lane.

Lane's bed felt like it was stuffed with hatred, but I hatched comfort in the oddities of the surroundings—including Lane and Declan. I've never laid so close to girls who weren't my cousin. The experience ended up being so benign, that I couldn't help but to get tangled up in it with Lane's amethyst sheets.

Lane only lived with her uncle, and their small apartment was stacked full of shallow memories. Her uncle was gone for the weekend, and according to Lane he loved to shower his boyfriend in nothing but getaways. It was clear that Lane had recently moved in, but it was also clear that her uncle was a bit of a simple dude.

Their apartment was small, and Lane confessed that she could always hear her uncle hooking up with his guy whenever they were around. Lane said that even though the apartment was cramped, she still had more room than she had in her old space in the city. She told us how she gets along with her uncle because he thinks things through, and she pretty much left it at that.

"Do you think Milo likes me, when I say like—fuck that, you know what I mean," Lane leaned forward and reached for her charging phone. "Black Beauty, full transparency, I'm talking about Milo Hunter."

Figured, the unauthorized continuation of Elly.

"Yeah," Declan was lying. "Why wouldn't he?"

"The other night I saw him and he was looking at me, but not in the way he usually does," Lane was speed texting, her bangs dispersed to each of her temples.

"I totally get that," if there was anyone who wouldn't get it, it would be Declan.

"It was as if he was making eye contact just to make eye contact. OHMY-see! Let me read you this."

Lane began filling us in on the external details of the text convo; where she was at and why she texted him first. I stopped listening way too late. Instead, I thought about my conversation with Elly, and how he convinced me that I should be here right now—that friendships oil the recluse. It takes more to enamor me with the jarring pretense of white-girl raillery, especially when the end goal is a fantastical broadcast brought to you by me.

"I think Milo likes you more than he thinks," Declan hummed.

"He's a little dumb but I freaks with it. BB, how do I get a guy to anchor my G?" Lane directed that sentence at me.

I have to shit. "Uhm. I'll be right back."

The bathroom was old and un-renovated. My unclothed feet caught frostbite just from walking from the doorway to the toilet. I could hear Lane still going on about Milo from the bathroom door, and I wondered if she knew that Milo was cheating on her. I don't think my introduction to sleepovers would be the intervention Lane needed regarding her relationship. I made my pee go a little faster so it could shoot into the bowl loud enough to block out Lane's jabber.

I forgot my phone in the room, so I was left to stare at the shower curtain. A cotton fabric full of matryoshka dolls that looked like it needed a quick spin in the washer. There were these funny knickknacks all around the bathroom. Each toiletry item had its own porcelain encasing, and the mirror clashed with the general mood of the room. Eventually I stopped peeing, but the longer I stayed, the more I'd find. Like, cast iron sculptures of mice. Bizarre.

"Hey Basil," a knock came from the outside. It was Declan's voice.

"Give me a second," I wiped before pulling my trousers up, walking over to the sink. "You can come in."

"Sorry, I really have to go! It must've been the beer," without stalling, Declan threw herself onto the potty and belted a sigh. "I hope this has been fun for you."

Oh, so we're gonna have a conversation.

"I'm having a great time. Are you?"

She nodded, looking up at me. "I am. It's nice to spend some time with you, now that I know you're dating my brother.

"It all happened so suddenly. Elly is the first boyfriend I ever had, so I'm not sure if I'm doing this right."

Declan shook her bum over the toilet before snagging some paper. "Really?"

"Yeah," I replied. She lifted her boy shorts to her waist, crowding over me by the sink.

"If you don't mind me asking, why do you like my brother, Basil?"

For years, I woke up and I went to school. I never asked how I got there, or what I was doing there—but I accepted my environment for what it was. Cool. In front of me and beside me, students conjoined and confided in each other. Everyone had this verbiage that was too alien for me, and if it were explained, I wouldn't get it anyway. I wasn't caught up on the insider, I wasn't even the inside joke. I was never harassed or bullied, I wasn't notable enough for that. But, I continued to go and be present, no one asked who I was and I grew to learn that it was because no one cared.

My cousin was the only friend I had, and when my parents found that out, they adopted a bunny. Taz started making more friends at school, and when she was invited to her own play parties, she had to take a rain check for mine. My parents tried to conceal it, and by doing so, they replaced the friends that I never had with friends that I'll never lose—them.

Elly. He never called himself a friend, but that was never his intention. He saw me on the edge of a cliff at a bonfire, making out with a boy whose tongue felt like a wrung towel. He noticed me there and made the crowd notice too. When I'm at Villeton people fight the urge to ask me who I am, and why would Elly Hayes pick me? Now his sister is asking why would I pick her brother, and if that's not a token that we're meant to be —I don't want it.

But for the sake of time. "He's just really nice."

"Wow, no one has ever described my brother as being *nice*. That might be because you see the good in people."

I snorted. "You don't know me well enough to say that."

Declan moved a strand of hair from my ear and touched my helix with her murmur. "I know you more than you think."

Back in the room, Lane was still going off about Milo. While Declan and I were in the restroom, it came to our attention that Lane and Milo had agreed to take a break. Five minutes after that, Lane texted Milo asking him if he still needed an ounce. Milo, who has no money because he's a high school student, responded saying yes but only had one form of currency. Lane was totally alright with Milo selling himself out for drugs, and they were back to aggressively texting within minutes.

The way I interacted with Elly was polar opposite to how Lane interacted with Milo. My conversations with Elly were a bounty of what-ifs and very-likely possibilities. I was his, but I still took the time to float along in his conscience. Right now, I'm pretty things and costly g-strings. A set primped with the versions of me that for some reason, he draws out so painlessly. Being in his movie was a disheartening thought, but why did it tinge me so noticeably lively?

"What were we talking about?" Lane finally put her phone down, and curled up next to us as we got back in our assemblage.

"We were talking about, should Lane get Declan another beer?" Declan giggled.

Lane laced her arm around the two of us. "Piss off."

It grew silent. I listened closely to the noises pouring in through the window. It was raining outside, and the drops tapped on her window sill—*plop-plopping* and cleansing the pensive moment. Our exhales all combined and mixed with the rain's chatter. There was something about the suddenness of the storm that humbled each of us, making us forget about routines. I could feel Declan's hand rustle into mine and we saluted indolence.

"Do you think Betelgeuse knows any of our names?" Lane exhaled. Nobody answered her but I knew it was on all of our minds until we drifted to sleep.

Cold palms ran up my back in the middle of the night. Through Lane's fine snooze, I knew she was fast asleep, but the hands continued. They scratched on my spine, and found their place at the tip of my abdomen. I was uncertain whether I should turn around and ask Declan if she was afraid of the dark because sometimes I still am.

"Your skin is really soft, Basil," her exquisite voice hide beyond my cochlea.

"I thought you were sleeping."

"I couldn't sleep," the more we spooned, the warmer her body became. It was nice? "I hope this isn't weird...me cuddling you."

It's so weird.

"No, it's okay."

Declan smells like Elly, but with a mixture of lavender.

Easy now.

"I sleep with a stuffed animal," Declan sneered. "You are almost identical."

"I resemble your teddy bear?" I turned around to give her a noticeably daunting look, but I could see that her eyes were shut.

"You resemble comfort," her eyelids drifted up and grinned at my appearance.

I removed Declan's limbs from around my body and created inclusions between her arms with mine. I started to wind down into her, and collect her narrow back with my hug. She sat limp and immobile until finally giving in. She felt like Elly, or at least what Elly *could* feel like. I washed my face with her hair texture that matched Elly's. Soon enough, I was sitting on top of her, dissolving in our wreckage. She was Elly if I closed my eyes.

"Basil, are you there?" She muttered.

I gently stationed my hand on top of Declan's mouth. The pace of her heart was like Elly's, chaotic and enticing—but also a little too hot. Her smell, herSMELL, like Elly's. Smelling like Elly. Elly. Elly. Her exterior, so ripe like Elly's when he is near me—next to me. The outlining of her lips linking with my fingers, almost like Elly's, but too plump. If I squeeze tight to try to remold them, they could almost be perfect. They could almost be Elly's lips.

I rocked on top of her. I listened out to see if Lane was still asleep, and her back was fully turned to us. Declan suppressed her urge to scuffle. My merciless glare couldn't get enough of the way she became dormant. I didn't want to be that to her; to be the thing holding her down when only seconds ago I was her designated plushie. My frailty was my coating and she bypassed that. Some way, she did this all on purpose.

I think that if I imagine hard enough, Elly could be here.

"Basil," she groaned. I released her voice. "Can you bake for me sometime?"

"Yeah," why does she say the things that I wish Elly would shout?

Chapter 11

;D

Elly: Basil.
Elly: Are you awake?
Me: yeah
Elly: Can I see you?
Me: yeah
Elly: Thank you.
Elly: Are they asleep?

Baby's-breath vines spun around the rearview mirror. The middle of the night has an irresistible stench, and I imagined myself smoking on it. The car became a pawn to the flower's odor. As soon as I entered the vehicle, it washed out the fabric softener on my clothes. Elly watched me stew in it. He admired me for a little before driving off.

"I was going to take you back to my place but my parents are still awake," a herd of birds flew in between the stars. I couldn't find him yet.

"You wanted to go back to yours?"

"I wanted to do some test shots."

Elly was always so focused when he drove, a much better driver than Wesley. I remember being in the car with Wesley on our way to the bonfire and practicing my faith like never before. Wesley drives like the road is coated with marshmallows and gummy bears—which in his mind, I'm pretty sure it is. Elly drives like he wants to be here, but also it makes me wonder if it's him trying to prove that to me so I don't run away.

It was never the appropriate time to ask Elly if he's okay. I never captured it as a discovery in the middle of the night. Through all the rumors I've heard of him, the one that created a splinter in my lifestyle was him trying to leave us all behind. How could someone that seems as if they have everything in front of them, can see nothing at all? It wasn't like Elly was trying to put on a happy face either, maybe it would make people feel too sorry for him.

I'll let it go for now.

His hair was pushed back into a sorrowful bun. I've never seen his face like this before. I should've made more of an effort to appeal to the scenario. A linty sweatshirt and thigh-high platforms. I wanted to be cool and *girly*, but how does that even transcribe? Feminine energy pretends to be conceivable.

"Is this a good time to make-out?" I was kidding, but not. I rubbed two hair coils in-between my fingers. Declan had left a mark on my pointer, the fresh tear is what kept me awake.

He stopped, not expecting that at all, and honestly—me either. "I can't kiss you."

"Why?"

He proceeded. "I'm nineteen, Basil."

"I'm your girlfriend and I give you consent. Why even ask me out?"

"I needed reasons to be around you."

We stopped again. He made a U-turn by the hospital and began driving back towards Lane's house. Or where I thought we'd be going. He closed his eyes and opened them. Then closed them once more and opened them again. Then repeat-repeat, I concluded we'd get into an accident. I accepted I'd die like this.

"For what? Just for the film? That's all?"

"No."

"I need you to give me something, Elly," I demanded for once—it was the restlessness talking.

He pulled into a supermarket parking lot. We brewed our thoughts in the baby-breath's mist; it was hella calming. My phone started to gyrate inside of my boot sleeve. I pulled it up and saw the *Dec* being highlighted. I peered at Elly and he saw it too. Why did I feel guilty? I allowed the phone to slither deeper into my shoe. I decided not to mention it unless he did.

"You should let her know where you are," and he did.

"She can wait," I sighed. "Will you give me something?"

"When I was your age kissing was more than a statement."

"Don't speak to me as if we weren't in the same high school at the same time."

He sneered. "I know."

We chilled with the windows rolled down, each of us making up our own internal narrative of the moment. Elly retrieved a candy bar from his glove compartment. He unwrapped it and offered me a piece, I declined. He pushed the whole bar into his cheek and gnawed down until it was smooth enough to swallow. He took out another bar and did the same.

"My mom used to give me candy when I was a kid to make me shut up," he hardly said anything that didn't pertain to the film or the way that I looked before, so I wanted to take this for all it was worth.

"Are you telling yourself you need to be quiet now?"

He smirked. "I don't want to say the wrong thing to you."

"Up until now, you've said all the right things. That's why I'm here."

A brisk paw met my knee. His fondling eyesight tinted the car's windows and darkness sunk in. He unbuckled his seat belt and it relapsed from our apprehension. He elegantly maneuvered himself to face me, I still had a difficult time redefining our eye contact. I think I thought that I wasn't really allowed to. Like, he wouldn't let me.

I gulped in the fat from my bottom lip to keep me from smiling. The peak of his nose pierced mine, and I could predict his tongue's aftertaste at this point. He jittered before chafing his mouth to mine. His skin was unreal, it felt like dandelion fluff that never flies away in the jealous wind. I was digging a grave for the siren that leaked at the bottom of my throat. His other hand slung around my waist and hovered me slightly above the passenger's seat.

"Explain to me," he spoke. "What is this feeling that you're experiencing?"

"Shut up and kiss me already," I mouthed. Our lips were so close, he could mock my speech.

"Is it warm? Does it make the sky lose its ability to cast moods?"

A ripple of singes made my skin writhe in misery. It traveled up my legs and through my arms. I couldn't tell if there was something on me, or if the heater had been turned up to unbearable. It was a sensation that was planted in my bloodstream, and I wanted nothing else but to get it out. NOW!

"Elly, stop."

"What would you do for it? Would you forget who you were?"

The burns had names on them. They had mistakes and rues. It was all over. Teeming now from my shoulder tips to my neck. It was a pitiless agony that impaired me the more Elly came in.

BURNS!

"Stop it!" Fire built up in my nervous system and plagued my judgment. I could see him casting these scorches onto me, and injecting them through the layers I had. My body was shaking from horror and confusion. His eyes were a leaky-torturous blue, and they told me they saw me for exactly what I was.

"Would you surrender who you might become?"

"ELLY!"

My nails defied his posture, clawing into his ribcage and forcing him to trip back into his seat. The strike caused some of the flowers to quiver and break from the stem. My body returned to normal with no traces of smoke or ash dawdling.

"What was that?"

He let his hair down and massaged his scalp. "What?"

"You burned me, Elly."

"What are you talking about? No, I didn't."

There was no lighter in his hand, and if there was one there—he was super good at being deceitful. If he had sparked a flame, there would be clues. There would be scars left on my skin, and the only thing I was lacerated from was his missed touch. Shit. Is this what it's like to be in love and to be completely dependent? I think I'm built too well for this sort of thing. How could I have imagined all of that?

"I thought you wanted to kiss," his stare was back to normal.

"I did, but clearly you didn't. You started asking me questions right before we got the chance," I couldn't feel anything anymore, not even him.

"I wanted to get you ready for the film."

"Can we take, I don't know—maybe five minutes to not think about the film? Why is everything about the film?"

He twitched.

"I'd like to think the film is what brought us together, Basil," he looped his hand with mine. "I want it to be good— for you."

The moon made a fierce playlist. I unlocked my seat's lever and jostled backward. I could hear another car pull into the lot, its engine was wasted and belligerent. Elly's attention was stolen by the stranger's prominence. His lips curled and became a disastrous simper. His knuckles rang from the crickets that resided within his fine fingers.

The tempered motor paused. I was now listening to the car's door croak and sway open. A nasty thing. Whoever-it-was escaped, they had on heels or something with a sole that impolitely exhales. Their direction was boisterous and aimed; they were coming to us. Elly's smirk was now a pretty-please teethy smile.

"I think I know her," he exclaimed.

Humiliation had a certain grime. It was almost like it festered from chosen ignorance. I don't think there's a way to lose it. The kind of funk that won't wipe away with a damp toilette. A shrilling voice in a crowd of meekness, purging from an afterthought. I think I clogged the drain with the front I put on. I can, for the most part, always push a smile but I can't stop my tongue from falling numb.

"Hi Declan," Elly whistled her name. She stood by his window; the glass still pulled down.

Declan's shriveled strands made fun of Elly's bun, but they were true visions of each other. However, Declan's hair held a particular privilege that Elly's killed itself for. It kinda started to make sense.

Or I'm really good at faking it.

"Basil, I thought something happened to you," worry was all over her powder blue eyes.

"She's fine, she's with me," Elly gave a mirthless smile. "You can go back to your sleepover now."

"Do you want to stay here or come with me?" Declan's breath scratched at the jeep.

"*Il vaut mieux être en bonne compagnie que seul,*" Elly hummed.

This was the first moment I had with Elly where we were completely alone. I always discovered people on the other side, nipping at the ends of my flower bud—my baby's breath—my time. There was something I needed to find out that was implanted in our soft tension. The hesitations that stained the hours I was left to myself. I can't be alone again, not after I've had Elly Hayes.

"I'll stay if you kiss me," and there it was, my first ultimatum.

Elly's cheekbones became poisoned with a thirsty red. He laughed at me, "I'll see you later then."

Declan told me that the car belonged to Lane's uncle. Lane described her uncle as being a scholar, but I assumed that a person with such divine intellect would at least have a well-functioning car. My dad blew enough cash into the wagon we had now, which he says is the reason I don't have my license, but I truly believe it is their way of quenching my independence.

"I wanted to ask you a favor, Basil." Declan drove so politely, despite the lingering vile atmosphere. My eyes couldn't help but to be closed.

I don't think anyone has ever asked me for a favor before, totally scratching out my parents. "Sure."

"The Cheer Babes are having a fundraiser, and I wanted to know if you'd be willing to donate your baking talents— maybe with some Villeton themed cupcakes?"

jusssayno.

"You want me to do it? That's so flattering."

"I couldn't stop thinking about the way your mom talked about your baking skills. She speaks so highly of you."

"They're a smidgen above mediocre," I giggled and opened my eyes. Declan's complete attention was firmly rooted to me, forgetting the road ever existed.

We stopped.

"Can I ask you for another favor, Basil?"

"Yeah."

"Can we still be friends after this?"

Right before the kiss, the passenger's seat told me about the mysteries that injured the interior design. It spilled the scenes of Lane and Milo Hunter dusting off the fragments that held together their relationship. It gave me reasons as to why the woven cushion had grown exhausted from thirty pound anthologies. It said too much. But one thing it couldn't recover from, was the stress of bitten lips when they hold more than secrets.

Chapter 12

;0

"Hear me out, the femme movement is dead," it was 11am, and Lane was already on the go.

Declan swung a throw pillow in Lane's direction but instead hit the fridge. "Be careful."

"How could I believe in a movement where the only way to successfully gain equality, is to obtain the acceptance from a man. Who the hell is a dicksie to solidify my acceptance?"

"Lane, for someone with the academic success that you have, you can sometimes sound really stupid."

"Dec, are kidding me? Have you even read the article by QonciousQueef? They DEPLORED feminism! BB, tell me I'm not the only one with this logic. Also, feminism doesn't do bull for black women."

Declan was now tiger crouching in the armchair. "Feminism wouldn't have to be a movement if men didn't suck so bad. Think about it, Lane! At one point in time, men were so bad at being men, that women had to step in to save them from themselves. And the minute we did, they said—wait, women can't compromise our masculinity!" Declan wasn't much of a talker, but when it came to passion, she wasn't short to show her wings.

I should know.

"I'm not going to come to a conclusion until Black Beauty chimes in!"

We were all unwinding in Lane's living room. The kitchen was separated by a slender island; where Lane stood slim and sleek in her tank and sweats. Her uncle was still absent, which left Lane feeling even more rebellious than her usual self. Her version of rebellion included using her uncle's Japanese imported china and arguing about feminism. They had no dining table, but an extremely spacious glass tabletop that was held up by stacks of hardcovers.

I don't know if rooms have people preferences. If my room could talk, it'd probably have some kind of dad-block, or maybe even vegetarian-stopper—I hate vegetarians, in theory, they're smooth, but in practice they're ruthless. The room that I'm currently in holds a bit of dread that competes with assertion. I'm really not into that, and particularly when I'm miming my drawbacks through Lane's graciously burnt omelet.

I wasn't ignoring Declan, but I tried my hardest not to say anything that would catch her interest, or make her want to respond. All my responses this morning have been brief and calculated. I was doing a remarkable job, right up until Lane decided to bring up black women.

"I don't know. I'm not really good at talking about this stuff," and my parents would kill me if they heard me say that.

Declan rolled her eyes, not at what I said, but at my cheating out of the conversation. "Black feminism was a crucial part of feminist history—still feminism. Even queer liberation—still feminism and freedom of expression."

"I really wish Wesley was here sometimes because at least I know he's too much of a doof to have an argument about this stuff," Lane whistled. This wasn't even hard stuff to argue about it, but I shouldn't be the one giving out degrees.

"Are you saying you miss Wesley?" Declan asked.

Lane squirted some easy cheese in her mouth. "I guess I do miss that pimple-headed mofo. Y'know, what I was thinking? It's been a while since the three of us have been to Eight Ball."

"Oh my God—yes! Basil would love Eight Ball," Declan smiled. Post shower varnished Declan in magnificence. She sat parallel from me on a wine armchair, I took the hunter one. Her crinkled hair flopped over her grey sweatshirt, leaving damp striations around her chest.

"Elly was talking about going to the city next weekend. We should drop by Eight Ball," Lane flung a cheese cracker at me, "You jello, BB? I just mentioned Elly and you didn't spazz."

no.

"Sorry, I'm kinda tired. Prolly need some water or something."

"I'm making coffee! That'll wake you up."

Declan looped her eyes around me before heading to Lane's room. Lane creased her nose up at Declan's escape. She removed two carved wooden mugs from the cabinet and charged them up with coffee. A small blob landed on the countertop and Lane slurped it up with her tongue, which I now know is pierced.

I don't care if people wear makeup, but seeing Lane drowning in her freckles made me question who else in Villeton is hiding. I had no clue Lane had even more freckles than Wesley, who prances proudly in his dotted face. Her blonde hair struggled to hold itself in its drowsy ponytail; budding from coffee roots.

"Here you go, BB!"

She dropped the cup in front of me, and without hesitation and fear, I choked it down. My tongue ached from the fierce temperature, but I knew it would only last for an hour or two. If I'm lucky it will last the entire day, and anchor in my attention. Maybe the caffeine will give me the boost I need to get away.

"Damn! Don't burn your tongue! Were you thirsty?" Lane unwinded to the floor.

"More than I thought," I answered, and she gently punched my knee. "Lane, I have to tell you something."

I was going to tell Lane about Declan's kiss. I needed to tell someone or I will end up telling Elly, and I wasn't 100% sold on telling him yet. Lane and I weren't close, but she was too unrefined to not be upfront with.

"I think I know what you're going to say."

Declan beat me to the punch? "You do?"

"Duh! Do you think I'm that much of a sleeb to not pick up on social cues? I'm not Wesley for God's sake."

"Is it really that obvious?"

"Yeah, you always look like you're about to puke," it's that apparent, huh. "You have my word, BB. I won't tell Elly."

"Thanks Lane, I want to tell him at some point. I'm just not ready yet."

"I get it! It's a lead role packed full of nudity. But, I think you're the perfect fit to play Tartula. Don't give yourself a hern over nervousness."

I really need to get better at explaining myself. Lane thinks I'm having second thoughts about playing Tartula, which I always have, but it's not at the forefront of my mind. Wonderful—Lane reminded me that I should be stressing over issues that I really should be stressing over. A kiss with Declan in Lane's uncle's car was in actuality, the least of my problems. If this is what it's like to be a Villetoner, where is the line for expulsion?

"You gotta tell me one thing though, Black Beauty."

Sigh. "Sure."

"Are you really a virgin, or are you flippin' my burger?"

Uh. "I've gone to third base, but I've never had sex. So to answer your question, yes—I'm a virgin."

"Oh! Have you ever hooked up with Milo Hunter before?"

I coughed. Some already digested coffee flew up. "What? No. Aren't you two kind-of together?"

"Yeah, but it's not unusual I find out he's banged my friends," she called me her friend. "Him and Dec hooked up before."

"Seriously?!"

I wanted to be more surprised, but I wasn't. I wonder how many times people look at Lane then quickly goggle at

Declan. Lane was always the sidekick or the one who was adjacent to the person that broils under a spotlight. Even now as Lane spoke to me, I couldn't stop myself from thinking about what Declan was doing. My intestines urged my nerves to reveal the instances of last night, but wouldn't I be part of the reason Lane stays the subcategory? Prolly.

Lane took a chug of her coffee, then wiped her brown mustache from her lips. "Yeah, but it's drippy. It's one of those things that come with being her friend. She was kinda the first friend I made when I moved here, so I can't complain too much."

"Oh yeah! You moved here from the city, right?" I asked, Lane nodded.

"Good ole NYC."

"Do you miss it?"

"Do I miss sleeping in a two bedroom apartment with a million little nip-titters? No. However, I do miss taking the train and slerbin' churros off the little Mexican ladies."

It got quiet after that. We continued sitting next to each other, not saying a word but casually forwarding funny images to each other. Lane would get up and go to the kitchen to retrieve something crunchier than her last snack. I think Declan had fallen asleep because an hour had gone by, and I could now hear the turning vents come from Lane's apartment heating. Lane would mutter some lyrics under her breath and I thought about telling her she should be a singer, but too much time had passed before I could mock up an appropriate compliment.

"Are you excited for this weekend?" She cracked the silence.

"What's happening this weekend? Eighth's Hall, right?"

Lane quacked. "Eight Ball, you sleeb! But no, I'm talking about The Grand Babette."

"The Grand Babette?"

"The nice-ass hotel downtown. Aren't you part of the group texts?"

"No," my stomach was now in my uterus.

"Elly booked a hotel to see if it's the *one*."

"Why do we need a hotel? Isn't Tartula some kind of nature nymph? Wouldn't a hotel be counterintuitive?" I was SHIVERING.

The ceiling was attached to a booby trap. The gallops from the upstairs neighbors discharged along the drywall. They spelled something out to me, it was more than likely Elly's full name; the name I can't say. I lifted my arm to wipe it off, but it continued to mark up the entire wall—up and over the kakejiku wall scrolls. Why does Lane's uncle own so many Japanese artifacts? Why does he fantasize Japanese men?

Lane's phone wafted up, making spirals above her head. "You're added to the group chat! As the creative director, I have to say I agree with you, BB! I've got to tell you that I've had a more avant-garde location in mind."

"Lane."

"But I get it," her laugh left blisters across my chest. "He wants it to be more discreet and off site."

"LANE," the bones in my fingers couldn't hold themselves upright.

"Are you okay, Black Beauty? You've got that same puke look on your face that you had earlier."

What the pineapple soda was going on with me? My heart was digging a hole up my throat, and I was doing my absolute best to keep it from propelling out. I think that Lane's uncle's apartment may be haunted, and Elly is the instrument that we need to bless it properly. I had to get my phone—where is my phone? My phone has Elly in it. Ineedmyphone. I haven't spoken to Elly since last night! Where is my my phone?

"It's right here," Lane removed my phone that had turned into a ceiling fan above her head.

"Did I say that out loud?"

"Hm. I think I know what's going on," Lane spider crawled up a bookcase.

"Lane! My body doesn't make sense!" I leapt up and dogtrotted through the ro

o

m.

"BB," Lane's arms distorted themselves. "I put a bit of cannabis in the coffee."

"What?!"

NO.

"BB, you'll be fine. Okay?"

I had to let go of all of this hair; it was drugging me down too moroseLY.

BASIL.

The room was like, like a, like the Metropolitan Museum on a mid Saturday. Except the artifacts all spontaneously crowd around and perform a lackadaisical jig. Lane's apartment was a facsimile of the Metropolitan Museum, except the artifacts perform a lackadaisical jig. Lane's apartment was like the Museum. What Museum?

I'd like to go to Holland someday.

When I was in fifth grade, I told my mother I hated her because she came to chaperone the school trip, but I didn't hate her. I DIDN'T HATE HER. I didn't want anyone to see her bob cut box braids with bangs! I thought that if they couldn't see her, they wouldn't assume that I went home and listened to R&B through the surround sound of my upbringing.

My pores began to vibrate. I know this is what death felt like. When I first met Elly, he told me that sex was the closest thing to death, but the closest thing to death was devouring a canni-coffee at the break of day with a group of girls; one who is going to film me naked, and the other one who would probably love to see me naked.

I have a stringy labia that un-aligns all my panties on purpose.

The boy I went to third base with was from Mallory Prep, and I only stayed because he gave good head. I wanted him to forage through me and swallow me whole. I wanted to feel it at my pit until no one else could see me this way again. In my head, I would call on him and he would answer with lips full of the things I've never planned to lose.

"What's going on?" DECLAN.

"She's paranoid! I gave her some coffee."
"Why didn't you tell her, LANE?"
"Dude, I'm fucking sorry. I'm sorry, BB! I didn't know she
would act this way."

I used to want to look like Declan. Villeton is only brutal
to the in-advantaged, everyone else is a fallen backdrop.
"We need to give her some milk," Declan was doing a
handstand. I always thought of her as the best Cheer Babe.
If Tartula was really a person, she would fall captive to
the internal *zizz*. She'd like it. Fold it into a reason for everything
that has progressed in herself. *It's a coming of age story*, I was told.
Tartula doesn't mind making the story about her, but she
couldn't even be the title of the film. What's the title of the film?
I never know where I'm supposed to be.

"Basil, you should sit down."

I can't sit down because my feet turned into pulverized
coal. If I make any sort of movement, I'll have no feet at all. It's
comical because I used to pretend to be a mermaid, with gills
made of fountain pennies—capturing wishes as they sink to the
bottom.
Like Elly.
"You shouldn't have kissed me, Declan."

I was now sobbing. Whenever I cried people told me I'm
beautiful, I think that's what I hate about it so much. Lane
looked gross without makeup in the morning, and I leave mine
on so no one would ever look at me the same way I looked at
Lane. Now it's painting my nails as I claw at my wits.

"Basil," Declan began to melt.
"You two kissed?"
"Yeah, we kissed last night."
"Dude, she's dating your brother. That's almost like kissing your brother!"
"They've never kissed."

"YOU KNOW ELLY WON'T KISS ME!"

"I'm trying really hard not to get in the way of what you and Elly have, Basil," Declan was a puddle on the ground, pooling herself out.
"Then you should know more than anyone how much he means to me."
"I do know. I also know how much you mean to him, and that was exactly why I didn't stop myself."

Chapter 13

:c

KECKKKKKKKKK!

Chapter 14

: |

I either love bright food or foods that could kill me instantly. My dad was always a better cook than my mom, but my mom always made the food taste better; neither of them were consumed by presentation. Sections of my soul wished they sought after that kind of effort, and I wanted something besides myself to become obsessed with. It has ended up with me putting my worries into my dishes but also being my own judge.

There was a bead of sweat hanging at the base my tailbone, def rimming my crack. My kitchen pampered itself with the steaming streams that came from the oven. The room was beginning to lather in the soft early morning blues. It made me miss the night, but also made me feel proud for getting through. I was on my last batch of cupcakes, and the sun was thanking me with today.

"Just a few more minutes," golden and greens dressed my palms. The frosting admitted to me that I am only a high school student, and yes—I go to Villeton.

I stole a spoonful from the tub before inserting the frost into my piping. The lemon tang stood out a little more than I had anticipated, but there was nothing that could more accurately illustrate my feelings when it came to Villeton. The harsh interludes of sweetness, a dreary tart but a lot of aftertaste.

"You're still awake?" My mom had on her purple cheetah bathrobe and cat eyeglasses. How glam.

"Yeah. Trying to get this done."

"Is there anything I can help with?" She filled the kettle. That was her pretty much saying she didn't care to help, and mornings are reserved for coffee.

"I'm almost done, this would be the last dozen," the tank top I was wearing displayed the scars I had accumulated through the night.

We each continued our duties, the bubbling water replaced the typical wake-up radio station. My cellphone beeped and before I assumed it was my baking timer, it beeped again. I looked at the screen and found Elly's name relaxed at the top of an unopened message. Tell me what feels better than that?

"Why are you smiling?" My mom smiled while asking.

Elly: It's been too long.
Elly: I'll see you tonight.

Tonight was the night the four of us were going to drive down to the parts of NYC people knew the names of. It would be my first extensive night alone with Elly, and though there was an objective at the end, there would be me. I had done absolutely nothing to prepare for this moment but occupy the bathroom a little longer than usual for shaving purposes. I felt a rapture rupture through my skin, and it reminded me of baking.

I was still running from the kiss I shared with Declan. I knew this was something I had to tell Elly because I wouldn't want him to find out any other way, but I wasn't sure if I should. No matter what corner I welcomed myself into, Declan was always behind me. She was on the other end of a friendship that I slipped into, and I couldn't get past her impact. I wasn't sure if I should tell Elly because I liked it.

"Basil?" My mom called.

I had to write back.

Me: Can you come to the bake sale

"Excuse me, Basil."

Elly: Did you think I wasn't going?

"Basil!"

"The cupcakes!"

I was able to rescue the babies before they were an undesirable dijon. The smell was supple seduction and it took every overworked muscle in my body to not give in to it—to not take a bite. I was so greedy that I couldn't apprehend the seconds before I had my hands around the dish, that was now burning my phalanges. The feeling hijacked me to my moments alone with Elly in his car, and right before the kiss we never shared.

"Basil, I'm speaking to you."

Oh. Mom. "I'm sorry, what did you say?"

"I asked you why are you smiling? Are you talking to your boyfriend?"

"Yeah, I am."

Nothing.

"I can't wait to meet him! How was last weekend? We never got the chance to talk about it. Every day you've been coming home and going straight to your room."

"I've been really busy with school work and trying to mentally prepare for last night. Obviously I didn't prepare much because I just pulled an all nighter."

My mom had an advantage over me. She could look at me and know something. Sometimes, I wouldn't know what she was referring to, but she would and then it would come into fruition. I was puffing up my chest to seem like I was doing alright, and hoping it would make her pry a little less.

"I heard you crying the other night," I failed.

As much as I would love to talk to my mom about my first drug trip, the trip itself wouldn't present the memory. I could only recognize my soles hopscotching up into my room because I was sure if the floor was concaving inward. The crying wove with my nightmares and fatigued the snippets of myself that were hidden beneath a purgatory. I think that instance was a big deal for me, or it could be obsolete.

"I really don't know what you're talking about."

"Did someone do something to you? Did you get hurt?" The only hurt I felt was the restraint that came from Elly, but how could I clarify?

"No one hurt me."

"What about your boyfriend? Elijah?" Nope.

"That's not his name, his name is Elly."

"L-EEE? Is that short for something?"

My tongue pivoted upwards, but my breath forbade the name. "Yes," change the subject. "I think I love him?"

Wrong change.

My mom heard what I said but I don't think she *heard* what I said. She stirred her teaspoon around the brim of her drink before wandering into a laughing spree. It was adorable for about ten seconds until her body couldn't hold her hysteria. She slanted onto the kitchen island for composure and left my side of the conversation fending for its integrity.

"Why is that so funny?" I had to know.

She managed to turn down the tease. "You know who I love? I love your father and you, and I didn't start loving your father until after I had you. Remember when we talked about experiences?

"How could I forget."

"Love requires an experience. You have not experienced enough with your boyfriend to know that you love him."

I took my spatula from the countertop and began icing the batch of cool cakes I had. This was a signal to my mom that I was finished with the conversation, and she may go upstairs to watch infomercials. I was becoming antsy, and it showed on the way I smoothed out the edges of the cupcake. I couldn't let my emotions ruin this—this is the one thing I know I have.

"Look at me, Basil."

"Let me finish this, please."

I was almost done, I only had anther dozen to go and I would officially be finished. I had tonight on my mind, and it's what controlled my stamina. If Elly was in charge, I could bake another sixty cupcakes without knowing tired.

"You have frosting in your hair," she was now doing that thing she always does, which is to irritate me even more to get me to talk.

"I know. I really need to wash my hair, but I know it's going to take forever to dry. Mom, can you help me blow dry it and then straighten it afterward?"

She gasped. I tried to casually ask without it becoming the revolving point of our conversation. For me to ask to straighten my hair was to ask my mom to put a knife to her ovaries. She thought that straightened hair was me admitting to myself that I would rather be anything other than black, and it was her liability.

"You haven't asked me to do that since you were in elementary school," she turned her back to me, now working something out of the fridge.

"I don't know. Sometimes I want to try different things. Is there something wrong with that?"

She rammed a box of eggs onto the marbled countertop. "Basil, how many eggs are in the carton?"

"Like, three?"

"I tell you again and again, Basil. Once you see the eggs are coming to an end, you go out and buy a new carton. You get a weekly allowance, and you need to start using that to fund your baking expenses!"

She was upset. "Okay."

"You don't need to straighten your hair. You have hair that I wish I had. It's long, it's full of all kinds of textures and bodies. Your hair is your present to me as your mother."

JADE BROWN

My hair has a mysterious quality that even I'm trying to figure out. It guides me through my life, sometimes speaking to me from a fourth grader's heckle, telling me to go back to the jungle I came from. But, my hair is also something that Elly can't stop gazing at whenever we're together. I like that my hair intrigues him, he really intrigues me too. I'll mess with the strands only to apprehend his attention. Look at me, Elly. Look at me.

"Basil!"

"Huh?" My mom placed the egg into a pot of boiling water. I don't recall her filling the pot, or retrieving the egg.

"There you go, zoning out again."

Elly: Talk to me.
Elly: I need to see you.
Elly: I can't stay away this long again.

Elly, I know. Elly I won't let that happen again, and tonight, I will tell you how I feel. I will tell you what slipped during my frivolous conversation with my mother. I will explain to you why you give me the determination to bake, and to bake for the one place I can't stand the most. Elly, you make things so tolerable. Tell me how you do it. Tell me that you'll feel the same about me—tell me exactly that. Tell me how you don't want me to play Tartula because I AM Tartula to you.

Me: It's been so hard.
Me: Tonight is going to be our night

No matter the circumstances, Elly and I were going to do more than kiss tonight. Elly will see me for the woman that I've

120

stepped into. He will acknowledge my maturity, and reconsider all the doubts he's had up to this point. Wherever it happened, it wouldn't matter. As long as I'm with Elly and he is with me. I will give myself to him, just as he's given his severed soul for me.

"Basil!"

"SHUT UP!"

My hair was plaited into two oversized French braids. I was breaking every culinary rule in the book, but I unbounded the twists from their formation and raked them loose. The whiff of unwashed scalp replaced the trail of fresh new cupcakes. I took a coil and elongated it down past my nipple. I fluffed it through some more and my mom was on the opposite side of the island, astonished by my impromptu acts.

It's in the hair somewhere. The soliloquy that abides by my connection to my mangled birthright. It has to be the answer to something. It can stop something, it can start something, it can become anything if it buds straight from colorful concepts. It is who I am, so I should have no problem addressing it outside of its mane.

"If you talk to me like that again Basil, you can go and find a new place to stay," my mother immersed in her coffee breath.

Mom, I already have.

Chapter 15

:x

Before it was me and Elly, it was Elly and Pavia.
His real relationship.

"What's wrong with her skin?" A boy laughed, pointing and screeching.

This was back when I was a freshman. The sophomores were celebrating their spirit week, and as a result, they teepee'd the freshman hall with streamer spray. I was hiding behind a vacant classroom door with a group of students who feared for their lives. I thought the strings were a parade of colors I'd forgotten.

"She's albino," someone answered referring to Pavia, who had the essence of the sophomore's leader.

"She's ugly as hell."

"If I were you, I wouldn't talk shit about her. She's Elly's girl."

Then it stopped. The guy ceased his attack on Pavia and after another twenty minutes, and a few teachers intervening, we were out of the classroom.

It was after that incident that I started noticing Pavia a lot more. She was so cute, so girly—so likable. She had this way of talking that made people want to feel sorry for her, but they weren't because she was so damn charismatic. Whenever she would complain about problems regarding her eyes, someone was on it—ensuring she wouldn't go blind. If she dropped a notebook in the hall, it would be less than two seconds before the entire hallway was in a frenzy trying to rescue the book.

"It's only because she's dating Elly Hayes, there's nothing else special about her," some rando would say once in a while.

"Yeah, he probably feels sorry for her."

I never saw Pavia and Elly together, but it was known that they were. Pavia would remain in a good mood, jumping around Villeton with her yellow hair wafting behind her. She was a Cheer Babe, so she wore her uniform ritually, and the gold brightened and shined on her skin.

Positive Pavia.

Perky Pavia.

Precious Pavia.

Then the break up. She was out of school for two months. I overheard her parents sent her to Mexico, and we all know what happens when kids get sent to Mexico. I don't, but I acted as if I did. Apparently it was Elly who broke up with Pavia, and seeing his face stunted her exhausted perfection.

Basil Baked These!
150 Villeton Themed Cupcakes
50 Chocolate Molten
50 Lemon Curd
50 with Nut Butter
With like, Zero Cross Contamination

The lighting in the gym was a neglected technical difficulty. My setup was humble—a golden plastic cover to match the Villeton colors and a handwritten sign designed by one of the Babes. *Basil Baked These* was never discussed with me or if that was my preconceived brand, but I had to commend the spelling. The afternoon had wrung out all of my customer service and mercilessly spat me to the brutes.

I was a lone vendor with the occasional assistance from Pavia, who was as nice as I expected her to be. Her high-waisted cheer skirt was pulled up to the point it exposed the bottom of her bloomers—which exposed the bottom of her ass. It was a sales tactic I was both envious and repulsed by. Not because I wanted to body shame, but because there was an unnerving module between the cakes and Pavia's rear end. Everyone wanted to be around her iced skin, which shifted to a rash red when grazed by boy shorts.

"You've had a line across the gym since 2pm. Is she really helping?" Declan stood at the corner of my display with her cheer outfit almost completely covered by a blank long sleeve.

She was too nice to admit her dissatisfaction with Pavia. "It's all good. We're on the last tray."

Pavia went into a drawn out conversation with one of the jocks, who was craftily checking out both Declan and me. Pavia was a people person though, almost like the nearly burnt crust on an apple pie—abnormal but hella ambrosial. She knew how to work with what she was given, and I couldn't be mad at it. I could only sit and list out all the reasons Elly was with her.

I was desperately anticipating his arrival. I knew the second he'd appeared, I'd omit my fundraising duties. The week was so vicious in the way it kept me farther away from him but also dangled him in front of me like some farm-grown carrot. I was pulling knots of hair out, which was now straightened streaks that smelt of hot combs and hair grease.

"I want us to talk, Basil," and there was Declan. "I know you've been avoiding me and you have every right to. I can't stop thinking about the kiss that happened."

Neither could I.

"I think I have to pee," I sorta shouted.

"Ohohoh! You have to use the bathroom, Basil? Go ahead and I'll watch the stand!" Will you, Pavia?

She bounced up to me, shoving me off with her butt-bone. "Are you sure you can handle it by yourself? The line has been nonstop."

"Basil, heheHEhe," she twitched. "You are so sweet! But of course you are, look at all the things you make!"

"You're really sweet too, Pavia," I returned and Declan finger-kicked me.

Pavia's glimmer buffered before she twisted me to the exit. "Shooo-shooo! I got this!"

The roots of my hair reminded me of my argument with my mother and curated a headache. I wanted to deep dive into the pool of water that overflowed from the bathroom's sink, but shrinkage was a real thing that I couldn't explain upon my reentry. I was too sick to pee, my mom's temperament made use of the space around me. I could use the by-chance distractions that came with Elly.

"Hello," who says *hello* anymore? A girl entered into the bathroom and dipped her hands into my sink. She was a little taller than me with dark features and olive skin. The area between her nose and right ear was marked with a sudden bright pigmentation.

"Hi?" I didn't mean for it to sound as rude as it came out.

"You're dating Elly, right?"

Sometimes. "Yes."

"How?" I wish this was weirder for me.

"He asked me to be his girlfriend one day. Not verbally, but he wrote it in the school's front lawn. It was kinda cute."

"Yeah, I know. I saw."

"Oh?" The lag between one sentence to the other concerned me. I almost had to check to make sure she wasn't a hologram.

"I know this is a weird question, but what I'm asking is —what I mean is, how did you get him to like you?"

I said yes to be in his film? I couldn't answer her question, so we made unwavering eye contact for a few before I began to nervously squirm. I was trying to place myself in a different environment, the one I stumbled into had not prepped me for this level of interrogation. It was a question that tarried my sanity because I didn't have the answer for myself.

"I was just me," was all I could come up with.

She inched closer. "I've been to his house. We used to have sex in his narrow room with the white walls and the bed by the window. When you look outside you can see a grey Acura and a hula hoop."

She's seen Elly's room before me? "I'm sorry, but what are you getting at?"

"He used to put together sentences in my head that my mind couldn't make up."

"I'm going to go now," I left her by the flooded sink. She stayed behind.

"What makes you the star?"

No one missed me at my station. From my basic math, I could tell Pavia hadn't sold one cupcake. We were coming to the home stretch and I had a long night ahead of me. I had my backpack stuffed to the zipper and a hotel in downtown New York City that was about to know my name. I needed these cupcakes to squeal for their next consumer. I needed to be with ELLY.

Elly.

He strolled up to me. It's been a week since the last time I saw him, and then I was half asleep almost being burned alive by expectations. He looked so different, but also the same. Each time I saw him, he had an airy facet that I'm assuming I was the reason for. Nope—he only gets better. His hair had a ravishing recoil that made eye contact with me before his eyes did.

Those eyes.

"Your hair," I forgot how tall he was. "It's so different."

"I straightened it," I wheezed. Each encounter I unraveled a new feature of his—from his lopsided teeth to the small stubs of hair between his brows and lazy shoulders. It made him sound atrocious but it was the smaller atrocities that made him look so real.

"I have to get used to you," misplaced language weighed down his tongue.

I could see the creases in Elly's fingers tighten up. He was not into the social dilemma and honestly, same. I wanted to dodge the false innocence from Pavia alongside Declan's passivity. It was too cruel. Not to mention the never-ending line that wanted to suffocate me into a different person. I wanted to cut it short to get away with the person I came to love. Love? I think it's that.

"How much are your cupcakes?" He lifted one up and sniffed it.

"They're five dollars each."

He picked up a cupcake and handed it over to me. "I'll buy one if you eat it too."

There could be worse things he could personally request. Like, be in a porno. "Uhm," I've yet to have one anyway. "Sure."

The cupcake unpeeled the liner off of itself. It had a natural luminosity that encompassed all of Villeton. The golden hallways that swept across the building and told me I didn't belong—stitched with a warm green. It was a troublesome moment trying to fit two and a half years of high school life into a cupcake, but it was also really easy.

I timed my first bite with Elly's mercenary exhales. I could watch his lips on a projector—nothing moved like his vowels. The filling dispersed towards the back of my throat, numbing my tonsils with its taste. This was the lemon curd. Bitter, spontaneous, but also stunning. My baking was better than I remembered, but still not as good as the still portrait of Elly in front of me.

"Can I try some?" I dropped the remainder of the treat in his palm. He thrust the rest into his mouth without a huff or an audible swallow. "Wow."

"Do you like it?"

I could see it. "I like it very much," the stroke of merriment in his eyes.

"Where's Lane and Wesley?" I could see Declan making her way to us and I wanted to get the question out before she did.

"Lane doesn't go to school, and Wesley is babysitting until you're ready to leave."

"Is he driving?"

"Yeah."

Declan joined. "Oh yeah! Y'all are going to Eight Ball tonight, right?"

"Yeah, are you still coming with us?"

Declan caught Elly undeniably checking out of the convo. "Yeah! I'd be happy to," and she really didn't care.

"ELLY!"

It was a chilling shriek. I couldn't catch the name until they went for it again. "ELLY! IS THAT YOU?!"

It was Pavia. It was somewhere in a flickery font stapled to her prerogative. She was charging towards the thing she had lost and found and then lost all over again. I could see the name surging through each indigo vein. No one knew how to respond, or if they wanted to put an end to something that couldn't start.

"What's wrong with her?" No one could hear me past the silence. The line that curved around my station had become a speechless mob awaiting Pavia's downfall.

Declan surveyed Elly and went back to Pavia. Elly could not be read. His face was a glistening monotone and eerily brought grace to the spectacle. Like I waited for him to inhale my cupcake, I waited for him to say something. The company we were in expected the same and everyone's eyesight pin-balled to me, then Elly, and lasted at Pavia until they decided she wasn't going to change.

We had to change.

"Elly, what's going on with her?" I repeated myself. Pavia was two feet from Declan who shielded both me and Elly.

"Pavia, I think you should go to the restroom," Declan spoke with a cooled tone that only Pavia could hear if she listened.

"YOU'RE ALIVE!" She leaped forward with some insane might as Declan blocked her with a hug. "eLLy!"

"Do I know you?" His mannerisms told zero lies. He couldn't recognize her.

If puzzles had words, I'm sure they'd be tongue-tied; Elly was two in the same. Pavia disregarded Declan's hold and continued to hoist herself towards Elly. He cocked his head at her dance movements—Pavia was def a Cheer Babe right now, and nothing was going to stop her from her ultimate riot. I could hear Declan grimacing underneath Pavia's body weight. Though Pavia was smaller than Declan, nothing could break her challenge.

"Elly! I tho—I thought you were gone forever. That's what they told me. I thought we'd never be able to talk again, but you're here! You're right here, Elly!" Gallons of tears gushed down Pavia's face. "Do you know me?"

His pupils shook in terror. "No."

Pavia unlinked Declan's arms, her body was like a withering Raggedy Ann. "We dated. We dated here, at Villeton, for a really long time."

"I've dated a lot of people," he responded.

"NO!" Pavia went for a strike, but Declan impelled it with her grip.

Was no one going to explain to me what was going on? Pavia was unrecognizable. Her mascara had turned her face into a blank canvas. The light brown smudged and mixed with the rest of her shades—the rose blush on her cheeks, the turquoise above her eyelids, it drew down to her chin and onto Declan's white shirt.

"Who is she?" Pavia stopped moving. Her legs had become motionless and stiff; her finger jittering until it landed at me.

"This is Basil," Elly swung his arm across my shoulder. "She's my girlfriend."

Pavia broke from Declan's hold and glided from her destination. She was no longer targeting Elly, all of her attention went to me. My joints couldn't acknowledge the potential ass kicking that was coming my way, but I was almost awaiting it. I wanted to see something happen. She stepped forward with a calm wetness beneath her lash and a buttery vexation. She was about my height, but her sneakers gave her about an inch over me.

She was close enough to lick. "WHAT MAKES YOU THE STAR?!" A fleck of spit hit my left dimple before she bolted out, and before I could apprehend the collision.

The cupcakes dissipated once Pavia vanished, and all the hours I ditched sleeping finally caught up with me.

Chapter 16

:V

The rolled down windows dampened the 80s rock, and Wesley was really the only one singing it. His hair lit up the front seat of the car where Lane was cruising shotgun. Declan was passed out against Elly's shoulder, and both of our focus were preoccupied overlooking the Triborough Bridge. The lights were soft and made the backseat way more romantic than it should've been, or I imagined it to be. Wesley had almost no understanding of velocity and sped past any car that dared to go faster than him. I knew my parents held out on allowing me to drive, but Wesley was the raw pamphlet of exactly why I shouldn't. The other cars were scared of us and they had every right to be, we were hauntingly dangerous.

"Don't think about that," Elly whispered, but it was the first time that evening I had stopped thinking about what happened that afternoon.

I wanted to speak to Pavia or even the bathroom girl with the mark on her face after everything happened, but I couldn't find them anywhere. Everyone continued to laugh and talk smack about the bake sale, but the confrontation never existed. No one was brave enough to let it leak past the insouciance that elegantly became the aftermath. I was searching for that conversation but was holding in conversations I haven't had with myself.

"We need to discuss what happened," I remarked.

"Basil, let's have a good night, okay?"

"Yeah BB!" Lane had no idea what we were talking about, but she was hella high already. "Let's get crazy tonight!"

"Crazy is a bad word!" Wesley poked out his bottom lip. "It insults crazy people!"

"The way you look insults crazy people," Lane snickered. "Naw but forreaaal. I'm tryna to get balls DEEP tonight! I'm tryna to get smashed tonight! I'm tryna not to know my name tonight! If I end up at the exit, that means I purposefully took the wrong LANNNE!"

"Boom!" Wesley cheered.

"Let's just go straight to Eight Ball before we head to the hotel, Basil is having a rough night," Elly massaged my neck with his thumb and index.

"I need to talk to you, Elly."

"*Deixa para lá*," he answered.

The look on Pavia's face sat on my lap the whole ride. There was something unnatural about it—a face that a person can't make, it is induced. I was never one to become queasy, but thinking back on her glare made me excruciatingly nauseous. It was the evolved translation of Maude's, minutes before Elly asked me to be his. They had something against me, and they all wanted me to rot in their despair.

Elly was sure it never happened. If I uttered a word, he was tipping the subject over with a bland comment. He knew that I was uneasy, and he figured strobe lights and an IPA could brush it off. A few drinks could make me soft again, and the music might take hold of my anxieties. Everything could be okay if it's only ignored. Why am I making it okay?

Lane slurred a lot of ridiculous jargon for the rest of the drive, and Wesley would often correct her—which Lane hated. We ended up somewhere in Brooklyn beneath an above ground train track. I could tell it was Brooklyn from the late night bodegas that held stale fruit, and the way my parents described it, but with a few more white people.

A magic eight ball hung above a small but packed black brick entrance. The eight was the only part of the sign that was working, and I wanted to know if that was done on purpose or for aesthetics—we're in Brooklyn, so everything was an aesthetic. Dry ice polluted the only window that gave bystanders the proper peek inside, and before we exited the car, I could see how sardined it was. If this was how all the bars in my life would be, then they are precisely how I imagined and nothing I was missing out on.

We all huddled up before reaching the bouncer, who was quick to eye our shenanigans. She looked hella like my aunt, but with more bust and sass.

"ID's out!"

"Yooooo! Wassup Mona?" Lane saluted the bouncer who was not into it.

"Who's that one?" Mona picked me out, and it wasn't hard to from the cluster I was in.

"This is Basil, she's with us!" Wesley coddled Mona in his arms, and Mona looked accustomed to it.

"I don't know her, I need to see her ID."

"Mona, this is my girlfriend," Elly was holding my hand as we waited for Mona's facial expression to shift. It didn't. "She forgot her ID at home and you know we live in the middle of nowhere."

"Yeah!" Lane added. "You know we live in the greaseburbs!"

Mona tittered. "Yeah, I know," Mona and I both knew that I was underage, but Mona and I also knew that Elly's charm was compelling. "Go ahead."

Lane quickly skid past a couple who were tonguing each other down near the bar's window. She dug out a tiny palette from her jeans and splotched a heavy dark grey at the top of her lids. She proceeded to add more layers until it was too hard to tell if her eyes were closed or not. She took out some glitter and dashed it on the ends of her eyelashes, finishing up with a deep red lip to match her cropped woven tank. She looked kinda sexy —in her Lane-ish way. Declan chimed in, removing her cheer skirt right in the middle of the sidewalk, guys hooting and hollering at her revealing nothing but upper thigh. She had on a pair of black bike shorts, and once she deserted her long white tee, she unclothed a bedazzled sports bra.

I was the only one who still looked like a high school student, and I had nothing to uncloak to leave me feeling part of the pack. I flaunted a button down paisley print sundress in the middle of autumn, but it was because I wanted to look presentable for my first bake sale—and I'm not much of a fashionista or trendsetter when it came to presentation.

Wesley and Elly didn't change a thing, but they didn't have to, out of all of us they looked like the two who would own a bar like this—especially Wesley. Everyone outside Eight Ball sized up our group. I'm certain they knew that a bunch of high school students from rural New York just drove three hours to get drunk and maybe laid. And like, they were all totally right, but I had more at stake than my virginity—I had my relationship I built with Elly.

PINKBLUEORANGE.
Smoke.

"Dude, who is that?!" Some bro sitting at the bar with his other bro snapped a shot of Declan with his phone. We had just gotten in.

Lane jerked the guy's wrist until the clench gave him carpel tunnel, forcing him to drop his phone."Do you want to die?!"

The bartenders at Eight Ball were good-looking and vivacious—they were also the first thing anyone would see when coming in. My permanent walking stance had become the penguin waddle, and it was hard not to lose the rest of the group who were accustomed to the packed out scene. Every color in the room was dark and muted, but still bright enough to see who was who. Declan would turn every three seconds to make sure I was right behind her and eventually locked onto my forearm.

"Let me get a shot!" Lane howled at one of the bartenders.

"A shot of what?" They screamed back, charmed by Lane's candid behavior.

"Anything to wash this down!" Lane flashed a pill at the bartender who raised her eyebrow in amazement. "Make it three!"

"What is that?" I was the only one asking. Wesley had gone off somewhere and Elly...wait, where did Elly go?

Lane disentangled her tongue and placed the small round tablet right by her spiked piercing. She gulped it whole and passed one to both me and Declan. Declan slurped without question, and I–I'm not doing that.

"No thank you," I flung it back at Lane and she refused.

"BB, I need you to do me a quick fav. Reach up your crotch, get way up in there, and take your panties out."

"I don't do drugs, Lane."

"I don't do drugs either. I take medicine," she stole a cup of Idontknowwhat from a dude with a braided beard. "Now take your medicine."

ORANGEBLUEPINK.
Smoke.

Thirty minutes had gone by and Lane was profusely sweating and stancing. She held her arms in the air for ten minutes straight without catching a cramp, and that was how she communicated to me that nothing else mattered. Declan wasn't leaking like Lane, but she found her comfy medium and was making sure that even though she was sandwich'd between some aroused canines, she wasn't going to allow them to agitate her groove. Declan could dance. Like, I knew how to jiggle my butt fat, but Declan could control the orbit of her hips and knew how to emphasize the tempo with her isolations.

I couldn't stop looking at her, and I felt a buzz of perversion whenever I noticed. I summed it up to the drugs, but they had yet to kick in for me. Declan's neck glimmered behind her holographic top and it looked so edible. The music was a funkish-rock, the kind of music that no one couldn't dance to. The more time passed by, the darker the bar became, and the shinier Declan glowed.

"Why are you standing there? Dance Basil!" She tied her arms around my collar.

If I joined her, I wouldn't leave. Engaging with Declan right now would make me neglect Elly, and I think the side effects of the pill were already messing with that. Her eyes peered right into mine, we were almost the exact height. She dipped her head and gave me that *look*—ensuring me that all the slips we fell into were deliberate and premeditated. Her breath smelled like she chewed a pack of *ArcticAirs* but I know she didn't, but that's my favorite gum in the entire world, and if I could just kiss her again—

"I shouldn't have kissed you, Basil," she sang above the music. "It was wrong, and I promise I'll never do it again."

I could hear sounds extending from the lower floor that clashed with the upstairs genre. There were more people down there, and I know if anyone would enjoy being at the lowest point, it would be Elly.

BLUEORANGEPINK.
Smoke.

A dance floor enriched with bodies was buried at the end of a staircase. Blueorangepink smoke sailed up the steps and invited me to embark on its hypnotic venture. The rare moments I avoided someone's close contact, gave me a better understanding of nightlife and what lured me into it. There was a whiff of eroticism in Eight Ball—an eroticism between my freed destiny and conscious present.

"What are you looking for?" A stranger with connecting hexagons tattooed on his cheek stopped me. His clothing was stained and moistened. He sat comfortably on the rail of the mid-step, sipping on a half empty can of beer.

"You wouldn't know anyway," he was built, I could see it through his half buttoned shirt, displaying even more tattoos going down his sternum.

He had bleach blonde locks with shaved sides, and I don't like guys with locks because they always remind me of my dad—at least this guy's wasn't two toned. "Maybe I can help you find whatever you're looking for, they always say two eyes are better than one."

"I have two eyes, thank you very much," he laughed. He had a nice strum in his voice.

"You know what I mean. I'm sorry! I'm Marques by the way. What's your name?"

"Basil."

"Are you forreal?"

I could hardly hear him, I stepped forward a little more and he followed my gesture. "Why do you ask?"

"I've never heard a name like that before," his teeth. His teeth were so straight. "I don't think I've ever met a girl like you before either."

His teeth were nothing like Elly's.

"I have to go! I have to find what I'm looking for."

He reached for my arm but failed to grab me, I'm sure out of respect. "Basil—wait!"

JADE BROWN

Smoke.

It was everywhere. It came from the guy with the braided beard in the corner, the DJ hanging from aerial silks while hitting an opaline bong, and my ears looking for the sound inside of sound. It only took one person to funk up a dance floor, and that lone stinker was bubbling underneath the minimal pinks. Whenever the DJ scratched into a heavier beat, they would squirt the pit with more smoke and everyone would lose it. Time and time again.

Hiding in a pond of flailing arms, in the dead center— was Elly. His chin punctured the ceiling as his head tilted to a 90-degree angle. His hair brushed the top of his mid back and his white t-shirt was soiled from those gathered around him. The ambient blues iced his skin and hindered his path. It looked like he was ascending somewhere that was only made for him, and it made me jealous to think that I couldn't be a part of that.

"Why are you going so slow?" He asked me. We were disconnected by a chain of drunken college freshmen.

"I was looking for you," I slipped into his ribcage as the chain tumbled. He diverted his concentration to me, his pupil was the size of the earth and his iris was lavender.

"Were you? I saw you talking to that gorgeousgorgeous man."

"I don't even know that guy. He stopped me on my way to you."

The room became cotton candy. The crowd was now dusting each other with crushes and sweet nothings. The air had a freezing mist that turned into bubble gum when it hit the tongue. Elly enveloped me with his lanky arms. His body felt like powder and good intentions. I could hear his hums coming up from his diaphragm, and it warmed me up the tighter he pulled me in.

"What did you do to those girls, Elly?" The gum swelled in my mouth, blocking my articulation.

"Things that I would never do to you," his grasp hardened.

"I need you to tell me. We can't continue if I don't know!"

A cloud ascended above us and deformed the closer we became. Winter winds heightened the cloud's intensity with nasty courage. It bled out a hefty and resentful rain that soaked both me and Elly—though he had a forgiving air in his posture. The cloud had a vengeance against Elly in particular and seeped water out in a malefic manner. Elly elegantly held his breath and waited for the rush to clear his mind. I could hear his thoughts bellow out, and they were telling me how much they awaited this.

"Will you end up hating me too, Basil?" Elly spoke softly through a mouth full of raindrops. "If I showed your skin to your heart?"

The rain halted. The smoke came in again and dried up Elly's mistaken tears. "Can you say it now, Basil?"

From where I was standing, I could see Wesley fooling around with a soft goth in the corner. The guy had on a studded choker, cropped halter top and leather trousers—I could see the tip of his briefs read *stardom*. Wesley was talking into the guy's ear, telling him how much love he could disperse. Why was I able hear them? The guy was falling over from Wesley's dry antics. It behooved me that neither of them felt the need to be more discreet, but it also took me back to when Wesley did the same with me.

I gargled on a lost drop.

The orange dialed up and screeched over the amps. It was now an overtaking of scarlet and ginger-colored blood smearing across the dilapidated basement. The DJ created windmills with their body, polluting the smogged space with burning pellets. This was a feeling I've felt before, in a car I'd rather be in. I wanted to be on the outside of this photograph and figure out how I ended up blocking my face out.

"Elias."

The particles all formed together and created a tornado around us. Pink, orange, and blue became each of our names amongst the horde of flames. The tips of my fingers moved up and grappled the collar of Elly's tee. His height crinkled downward and stored us in the middle. His face in front of mine was a pastie caricature of my desires. In all that I could ever become, I still wouldn't amount to enough; that was the trammel of Elly's name, and that was the emotion that dug into me the entire time we kissed.

Each component of our kiss was interrupted by our disbelief. While Elly's lips blended with my own, my brain encouraged me that this wasn't happening. He'd stop, look at me and start up again, then stop. That was the only truth I had that it was Elly. WAIT. Yes, it's Elly. My hands couldn't clutch the trigger points that made themselves aware through our tangled extremities.

"You're my star," his breath shivered and spiraled around my neck. "Tartula."

Chapter 17

:[

The bathroom was made of stickers and signatures. I wanted to scribble my name across the top of the mirror to remember who I was, but Elly was too quick at bolstering me up on the sink. I awaited his trimmed nails to graze my kneecaps, but he wouldn't touch me in that way. I raveled my index around his collar, and ingested the last bit of breath I could steal from him. He made a ring around my waist and hard-pressed his belt buckle to my pelvis.

The occasion poured truth into my soul. The only flame that emerged was from the seared anticipation. I wanted nothing more than Elly, and this was my first chance at receiving him in full. The night had caved in for a sec to measure my maturity; I think this daydream might be mine to take. All my rules are out of the way, who cares—I make them up anyway.

"I think I'm ready, Elly," the sentence oozed from my hung lip.

"You're ready?"

"Yes! I think I'm ready to become yours forever."

"I heard you, but can you tell me again?"

I threw my head back and yelled. "I'm ready to be yours!"

This was the closest I had gotten to meeting Basil. She was daring, spellbinding, messy, and in-your-face. Def not boring or average, and more than her looks. She wasn't too pussy to sleep with her boyfriend in a sketch bathroom in the middle of Brooklyn. She'd say yes to disasters—only to see where they'd take her, and they continue to take her far.

It always was Elly. It was Elly who introduced me to the responsibilities that came with a crush. Crushes have to be earned, worked for, and established from something. I think that I could return all that Elly has given to me on this very night, and I'll keep returning, and returning, and returningreturningreturning. It was Elly this entire time—how could it have not been clearer? If everything irons out correctly, I could be looking at the last night of the life I knew. My ties with Elly were still under heavy scrutiny—by myself mostly, but I'm cool with dealing with the precautions later.

Let's do this.

I leaned up and dragged him in. I could hear our kissing from outside of the kiss, and understood how depraved our mouths were. Elly's breathing picked up the faster our lingos swirled and stretched towards each other's uvula. From outside the kiss, I would think Elly was hyperventilating or quitting oxygen, but the heavier his exhales, the faster and more rooted his grips.

Someone on the opposite side wanted to get in, but we couldn't stop—I couldn't. Elly fussed with his pants pocket and finally removed a condom. It was the second time I had ever seen a condom out of its foiled packaging. It was so ugly, but I think that's what's hidden in all that comes with safety. Elly's hands were quivering. Like, arctic trembles without a down-coat. His focus was imprinted on his belt and taking it off. He succeeded on the eleventh try and dropped his pants just under his gluts, showing me his bellflower briefs. I didn't want to be too invasive, but I peeped to see what was about to go inside. I couldn't. I dropped my head back before closing my eyes and listening to the sound of the condom unraveling.

Please, don't let this hurt.

"I almost forgot," I could hear grappling followed by some taps. "I never thought I could be with someone as remarkable as you, Basil."

My eyes opened to find a lens pointing towards my forehead. He twisted my jaw up and open. My viewpoint was so disjointed—Elly never looked charier. "What are you doing?"

"I have to capture this moment. You're becoming a star."

I simpered. "C'mon, stop playing around. Kiss me again."

He shoved his thumb into my mouth and to the side of my cheek. He rubbed the inside until sliding under my tongue—pinching into the floor. My tongue tried not to get in the way because it forgot who the host was. He dragged his finger out and left it on my cheekbone, taking his index finger and implanting them both into my dimples.

"You're so beautiful," he whistled into the opposite end of the camera.

"Can you put the phone down, Elly? I don't feel comfortable," my voice wrangled with his pressure on my jaw.

"I'd hate to make you feel that way, Basil," his demeanor had no meaning—he was working off of a principle that strayed.

It was beginning to hurt. His nails were inserting themselves without supervision, and though my dimples were deep, they couldn't withstand Elly's grip. Does he want to hurt me? no.

eLLY wouldn't.

"Let me go, Elly."

"How many times in your life can you say that you have fallen?"

"Elly!"

"Huh, Basil?" The camera whirled around the crown of my head before landing at the bridge of my nose.

"ELLY!"

"HUH?!"

I smacked the back of the case, causing the phone to drop into the piss brimmed toilet. Elly froze with twinkling fingers and a revolted disguise. His eyes closed, then opened, then closed, then opened, thenclosedthenclosedthenclosed. He was keeping something from me, and I wasn't sure it was something that I should've already seen. The pill I took before was starting to hit, and it couldn't have come at a better moment.

"I can't do this, Elly."

"What?" He shook, coming back into himself.

"I can't be Tartula."

His steps were severed by our augmented lust. His head hung downward, but his eyelashes cheated towards me, letting me know that I was still his vision. We both laughed to try and fill the unnamed air—storing our immaturity in the bathroom's gloom. His throat turned chalky and hoarse until he decided to no longer spare his synthetic happiness.

"Basil, can you speak please?"

A sticker engraved with a hashtag decomposed from the ceiling. Another sticker followed it, thus sparking a swarm of social media handles and bad logos. Elly looked past the chaotic whirl, and his words meshed into a new trend. I tried to see him out of it, but I decided that it would be best to leave altogether. The bathroom handle tried to convince me otherwise, it convulsed at first touch, but eventually surrendered me to an unknown outcome.

I need water. The immediate smog landed somewhere in my larynx. I had figured the pool of sweat would dry out by now, but it had nothing to do with my natural response to Elly, but my acknowledgment to catastrophe. I might be, maybe, maybe even—accepting a catastrophic result. If Elly was building up to that part, he was also loosening some energy that was stifled by his ambiguity. I still need water though.

"Hey, Basil! Did you ever find that thing?" Marques sat at a table with unfamiliar faces. Go figure—I must be the newest face around here.

I was finally past the crowd and the basement that captivated me, and now I was being welcomed by a hottie with a southern flair. "I know you?"

"Wow! You forgot me already, huh? We talked for a bit earlier. I'm Marques," I know who you are. "Why don't you have a seat with me and my friends. Y'all—this is BASIL."

There were too many faces to count or hack them from one another. Some faces were so involved; I'm talking about colors on chromatics on saturations. The only person I knew who was moderately eccentric was Wesley. Why was he the only thing I had? Marques was an ornate contribution to his tribe. He belonged to them. If someone saw me with my friends, would they think the same?

"BeautifulBEAUTIFUL name for a beautifulBEAUTIFUL girl," someone with black lipstick rose their drink.

"You're GWAR-GEOUS!" Somebody else screamed.

"Isn't she?" Marques pinched their shoulders.

"I'm sure she wouldn't want to be called a girl, she's a woman," this person had cornrows and a pleasantly stern accent. "Or person."

"Girl is cool," because being called a woman felt icky, and sometimes perverted.

"Oh shit! She came in with the group of white kids, right? She was holding hands with that fine white boy!" The black lipstick person talked about me to cornrows/stern.

"Can white people be fine?" The one white person at their table inquired.

"No! You have to see that white boy! I never knew white came in that flavor."

Marques covered his face with his hand. "Please Basil, excuse my friends. I try not to let them out too much."

"Eight Ball hasn't been the same since we were in high school. You know the owner is POC?" Cornrows stern commented.

"They're fun, I promise," Marques added. "What do you like to drink? I'll get you something. Maybe we can get some of your friends to come and join us too"

All the names next to the chalkboard drawn margaritas were phonetically challenging. The only drink I knew about was whiskey, but I didn't want to get any more messed up than I was. "I don't want to drink, Marques."

No matter how far I separated myself from Elly, he found his way back to me. It was either through Villeton, or through a group of college students who assumed I was old enough to be their friend. I couldn't be their friend—they never did anything for me, but Elly, Elly rescued me. And, I should be thankful for the personality he's given me.

I knew that if I would've stayed in that bathroom with Elly a little longer, I might've changed. I would've been the trope to his film festival glory, and we would now be on the cruising side talking about how it unfolded. It was a camera to a dimension that might take me for granted—but who am I anyway to be taken for? I don't think I know myself.

Elly.

"I'm still looking for it," I excused myself from the table and Marques' crowd. They were good, but they weren't for me.

My thirst for water left me as soon as I skated back down the steps. I could hear Marques and his friends call out to me once more before I was in the midst of the mob again. This time it was too familiar. It was a phenomenon now, mist and drinks flying through the poisonous lowered sky. I had to get back to Elly before he disintegrated into repercussions. I had to let him know that I loved him. That's what I told my mom this morning before I left the house; that I'm in love with Elly Hayes. I staggered through the millions of bodies that now made Eight

Ball overruled by stomps, trips and thrashes. The basement appeared so distant from the top floor, and I couldn't get to Elly faster. I lunged myself past each hole I could fit into, and I wanted to know when the butt nips and ass smacks would end. My dress was hooked in opposing directions, and I couldn't see who was pulling at me, but I kept in mind—only two more leaps to go and Elly would be face to face with my apology.

How could I do that? I left him bandaged with a disclosed gateway. He was the only thing that made Villeton feel like school, and daydreams feel like they could be rationalized. I am a punk if I ever knew one, and I stopped right at the peak of my novice breakup. He can forgive me for that—I'm sure.

Elly.

He said, "it's not nice to run out of things to say."

This high was different from the canna-coffee; this high made my encounters feel like intrusions. Elly was bare stares and arrhythmia, and the woman next to him was phlegm. It wasn't like Elly to resurface this way, but I'm also talking about someone I don't know at all. I think this high brings on delusion. Elly is kinda apparitional anyway.

The girl had a soggy face and white leather booties. We looked nothing alike, and I desperately wanted us to. Elly had his hand on her upper thigh, the same position we were in right before I was escorted out by my assumptions. She was studying Elly, waiting for him to assert himself as the guy who is just trying to hook up, and to ask the random black chick to leave. She wasn't aware that this guy doesn't allow things to burn out, he likes to watch them blacken.

"What's happening?" I coughed up.

"There's another bathroom upstairs," her lips were fake.

"Elly, what's happening?"

Purple bites swam from her ankle to her thigh, and her clothes covered everything from her corduroy mini to her scoop-neck. On the outskirts of her wounds were engravings of poetic slander. All I had to remind myself of Elly's handwriting was the day he grooved his girlfriend proposal into Villeton's lawn—I recognized it instantly. Her legs dangled off the curve of the sink and fished for each part of him.

"WHAT'S HAPPENING, ELLY?!"

It was all words. Constricting static that held up my fury. I guess I feel angry, but I also feel fruitless. I visually sorted through my breast and my purity that was hanging onto the past hour. I was exceptionally weaker than I came this evening and also battered by my own decisions. It's my fault, it's all my fault and I think I deserve this.

I'm sure he feels so comfortable right now.

"DOESN'T HE?!"

"Do you know her?" She noticed his stare was secured to the kiss mark that he left on me not too long ago.

"Of course I do," he blew out a mouthful of laughter and shrills. He knew we were perishing. "This is my girlfriend,

Basil."

I charged at her. My hands were small, but I had the grip of a python. This was now my territory, and she just insulted my prey. The marks went up to her neck, and I could see my fingers trying to erase them all as they crimped around her wrinkled throat. I lifted her head to me and tugged it back. Her head ricocheted from the buffed out wall, and her nose steamed from the blow. She clawed at my chest, but the bind kept her on the defeated side—away from both me and Elly.

"I love you too, Basil," he kissed my temples and relaxed his palms on my shoulder.

The lake was now in my eyes. The girl kicked and hacked up an ounce of spit, but her aim was too contrite. She started to shudder before her face turned to the color of her bruises. Elly fixed his chest into my back and we both pondered. His touch sprawled like vines to the ends of my fingertips. We held her together, and it felt like at last, we were a real couple. This high was particular. This high made a bar's bathroom smell like wisteria. It made Elly's embrace floaty and nonintrusive; almost like he wasn't there. But, when I looked behind me at the gentle sweep of cranberry that pranced from his smile to his cheeks, I knew something inside me was gnarled and misplaced.

"What are you two doing?! STOP IT!" Declan lifted both me and Elly in one hull—she looked strong, but she was stronger than that.

The woman released to the footprint sloshed floor, and panted until whiskey vomit poured to the ground. Declan threw herself beside the sick girl, rubbing her back until she could find her breathing once again. Lane and Wesley stood by the door with befuddled and unanswered expressions. Elly drew his hand into his back pant pocket, and plucked out his already recording phone.

"Fin," he moved the camera around the tight room and veered in my direction.

I stared the device down until I could see my reflection appear in the glass that surrounded the lens. Until I could see my reflection light up in Elly's eyes.

PART TWO

(OrLike, 3 MonsLater)

Chapter 18

:3

    I had this *thing* happen to me while sampling some of Lane's home-brewed ayahuasca. I was underneath Tartula's body. She was draping her purplish limbs on top of my comatose state, and her habitat was luxuriously green and meaningful. Ivy wielded between twigs and fissures, breaking the distinctions made between her body and mine. Tartula had the same smell of fresh nutmeg, and it told me she was harmless. There was nothing but us within the tight proximity, and she had no clue I was there to give some of her attention to. She was so much of me, but she was nothing but Elly through and through. I saw me when I looked at her, but her skin was slick with arrogance and tragedy.

She wouldn't let me speak to her, she held my breath under her matted hair. It began to lower into my throat, building a forest around my heart—not killing me, but rupturing what I had.

"SHE'S SO HOT, DUUUDE!" Lane held a palette of eyeshadow in her arm while Wesley maneuvered the brush.

"I always knew that!" Wesley sang, dipping the bristles into magenta and over my lid. "Basil is a princess!"

"You love to ruin a moment, dontcha?"

"What do you mean? Is something wrong with princesses?"

"Princesses are the white man's capitalist dogma."

"Just be careful not to overdo it," Elly flashed his camera phone into my iris—nearly blinding me. "Remind me again Basil, what did she look like?"

Watery skin that could fall off if she stood up too fast. Dark, nearly black lips with a deep philtrum. Her eyebrows were more sharp and defined than mine, still bushy and agitated though. She had crystals embedded in her dimples that flickered like diamonds. Her top and bottom eyelashes were indistinguishable from each other due to the volume. Whenever she blinked, a flurry of wind drew out and hushed my concentration.

But, as ambiguous as she was, the thing that ruled over the fascination of her was a rash. A monstrous glowing rash that blew up from the front of her throat to her chest. It radiated with a citron glint, that dimmed and became more exuberant with her breath. The consistency of the rash looked like it was totally disorganized, but the more I could see her, Tartula—the more the blemish contorted to a message.

A message I can't read.

Wesley pushed the brush to his butt-chin. "I think my work is *finito*!"

"What about her hair?" Lane croaked.

"You said her hair was unkept, right Basie?"

Rupturing what I had.

"Yeah, her hair was like, not done."

They each took equal turns staring at me, except for Elly, he stared thirty seconds too long. "She's exactly what I wanted."

We all ended up at The Grand Babette at some point after Eight Ball, but with migraines and amnesia. Lane and Wesley spent the morning pulling the car over to empty their vomit bag, and Elly and I were in the front seat playing telepathy. We knew what happened towards the end of the night, but the same way no one brought up Pavia's tantrum, was the same reaction they had to my bathroom quarrel.

I guess I'm okay with that.

Elly started changing too. He would bring me to and from school every day, asking about what I had in store—never knew what he was referring to. It was evident he wanted to make the boyfriend effort, and I idealized Elly's potential fear of losing me. He'd laugh more—like, a lot. He'd talk to me about things besides the film, for instance, his obsession with fish—discus, saulosi, peacock, and other types of cichlids. I never knew how much Elly loved fish. Maybe that's why.

It was our first serious meeting since Eight Ball, and Elly had proposed a makeup-sesh after my mini ayahuasca trip. He wanted to make sure that it was all captured on my face, and that every resurfacing of Tartula be documented. She hadn't come out much since the hallucination, but she has pleaded her case on the film, and why it was worth my junior year. It was sweet to have Elly to myself for a bit before we had to go back to the way things were before our kiss—the first and last kiss we shared.

"Do you have the card?" Elly slumped himself into Wesley's computer chair.

"I think I forgot it at home," Wesley whimpered.

"We are LiTeRallY in your house," Lane lifted me up from the pile of pillows, simultaneously pulling out a tin can from her back pocket.

"I need the card," Elly speedily typed something into the search bar. I was only half paying attention to the site, and that was cause my false eyelashes gifted me a quarter of my vision, but I could clearly see two models in impractical bikinis pretending to kiss. Advertising.

"Okay! My mom said they lowered the credit limit though, so be careful!" Wesley moaned, handing Elly a heavy card.

"It's not like you have anything to buy," Lane dry swallowed three tablets.

"I have things to buy! I've started knitting and good yarn is quite pricey!"

The webpage was sky-blue and orange accented with a 70s-ish white bubbly font. Everything was tasteful and complimentary until it came to the subscription page—which should've been an affidavit. This was an after-hours kinda gig, and I wasn't sure if we should leave the room or let Elly indulge in Wesley's wealth.

"It went through," Elly took a generous bite of a biscuit. "I think it's time you all meet Phat Pheasant."

I had baked Elly a paper bag full of assorted fruit biscuits that were meant to last him the whole week—if stored correctly. It was only Tuesday, and I could already hear the negative space crumple and crease from the lack of apricot biscuits. Whenever Elly would begin his sentence, he'd overcrowd his mouth with three cookies, choke for like two seconds, and chew them until he couldn't keep the drool from dribbling through his lips.

Elly jostled his seat further into the desk, taking another munch. "There she is."

I could see Phat Pheasant from where I was sitting. She was slender, the waist size of poor respiration, and a medallion-like skin tone. Her hair was plaited in rainbow crotched yarn, and she had a painfully symmetrical face. She was the universal amalgamation of attractive, the kind of girl people paid to be. All of her photos were replicas of the others, and after Elly scrolled for four minutes, I gave up telling them apart. Her camera was always angled up her backside, showing off her bird tattoo that flew up her spine.

What was happening? Just twenty minutes ago the attraction was on me, now it's split with someone who calls themselves *Phat Pheasant*. A pixelated dime who probably has a well-thought-out skin care routine, and a nail technician who she's on a first name basis with. How did Elly find out about someone like her—about a site like this? Is Tartula something that I'm going to have to share? Am I not good enough to carry this flick?

"You're prettier than her," Lane whispered into my nape. I could feel a few cookie crumbs scatter along my standing hairs, how did she get her hands on those? They're not for her.

"She's online," Elly smirked looking at Phat. Opening up a window that brought the entire screen into a chat. The bulky site logo read, *PLAYTHINGS!* ♡ in capital letters.

Phat Pheasant: cutie..thank you for subscribing! xx
Phat Pheasant: do you want to hop on cam?
Phat Pheasant: 10% off for new customers
Phat Pheasant: But since I like you so much...
Phat Pheasant: ill give you 11% off! xx

"Are we really going to see a nip broadcast right here?" Lane poured the remaining crumbs into her mouth. "I'm so fucking down!"

Elly never provided us with a Playthings overview, besides making sure Wesley's credit card wasn't maxed out. I've heard of the website before, from being the optimum eavesdropper that I was, and I surely was not the target audience for Playthings. It advertised itself as being sex positive and allotted financial freedom to all the sex workers on its platform without skinning them for their profits—which is cool. It was made for sex workers, but C-list celebrities and chefs also took to the site as an extra means to some moolah. It was *the* way to capitalize off anything, ANYTHING. I should be thrilled with my baby-step contribution to the site, but why does witnessing Elly type in Phat Pheasant's name send my insecurities into overload?

User00324: Sure.

The chat screen ballooned across the 27-inch desktop and turned black. Each of us held our breath as a small loading symbol appeared in the dead center of the page. It loaded through generations until eventually, there she was. Phat Pheasant. She looked like these dolls I played with as a kid that my mom despised—she called them *Horndolls*. There was a quality in Phat Pheasant that left me transfixed. I think it was because I knew my kitchen pastries would never afford me the luxury of looking like her. Wherever I am in my future life, even if I'm kneading dough for the president, I don't think I'll ever acquire the facial rejuvenation that Phat Pheasant took pride in. Good for her.

Good for her.

Phat Pheasant was at home, or what she tricked us into believing was her home. It was neat, and polaroid pictures of herself across the wall with a selection of body parts. Hand-drawn birds flying through a parakeet wall, and one self-help quote. That was the thing I needed to accept that Phat Pheasant and I weren't that different. The quote read, *"Shoot All the Bluejays You Want."*

Her hair was down and disheveled, her posture was burdened, and her expression told us she'd been online all morning looking for a treasure, and that treasure so happened to be Elly.

Phat Pheasant: your cute! xx
User00324: Thank you.
User00324: Tell me,
User00324: How do you like PLAYTHINGS?

Her website pictures were an oxymoron next to her webcam appearance, she was way more average than I considered.

She was enthused though; she liked Elly, but she also had to uphold her professional but kittenish quirks.

Phat Pheasant: I love it!
Phat Pheasant: how can I make it better for you?

She wore a bra with a front clasp. She moved her thumb along the bra strap, raising it up to show off her unaltered clavicles. I laughed at her stunts, as if she could seduce Elly. I've been begging for months.

User00324: You can stop.
User00324: I don't want to see you naked.

Phat Pheasant drew back into her wall. Her lip filler made her mauve smile indefinite, and I could see her nerve lock up the more Elly peered at the cam. She was hella interested now. She leaned out of the frame for a minute, got up, and then returned with a silk night robe paired with cat eyeglasses. She wanted Elly to believe he was dictating the conversation's ease, and she had no idea he really was. Her long coffin nails were beautified with chains and jewels, setting them on her mouth before deciding to type again. My homemade nails by Wesley were so much better.

Phat Pheasant: what do you want?
User00324: I want to know how you got close to two million subscribers.
User00324: I don't want the fake answer.
User00324: I don't want you to tell me how all you had to do was be yourself.

User00324: I could care less about you.
User00324: I want to know every marketing strategy you had up until this point.

Phat Pheasant became humbled by the immediate interrogation. Her attention went beyond her webcam and off into a canyon. There was someone else in the room with her, and that someone was giving her the direction to proceed.

User00324: You want money?
User00324: User00324 tipped $100! ♡

"She's bacon, dude!" Lane slammed her hand into the back of Elly's chair. "Look at her face! She doesn't know what to say!"

"She's sososo pretty!" Wesley was on all fours and crawled up behind Elly's seat.

Phat Pheasant: i see people in the room with you
Phat Pheasant: what is this?????
User00324: I tipped you money to answer the question.

Phat Pheasant's eyesight skewed. The more screen time she took up, the more hideous she got.

User00324: User00324 tipped $200! ♡

Phat Pheasant: did we go to high school together????? are you trying to blackmail me??????
User00324: Answer me.
User00324: User00324 tipped $300! ♡

There's really nothing special about her.

Phat Pheasant: who are you?????
User00324: My name is Elias.

No. She doesn't deserve your full name Elly, she hasn't earned it. HOW ARE YOU GOING TO DISCLOSE SOMETHING THAT WAS mine? It took me so long to have it, and to feel the composition of Elly's name. From how precious it was when it whisked out, to the coriaceous layer that remains on my idioms. ELLY. No. Don't do this to me, not for her.

Phat Pheasant: Elias

Don't do this to me.

Phat Pheasant: you must really love someone to do all of this

I heard Elly when he told me he loved me, but my memory and discernment were blotchy as hell. Now was his moment to redeem himself from the instance that could've vandalized us. Elly had become so selfless with me, and I was upholding him to an incalculable degree.

His fingers quaked and widened amongst the keys. He wafted them over without pressing down, his direction delayed on Phat Pheasant. The only view I had of Elly's face played in a forfeited section of Phat's video chat; it was so tiny compared to the landscape of her. Winter was assembling through our small town and into Wesley's vacant home, but it couldn't obscure the sweat that broke from Elly's hairline.

User00324: Show me.

HOTEL STUFF

User00324: Please.

Chapter 19

:B

It gets harder to sit by Elly. When I look at him driving, paying attention to the road rather than me, it's insulting. His eyes get so low whenever he refocuses, and his dark brown eyelashes look like seaweed against his water-like pupils. I thought winter would rob me of this picture, I presumed the bland night would contradict Elly's shine. Elly has always been on the paler side, but winter turned his skin to frostbite.

"I created the account for you," he lifted his chin from his zipped up black fleece. "Playthings."

"Oh—you really shouldn't have. Phat Pheasant seems really nice, but I don't think we could ever be friends. We're too different. Like, what would we talk about?"

"I agree," Elly simpered. "That's why she's not your friend, she's your competition."

"What do you mean?"

"Phat Pheasant now has the most followers on Playthings' website, and this is all before Tartula joins."

My anxiety caught hold of Elly's plan—why he had messaged Phat in the first place. "You want me to be on Playthings?"

"I want you to be Tartula on Playthings. One of the main factors of winning the Brunhart Film Festival is votes. We need an audience to ensure the film gets the proper engagement it needs to be considered by the judges. Playthings is a great platform to gain a devoted following."

I believe myself to have one of the strongest stomachs known to upstate New York. My stomach can probably hold a pep rally, that was how strong it was; I thanked it all on baking. Before I could plot together a recipe that satisfied my freakish sweet-cravings, I had to be my main taste tester, and there was a lot that tasted rancid in the beginning. I thought my stomach was a major heavyweight, until this moment. My stomach was not okay with right now, and it was holding vulgar conversations with me.

"People are going to see my face."

"What's wrong with that?"

We curved into my home's driveway. The sensor in the front-porch light fixture was wonky, so it'd go berserk whenever anything was relatively close to it. It wasn't the worst malfunction but could cause some serious damage to anyone prone to migraines, like me every day for the past three months. Elly yanked the keys from the ignition, and we both gazed at the flickering spectacle.

"I want to meet your family, Basil," everything always happens in Elly's car. "Can I come inside with you?"

We hadn't prepared for this. My parents needed at least one week and a five page synopsis before they could even consider meeting Elly. I also had to absorb the Playthings proposal. Being displayed during the festival was one concern, but now my face could be seen by thousands of subscribers—most of whose identity will remain anon unless they fork up some dough. I would be camouflaging through Tartula, but anyone who knows me would know *me*.

"Are you ashamed of our relationship?" He asked.

"No," the opposite. "You just caught me off guard."

"Do your parents not know who I am? Cause my parents can't wait to meet you."

"Really?" A hoard of goosebumps plummeted down my legs.

"Yeah, and they want to see the film too."

Goosebumps annihilated. "I don't think my parents would want to see the film. I actually think it would be best to not mention it at all."

"Why?"

"I don't think they'd be too happy about their sixteen-year-old daughter doing something like this."

Elly squinted, drawing his chin into his fleece again. "Do you think it's a bad film?"

"No! I-I don't want my parents to say no, or to try and take me out of it," it was more than that.

Elly had become a hurdle between my parents and I. He was the culprit behind me staying out late, coming home the next day, and straightening my hair—from what my mom gathered; she still won't let it go. They never patronized me about it, but I think as long as I didn't give them a serious reason to discipline my behavior, then it would be unnecessary. If Elly were to uncover the reality of the film to them, it would give my parents the right to take me from him, and I can't allow that.

My mom and dad used to balance on the window sill every night to make sure I made it up the driveway okay, but what they were really trying to do was get a good glimpse of Elly. Eventually, I'd only see my mom and Purple popping their heads out, and then one day I saw no one at all. The first time I noticed, it def busted the grain of excitement I had left coming home, and I began thinking to myself, why bother trying anymore?

It's time better spent with Elly anyway. "So, you really want to meet my parents?"

What if my parents think he's ugly? He's not ugly, but I know he is not the broad-shouldered, chiseled jawline, and clean-cut jock that my dad used to be back in the early 2000s. My parents are not the superficial type, but I've never brought a boy over who I wanted them to like so much. If I were to make any past comparisons, I could go back to the time when Wesley impressed my dad in the middle of the night, just by getting out of a fifty-thousand dollar vehicle—that is pretty superficial now that I'm thinking about it.

"I'm home!" The chandelier in the main hallway was turned off, but I could hear standup comedy blasting from the living room meshing with the smell of fresh popcorn. "I'MMM HOMMME!"

Elly's focus pinballed from one area of the room to the other. I grabbed his hand to lead him towards the sounds of a live studio audience, where my parents were cuddled up facing the flat screen. A blanket, my blanket, burrito'd the two of them into a filling of love and welfare. They emanated toasty twosome without a care; how can I ruin that for them?

"I'm home," I squeaked. My mom lifted the remote and paused the tv, interrupting her hold on my dad. She turned around to tell me to do something but instead noticed a tallish slender white boy holding my hand.

"Hello there," she whistled.

All my dad heard was my mom's change in delivery and knew something was up. "You must be the boyfriend. Nice of you to finally show ya face."

Elly's hand became clammy and difficult to hold. "Hello Basil's parents."

"Elly, right?" my mom stood from the sofa and walked over, pulling him in for a hug. He didn't return it, but I think it was because he wasn't sure if he should. "You look just like your sister. I can't get her face out of my head. Declan?"

"Mom, that's really weird to say."

"It is, isn't it? *Eeeck*! I'm sorry. Are you hungry?"

Elly's mouth was gaped. My mom shyly waited for his reply, but his stiffened eyes wouldn't break from her.

"I'm sorry. I really shouldn't have said that about your sister. I know. Basilene doesn't usually bring people over. Everything has been so different since she started dating, and I don't think any mother will ever be able to—"

"You're so beautiful," Elly dimly muttered.

"Oh!" The compliment made my mom ditzy with delight. "*Heee*, well—thank you! I haven't heard that in years!"

My mom is gorgeous, of course Elly thinks she's beautiful, she looks just like me. Elly thinks *I'm* beautiful. "Did either of you two cook dinner?"

"I made stir-fry," my dad stretched his back out over the couch's arm. His hairy belly button underneath his tee decided to moon all of us, and it was not only disgusting, it was offensive.

"Stir-fried what?"

"It's chicken?" My dad visually nudged my mom who confirmed the poultry. "It's chicken!"

"Basil, why don't you give Elly a tour? I'll setup the kitchen table and we can all eat together."

My room was the only room worth seeing since it was the only section of the house I was allowed to decorate. As lenient as my mom was, home decor was her forte and neither I nor my dad had permission to ridicule her interior artistry. My room lacked the extravagance and *va va voom* that the rest of the house had, but it was modestly mine.

I opened the door for Elly to walk in first, and his eyes went straight for the fuchsia flooring. He ambled into my four corners, tickling the walls with his index finger, prolly collecting dust because I deep cleaned once a year. His attention went to the mountain of stacked nail polish I kept above my dresser; I don't wear nail polish but everyone in my family gifts me nail polish for the holidays. He opened up the cherry colored tube and accidentally dropped a bit of it onto the dresser's painted wood. He smushed his nail into the red until he was able to swoop it all onto his nail bed.

"Why don't you paint your nails?" Elly waxed his entire finger with the gloss.

"Baking. Pieces of it can chip off and fall off into the dough. Not only that but my nails will end up looking horrendous after the constant kneading."

"I always liked how it looked."

"I can always start wearing it."

Elly placed the polish back on its tower and walked over to my bed in the center of the room. He hastily dropped his torso to his knees, ducking his head underneath the frame to see what was shoved into the cranny; nothing but a broken beater, some middle school clothes I've been meaning to donate, and a ripped violet chiffon table cloth.

"What's that?" He towed the chiffon out from its hiding.

"It's garbage that I'm too lazy to throw out," my room was full of garbage. It was never unpresentable, but there were too many things that I left for another day.

"Can I have it?"

"Sure," I shrugged. Elly dragged and spun the material into a crumpled ball.

"So," he unzipped his jacket, revealing his worn band shirt. "Should we have sex now?"

I leaned back into my room door, lightly shutting it with my hip. This wasn't the kind of tour my mom had in mind. "M-my parents are downstairs."

"What does that mean? You brought me to your room, so I thought that's what you wanted to do," he situated himself on my bed, he really looked like he was meant to be there.

"I. Oh. Okay," my mouth was so pasty and my lips were quenched. I moved toward him at the edge of my duvet. His eyesight clamped to me and lowered me in.

"Are you going to run away this time?" He laid back into the plush of covers. His brown waves departed from his cheeks and forehead. Elly now looked like he existed.

"No," we hadn't kissed in so long. The muscle memory in my lips were going off of daydreams.

Elly abruptly sprung up, taking me into his chest and flipping me over; he was now on top. He thoroughly studied my anatomy with his magnified glare—going from the dimples in my cheeks, to my neck, to my chest, and back up to my eyes. His hand rose up and caressed the edge of my hair, until he decided to comb through the curls with his fingers. His hand continued to move through until it was at the very end of the strands.

"Did your mom have hair like you?" He asked. Def not the person I'd like to think about right now.

"She did, but it was never as long as mine."

"Basil," he took down the bridge he created over me, and placed himself to the side of my body. "Can I be honest with you?"

"Of course, Elly! I only want you to be honest with me."

"If we were to have sex right now, I'd only think about your mother."

Something was fermenting inside of me. An anguish that was the delinquent of my life. My hands locked and hardened with an invisible success. My surroundings blurred and Elly's voice was just a muffled chime. The fuchsia on the floor went in and out of color, the saturation pulled out so much, it had become a dying lilac. It was all really beautiful for a second, and then it reminded me of the words Elly had told my mom. *You're so beautiful* stood at the bank of waste. I couldn't hold myself up on just a kiss from a fucking Brooklyn bar. How do I moisturize myself with the absence of my relationship with Elly? It's way too easy to think about that.

"BASILENE! ELLINGTON! DINNER!"

The spread was not the best, but my mom was a top tier finesser, so she knew exactly how to impress Elly with matching plates and imported silverware. Why is she so perfect? Our table could comfortably sit six people, and we were so used to having the three of us bunched up at one end, we had no idea what to do with the extra body. We waited for Elly to eenie-meenie the choices, and it resulted to him choosing the chair at the end of the right side; my dad's chair. My dad chuckled, mumbled something under his husky breath, and took the seat to the right of Elly. My mom positioned herself to the left, directly across from where my dad was. Now I was the odd one out. Any seat I chose would cause everyone to be off-balance, and I couldn't stand the whole time.

Maybe someone should leave.

"Why don't you serve the food, Basil?" My mom asked, unraveling her tablecloth to place on her lap.

"Sure," something I never do. I lifted the glass salad bowl and distributed portions to everyone's plate with Elly being first, then my dad, and finally my mom.

Then it came back into my head; the statement Elly made in the room. As I approached my mom's plate, a string kept me from willingly serving her. I clasped a conjunction of arugula and carrots, tossing them across her dish. I purposefully left out the cherry tomatoes because I know she can't live without them.

"Do you mind giving me some more parmesan slices, Basilene?"

I puffed. "Yeah, I can."

Elly snickered, lifting his fork to the ceiling. "*Guten appetit!*"

"Are you German?" My dad asked, he was already halfway done with his salad.

"Sure," Elly laughed, plucking a piece of arugula from the bunch and landing it onto his tongue. "Are you German?"

"Not at all. But, when I was younger I had a German teacher named Miss. Hahn—oh man, I had a crush on her! She used to bring us all this German cuisine and snacks. I remember once a year she'd come in wearing that little apron dress. What do you call those things?"

"Dirndl."

"That! She'd even style her hair into two thick braids that came down right by her sides," my dad implied. "It was a little much for the class, especially a little boy."

"There was a teacher at Villeton who was like that for me," Elly added. I lifted the platter overflowing with chicken, zucchinis and other colorful vegetables.

"Did they leave?" My mother questioned. Her voice had such an irksome quality to it tonight.

"No, they're still there. I left."

I filled my dad's empty plate with two large spoonfuls. He began eating before I had stopped to go to Elly. "What do you mean ya left?"

"He graduated," I inserted myself into their conversation. "He's nineteen."

"Oh!" My mom screeched. "That's a few years older than Basilene."

Shut up. "Yeah, Elly is in college."

"You'll be seventeen at the end of the year though! I guess it isn't so bad. Do you know when Basil's birthday is, Ellington?"

"No, I don't."

"It's late December. I almost had her on New Year's! Could you imagine? Welp! She's still a Capricorn though."

"What does that mean?" Elly responded.

This conversation was asking to end. Astrology only comes up when no one has anything left to say—anything good. The last time I checked my horoscope it told me I'd meet my *twin flame*, I was eleven. I had no clue what a twin flame could be, and I still think I don't, but it sounded tasty and custard filled, so I went home and tried to make pasticciotto.

"It's that silly horoscope stuff! You know! Wait, what sign are you, Ellington? When's your birthday?"`

Elly batted his eyes a few times, they clicked until he could finally remember. "June ▮."

"I don't think I know what sign that as, do you honey?" My mom looked at my dad who was already onto the next convo because no one cares.

"What are ya studying in college, Elly?"

"Film," perfect. Leave it at that.

"Oh yeah? You're a movie buff or somethin'?" My dad wasn't going to leave it at that.

I waltzed around the table, making double—triple rounds until I noticed that no one was looking at me; they had prolly forgotten I was the one filling their plates. Elly played his better hand to my parents, grinning and being attentive as hell. My mom had her elbows hiked up on the table, which is rude—shoving her cleav in Elly's untouched meal. It had never dawned on me how inappropriate my mom's attire always is. She can never wear a turtleneck or something that suited someone of her age bracket, like a mumu.

Elly started to chew on a strand of his hair instead of the food. "I'm really into Goblin's Guild, so I'm working on a project inspired by it."

My dad tumbled from his chair, knocking into me and my tray of horderves. "Ya got to be kidding me! What's your party's name?"

"Adventures of Freahyrst."

"That's my party too!" I haven't seen my dad this happy since he discovered GG. Should I make it stop?

"My screen name is Alilhaze," Elly answered and smiled.

"Alilhaze is dating my DWAUGHTER?!" Here we go. "Liv, tell me this isn't a small world! Now I gotta know more about this project of yours."

They were all laughing, cracking, and enjoy each other. I thought I would like this, and that I could submit a joke or two, but they're having fun all on their own. My parents are so used to being liked, that they can't read the room when their daughter is prying for recognition. Yeah—Elly would like my parents, who doesn't like my parents? They're so *hip* and *young*, and close to his age, of course they'd let our borderline illegal relationship slide.

"Tartula, the main character, is my absolute favorite," Elly's eyes tracked me.

"Oh! Is she the driving force of the movie?" My mom questioned.

"No because my mind won't leave her there. I wake up thinking how can I make this all be exciting for her, as exciting as she makes me," he dropped his eye gaze. "It's so hard to make the world special for someone," what is he talking about? Is he talking about me? Elly, you're all the special I need!

My mom held her hand over her ribs. "My God. You are such a romantic. I think you'll fit right in with our family, Ellington!"

Elly coughed.. "My name is Elias."

"NO!"

I had enough. The tray collapsed from my grip as chunks of chicken fell onto the table's cloth. Everyone jolted from their seats except for Elly, small shards of pepper were caught in his fleece. I still had to translate everything he said into my stubborn mind. "You don't get to say his name!"

"I didn't. You didn't...give me a chance to correct myself," my mom hoisted her hands out in front of her. "Thank you for correcting me, El-"

"WHY do you treat your name like it's nothing?" I looked over at Elly. The edge of his lip was snagged by the end of his angled tooth.

"You shouldn't talk to your mom like this, Basil."

"You know how long it took me to say your name? You know what it felt like when I finally had enough courage to say it?"

"I think you should say sorry to your mom."

"No!" It was growing. That thing inside that made me dislike myself. "She should say sorry to me!"

I can't help it.

"Basil, what is going on?" Her voice was a cacophony of fingernails dragging along my skin.

"You can't take me away from him!" I no longer have control over myself.

"Basi-" my dad placed his hand over my mother's shoulder to console her. I could see the tears form in her eyes and the way she looked at me, like she didn't want this for me at all.

Neither do I.
"sAy soRRy."
Mom.
Help me.

Chapter 20

:}

It doesn't feel right to be here for so long.

"How are the gingerbread men coming along?" Miss Lowe carried a bag full of sugar buttons and pastry tubes.

"Almost done! After they're finished, we can make room for the snowmen," I need to get going.

"I'm not sure if I deserve you, Basil," she squirted a bit of cream onto her tongue. "If you want some, help yourself! The school has to compensate me in some way."

"It's okay, I have to get going soon. My boyfriend is coming to pick me up at a quarter to seven," only to make sure I got to Wesley's in time to host my premiere live on Playthings.

I planned to be out of Villeton by 3pm, 2:45 if I managed to stealthily get past Milo's fan club and into my locker. Elly would pick me up by the front lawn, and we'd both race over to Wesley's place to start on hair and makeup. But, it wasn't like that at all. Miss Lowe caught me exiting Statistics, and thought it'd be a great time to ask for a favor—sure, catch me at my most vulnerable. She went on about how Villeton is infamous for scheduling things at the very last minute, including a holiday themed faculty meeting, and she needed my help. The convo shuffled back and forth for too long, me throwing a bunch of *I-don't-knows* her way, and her having to eventually knock off some TA hours. I wasn't sure how much more I could take of onlookers gossiping about my relationship.

"How exciting! Do you two have fun plans tonight? Catching a movie or bowling?" Miss Lowe grilled me. What does she know?

She emptied the candied buttons into a glass container, creating an ongoing *ding* noise. "No, we have to meet a friend."

"Wait! Aren't you dating Elly Hayes? Rightrightright, you are! How has that been?" I've never told Miss Lowe I was dating Elly.

"We're good," I refilled the pipe with more cream and continued lining the gingerbread's arms and legs.

"I used to have Elly as a student. Yup! He came to my class about three times the entire semester."

"This is my last one before the snowmen."

"He would always come into the class, no notebook— nothing, and he would count out loud the amount of students who showed up. Oh yeah! And, he would eat everything! He's so gluttonous, that one," she smiled to herself while sticking buttons to each little cookie. "I hope he's doing well."

I removed the trees from the oven and replaced them with snowflakes. They were our last batch before we could finish the decorating and hang our aprons up for the night. A couple of doors down, an assembly of whistling and hollering came galloping through the halls. The chants were faint at first, but the noise enlarged after minutes of starting. A crowd of golden and green varsity jackets mobbed the hallway as pompoms pervaded the air.

"I guess everyone's getting ready to go home but us," Miss Lowe joked. She's really not funny. "I know we've talked about this before, but are you still thinking about going to culinary school, Basil?"

"It's been in the back of my mind, I haven't decided yet," I took a sip of water and wiped my damp forehead with my shoulder.

"Well, there's a residency program that I think you should look into. You'd have to apply soon though because it would take place the summer before your senior year."

A summer away from Elly sounded disgusting. "I'm prolly gonna see if I can get a scholarship for a school in the city."

"The residency could potentially lead to a scholarship in Avignon, where you'd be residing."

"Avignon?"

"France. I think you have a good chance of getting accepted, you have a very special relationship with baking, Basil."

Miss Lowe knew I was giving her my best glum-gleam, but I was internally raving. France. This is the place I've asked my parents to go almost every summer vacation, but they would always end up choosing some tropical getaway with warm mojitos. France to me meant getting a step closer to culinary aristocracy, and that was a goal that wasn't going to be obtainable in my town. But, that meant my first boyfriend-filled summer would be a no-go.

"Basil?" That wasn't Miss Lowe.

"Is that Declan Hayes?!" Miss Lowe removed a cookie from our completed pile. "My girl! Come here, have one before a teacher walks by!"

"It's okay," she stared at me. I don't recall the last time I saw her. "How's everything been?"

I've seen Declan around Villeton, mainly dashing from class to class, always knocking into someone who didn't care because Declan Hayes just touched them. We haven't spent that much time together, not like we once did.

"Great. How's everything been with you?" I grinned because I was genuinely happy to see her.

She was dressed in regular clothes; a sweatshirt, joggers, and a baseball cap. Always like Declan to switch out of cheer-gear any moment she had. "You busy?"

"I'm finis-"

"Nope! She can go," Miss Lowe removed the tray of unfinished treats from my station. "Go—I'll finish up the rest."

"Are you sure?" I untied the knot in the back of the apron.

"I'm sure," she whispered. "Go have fun."

She cut her hair. Declan's hair used to swirl down her hip, but now it stopped at her mid-back. Am I a bad friend for not giving her a compliment yet? I like it. I couldn't tell until she started walking ahead of me towards the field. Getting to Villeton's football field was a conquest I could never fulfill—the entire sports wing was a myth to me. There were so many glass cases that held achievements and trophies like they were relics.

There was also this putrid smell right before exiting the school, which is only proof of how shit everything is.

Declan stopped and sat at the edge of a bleacher. The stadium lights blasted over the muggy grass, and a post rainy night sky made the clouds morose and fine. Declan scooched about a foot over to give me room beside her, but I instead took the damp bench above her seat.

"It's cold tonight!" I bunched my arms up into my coat. Declan peered out at the field. "How was cheer practice?"

"It's okay," she pulled her hat down. "Basil, what is going on?"

HELP ME!

"What?"

"You think I don't know something is up? Something is going on between you, Elly, Lane, and Wes. I know you're all spending time without me."

I couldn't possibly tell her, but I also didn't anticipate her bringing it up tonight. "Nothing. We're all just hanging."

"Lane and Wesley were *my* friends, and then all of a sudden they've started spending more time with my brother than with me."

"They are your friends! I think they think you're just too busy."

"I am, but you're the only person to mention that," she laughed, adjusting her hat further. "I'm sorry. I shouldn't have started off the conversation like this. I just miss hanging out with you guys."

I miss you, Declan.

"This might be a weird question, but do you even get along with your brother?" I asked. The remaining facial strain from her laugh calmed down.

She sighed. "I love my brother, but I tolerate him to be around the people who I do like."

I thought Declan's friends were nothing without her, I thought they were feasting off of her popularity—her reputation, but Declan was really nothing without her friends. She even cut inches off of her hair hoping someone would say something about it, and here I am—the friend who still hasn't.

"Have you heard about what happened to my brother, Basil?"

Yes. The car accident off the bridge. Elly Hayes being stamped as unhinged. "I hear a lot of stupid things that Villetoners say. It doesn't mean they're all true."

"It is true," she exhaled. "I was there."

"You were where?"

"The night of Elly's accident. I was in the car with him."

The story no one had the real answer to. It was the biggest rumor Villeton held onto that inherently wove to me. I was the girl that dated the guy who tried to off himself. According to everyone at my school, I could only be dealing with some form of mental illness or neglect to even consider dating someone who the town deemed as deranged. But, is everyone else not a little deranged too?

"You don't have to talk about this if you don't want to," I insisted.

Declan removed her hat from her head, fanning her hair with her fingertips. "I want to," she stammered. "Elly never drove into the river, he pushed the car off the bridge."

I stuttered. "Why would he do that?"

"I don't know, but I remember that night really well. He was extremely hysterical, and he kept yelling at me to get into the car."

"Hold on, Declan. He wanted *you* to get into the car—to like, push you off the bridge?"

"Yes," she swallowed some of her emphasis. "We were driving in his car and came to a stop at the bridge. He got out of the driver's seat, walked over to the passenger's side, and explained to me what he was going to do."

This. This—no, this is a facade.

"Declan."

"He told me there was something he had to do, and if it wasn't going to be me then it would be him," Declan's voice broke. "I still feel so guilty about it because I didn't listen to him, and he said I hurt him to the point of no return."

She started to shatter. I shouldn't see her broken over something Elly's done. Is she lying? This couldn't be true. Elly would never yell or tell his sister to do something that would sacrifice her life. Elly isn't a yeller, I've never heard his voice raise past a mumbling-octave. Elly is a good person, and he cares about Declan so much. If it weren't for Elly, I wouldn't be sitting in front of his sister right now trying to console her. She should be thanking her brother, but she chooses to shed tears over tall-tales. How could she do something like this to her sibling? I'd love to have a sibling right now because I don't think my parents will talk to me again after last night.

Help me.

"I'm sorry that happened to you," I rubbed her back. She sat forward, bringing her lukewarm tension to me.

"I'm not making this up."

"I never said you were."

"You think I'm lying."

I do. "It's just, why would anyone do something like that to somebody they're related to? And, why would you want to spend time around someone who threatened your life?"

"To be around you," she cried. The bleachers became rickety holding her voice. "Can't you tell, Basil? I like you! I've liked you since you were a freshmen. You're not someone who I want to hang out with from time to time—I want you to *have* my time."

With wet eyes, she stood and grappled the bottom of my jeans. She was so unreal up close, she appeared far. She placed her cap back on her head, and it guarded her peripherals from the waft of floodlights that traced around her. She grimaced at what she had done, and possibly everything she had said, but she wasn't going to let it stage her motives. She swam her tongue through and around the opening of her lips, softening them from the wintry tinge. I loved Elly more than my heart could account for, and I loved him so much I was in love with everything about her.

Declan's lips were just like I remembered. They were so kind and balmy, and they were highly permitted. I reached up, removing her hat from her head and lodged my fingers around the back of her neck. She was warmer than the manipulated kitchen degree—she was sensational. I counted the minutes I was aiming to stop, but they instead supplied me with more thoughts of her.

"Miss Lowe was talking to me about a summer residency in France before you walked by," it was the first breath we had taken since we started. "France is three-thousand miles away."

"That's amazing!" She scooped my face up with her palms. "I'm going to miss you."

"Well, I haven't decided if I'm going to apply yet," I loosened her hands and brought them back to my lap.

"Why wouldn't you?"

Elly. "France is too far away."

"Basil."

"What?" My phone beeped in my pocket. Elly was here. She kissed me one last time before standing up.

"I don't want you to be with Elly," she readjusted her tilted hat. "I want you to be with me."

I removed my phone from my coat pocket, I was already two minutes late to the message. "I can't leave him."

Elly: I'm here.

Not for her. Not for anyone.

Chapter 21

:#

Tartula:...
User00324: You look so beautiful.

Inside of Wesley's airy closet held a lair fit for a nature deity. Sparkles stuck to chiffon that dangled from steel coat hangers, and artificial grass coated the bitter floors. There were no vents or windows, but enough space to make me think this was okay—that I'm okay. Every so often I would max out the screen's brightness to see how much I could blind myself, but when my attempts were proven pathetic, I'd turn it down to remember where I was. My sockets started to disassemble, and I knew I was a muster away from calling it quits. But, how could I? Not when I'm seeping like this.

I held a lengthy trial with myself inside of Wesley's bathroom. Most of the time it was easy coming to his house; punching a code in at the gate just to get to the next level of pompous—it was never too much for me. Tonight though, tonight the furnishings couldn't avert from what I had agreed to. A mirror hung on every wall in the bathroom, and I had nearly no room to stroll from my reflection, or *hers*. From corner to corner to corner, there she was—Tartula. I had stopped speaking to myself a while ago; I was now adhering to demands.

In the past I've let myself down a bit, so much it had become suitable for me to let down everyone else. I knew there was always Elly, but I had to take into account that there was also Lane and Wesley—they truly believed that I was substantial enough to become a goddess when I could barely make it off of who I am. I'm the kind to always need something, or someone, to be that leverage that gets trapped. How can I succeed in this without them? How have I gotten this far knowing I'm not them?

Chat names all look the same after thirty seconds; they're just a *ding* when a tip hits. They're just a thing.

User00324: Are you crying?
User00324: You shouldn't cry here.

A string of remote-controlled fireflies twinkled behind me. They were fully under the influence of Lane, and she'd make them go berserk whenever someone felt generous.

User00324: I'm coming.

I shook my head to stop him. I'm not crying, I'm getting rid of still emotion. The false eyelashes I had on made everything appear choppy, and I liked that. "Elly."

Your Mic is Off ♡!

Drawing out the syllables in his name felt like pedaling up shingle. Everyone in the chat could still see me, and the private message between Elly and I flickered at the very bottom of the page, next to a still photo of who I was supposed to be; pink-tails, thick eyeliner, blinding grape eyeshadow, and lip gloss that was now between my teeth.

It was the first time I ever felt my backbone dissolve. I reached up to rip a piece of material from the decorated chiffon and blew my nose into it—sending bits of snot flying at the screen. The chat went bonkers as I did that, and it eventually occurred to me that anything can turn on impassioned beasts. The chiffon smelled just like Elly, and in such little time too.

"Basil," he balanced himself through the closet entryway, looking like serendipity. "What's wrong?"

Maybe I can make crying my passable temperament. Just earlier, Declan placed her lips on mine while her tears watered my resilience, and I doubt she ever hates herself when she cries. No one tells Declan Hayes who to be because no one expects her to be anyone but Declan. I wouldn't want anyone besides that. A part of me thought of telling her about the broadcast tonight just so she could be here; she has the kind of voice that makes crying not feel so bad.

I slumped my body forward—away from the laptop's lens. My arms crept up the grassy carpet in the direction of Elly's feet, and it almost looked like I was praying to him. How much would it hurt if I did? He crouched lower and lifted me up by my wrists, making a bow with them behind his back.

"Basil."

Elly smelled just like the chiffon. "What?"

"I love you."

My sobs broke the barricade to my humility, and then I knew I was doing fine.

"you do?" I shrunk even smaller. "What is there to love?"

"Everything."

"answer me like I'm something, please."

He groaned, and then passed it up with a smirk. "There is a box full of things that I don't know how to deal with."

When Elly talks, there is always a misty gas that revolves around his springy curls. Some days it's a blueish-jade-like color, and other days its more of a cyan. Today it's a modest periwinkle —congratulating Tartula.

He continued. "My brain breaks everything off into subcategories. I want people to see this part of me, I don't want people to see others," his voice was so different now—so unfeigned.

He was trying to speak to me without the modifications. No Lane or Wesley bickering behind closed panels, and no Villetoners swaying my ambitions.

Elly tell me. "Then, there's you Basil."

The periwinkle fog casted a helmet around me. "Uhuh."

"You're a part of all that I don't dig into. You're so valuable to me, and I'm going to keep you safe there."

"You think I'm that precious?"

"Without you, *Sounds of the Noir Amulet* wouldn't be."

The title. It was my first time hearing it.

"Hey, Black Beauty!" Lane shouted. And I thought this was a private moment. "Don't be nervous. This is bagels—you're going to do great!"

"Yeah!" Wesley tacked onto the reassurance.

Elly arched over and brushed my forehead with the tip of his nose. I tried to laugh, but his lips borrowed my amusement.

He laughed for both of us. "Look at how many people want to see you."

6.5k Members Joined!

CHrisCOOl: Where did she go?

VkngS24: Unmute your mic

CornDog70: god bless her

Philuck: DEJA ME VER TU CULO

PopRockGoth: She's hot.

Burnbam004: private pls

PopRockGoth: Come back lol.

MerylCreep: Can you unmute? Would love her you.

StreetSAVY: I need that skin again!

StreetSAVY: StreetSAVY tipped $20! ♡

"These usernames are stoke as hell. Hey, do you think we can we get these sleebs to pay with septiccurrency?" Lane cackled.

"They miss you, babe," pink shimmer now took up the top of Elly's lip.

Babe.

8.2k Members Joined!

Burnbam004: hot

Burnbam004: pls give m e call 4 private
PopRockGoth: You're back!
CornDog70: wb
CornDog70: wow u r beautiful
Philuck: QUE BELLA!
CHrisCOOl: Are you new
CornDog70: shes new
CornDog70: id remember a face like that

Babe.

Tartula: do you want to know something about me
Tartula: I'm going to be in a movie
CornDog70: tell us more
VkngS24: Name?
Druggymith: Thats so awesome!
MerylCreep: Tell us the name.
StreetSAVY: How much do you need?
K0RN4LUV: d do anything to see u agn
Burnbam004: private pls I tip well
PopRockGoth: You're an actress?
PopRockGoth: You've got the face for it.
User00324: How can we support the film, Tartula?
BlameLane: do you need money?
BlameLane: or do you need votes? :#
Tartula: Both.

Elly spoke like my mother. Not like, the kissing part, but him trying to cheer me up when I made hills out of my fears. My mom does the same thing. I psych myself out not only with baking, but every time I realize I can't be safe as the wallflower.

My mom is the opposite of me, and she's so good at making it appetizing with encouragement and cheer. I know that I will never be the person she was in high school, and she will never outwardly admit that I am the daughter that she didn't imagine. I'd rather not think about her after what happened at dinner the other night, but she's my mom.

NO.

She's the person trying to take him away.

10k Members Joined!

Tartula: sounds of the noir amulet
Tartula: make sure to vote at the Brunhart Festival
Siskeeper: sure!
CornDog70: I will
PopRockGoth: I've heard of the Brunhart Festival.
PopRockGoth: Do you live in New York?
StreetSAVY: !!!!!!!!!!!!
BlameLane: who cares?
Tartula: I do.

Babe.

SINFINSTER: nigger bitch
SINFINSTER: nigger
SINFINSTER: ugly nigger

They stood out like a bad memory, and in there I was revived. I am the little nigger bitch waking up in the morning to find frays of where I left off. The times I told my classmates that my father was half white, or the many times I told myself that my skin color would grow out. I thought hoop earrings were a *black* accessory, so I refused to wear them in my middle school graduation photo—they'd all find out. I think I forgot all about that this time—the smoother my performance became, and the more fascinating I had become. Inside of the kaleidoscope of my infirmity, was still the nigger bitch. Going strong, but still not gone.

PopRockGoth: Disgusting.
JEEFUS: bruh
JEEFUS: gtfo
MerylCreep: Let's dox them.

"Dude!" Lane yelped. "Let's block this trag."
"What a meanie! I'm so sorry Basie, don't listen that guy! Yuck!" Wesley included.
"Let them stay," Elly declared. "Look."

CornDog70: CornDog70 tipped $50! ♡

It's all for me.

battlebright: battlebright tipped $220! ♡

"They're banking hard!" Lane pressed her phone into her nose. "Look at these sleebs blow! This must be the price of white guilt."

PopRockGoth: PopRockGoth tipped $75! ♡

Burnbam004: Burnbam004 tipped $500! ♡

Kingstiff: Kingstiff tipped $340! ♡

    I must be great.

    Babe. Do you finally see how great I can be? I'm a high-rise billowing over SOS missiles and grenades. I'm accelerating and expanding, and with you—with you Elly, I can take it all hostage! The two of us will no longer have to spend hours parodying the series of our love story. This is rEAL! Here comes that adrenaline you scrapped from my skin in your jeep (Declan's). That HOT censored steam plaguing that girl who was too shy to make you mine; the girl who couldn't say your name because she couldn't accept how it drained her taste. Let me be your movie star inside the shutter of your imagination, and cast me into a satellite for the world to televise.

    Tartula, I think it's time for you to come alive.

Tartula: do you love me?
MerylCreep: Yes!
K0RN4LUV: more thn anything
K0RN4LUV: unmute
Tartula: TELL mE.
Tartula: ShoW mE
DreadsDead: hey
DreadsDead: I think I know you
DreadsDead: your name starts with a B

    It's dying.

    "Uh oh!" Wesley yelled. "Mayday mayday!"

    "Shit. Log off, BB!" Lane trampled into the room, stumping her toe into my small setup. Particles from her drink splattered across my knees and onto the touchpad—waking me up.

"Someone knows you," Elly was simpering. "Invite them to a private then."

"I thought you said no privates," Tartula.

"I want to see who this is."

"This dude could be flipping our burger. You can't just put BB in a chat with them—it's dangerous!"

"Lane," Elly crouched down and yanked the can from Lane's grip. "Why don't you go take a walk?"

Lane's fingers trembled in a still motion, outlining a drink that was once there. Elly loomed over her until Lane finally dismantled the gaze. She shot up and made her way out of Wesley's room, crashing the door behind her.

"Invite him to a private, Basil," he scattered over, snatching the mouse from me to click on the unknown user. "Don't you want to know who it is, babe?"

Chapter 22

;I

DreadsDead: I can't afford your rate
DreadsDead: so let's make this short
Tartula: How do you know me?

Elly was typing for me. This person could be anyone; it could be someone who I go to high school with, and they could blackmail me for the simple reason of me dating Elly Hayes. If Villeton gets a hang of this, my rep would be as dead as this person's lame username—we could all get expelled. My parents would catch heed and fully disown me, not like they already have, but they actually *will*. I'd be an embarrassment.

DreadsDead: Can we video chat?
Tartula: Sure.

Elly went behind the monitor, leaving the circular cushion that was originally Tartula's wide open. I leaned over, looking up at him before I decided to click the video chat icon. He twisted his legs up into his arms—worry was nowhere on his bones. He did to me just as someone did to Phat Pheasant the time we video chatted with her. Someone besides the host was pulling the reigns, and the other person in the chat had no idea. They'd assume I'd be doing all of this for greed, and I'd have to be alright with the contrived spotlight.

The small chat window hopscotched across the screen, expanding over the blinking chat messages. A guy in a heather grey hoodie sipped cola from a cardboard straw and sized me up before I could interpret his rationale. There were a handful of black kids that attended Villeton, and he def was not one of *them* —I'd be able to recognize any of those kids before I could break apart some family members. We each strangled each other with glances until I noticed the beehive tattoo on his cheek. Where is that from, and why does it make me blush this way?

Oh.

DreadsDead: I thought we'd never meet again
DreadsDead: can we turn on our mics? If that's cool with you...

I started to type *no*, but Elly quickly reached over and unmuted the laptop.

"I forgot your name," I blurted. It's Marques.

"You can call me, Marq. Basil, right? That's probably the only thing I remember from that night at Eight Ball."

Elly blinked. He unrolled back into the closet wall and watched me continue.

"Is someone in there with you?" Marq commented, veering closer to the frame. His hoodie was pulled up completely, concealing his forehead and eyebrows—this must be his online outfit.

"My friend," I lied. "She's laughing because she was there that night too."

He unveiled his perfect smile. "What are you doing on Playthings?"

"I'm starring in my friend's movie, and we needed the votes for the festival," I was SWEATING. I knew that Marq and Elly could both see the forest of water cascade from my hairline.

"Really? I would love to go to your premiere, or support however I can," he bite his lower lip.

"I don't think you should."

He choked. "Why not? I actually really like you, Basil. I was upset I never got your number that night."

Elly fiddled with his pants cusp, pretending to leave me out. "We can't meet again, and I'd really like you to not tell anyone you saw me here. Or, say my name—please stop saying my name."

Marq was good looking, but to look at him, I had to gawk in front of Elly. Elly was off counting the strings at the bottom of his distressed jeans; he knew that I could never tear from the plague of this crisis. It devastated me to know that someone I met inside of a dark club could point me out underneath gallons of highlighter—if he could, anyone would be able to. But, Marq has to understand that I'm not who he thinks I am—this is just a coat I put on when Basil is too cold. I'm sure he's still excited to extort me for the little I've salvaged.

"Can we meet in person again?" The connection cut out for a second, but Elly heard Marq through the echoed fizz. He looked away from me.

Relationships are forged to heal infatuation. I know it because I'm looking at Marq and discovering Elly. Elly wrenched a strand from the bottom of his pant and twiddled it in with his hair. It's my mistake to not always be available, but I'm determined to make all that Elly is for me.

"I'm sixteen," I replied. Marq turned his camera off and I could hear rustling behind the hooded screen.

"Sorry," the rustling continued. "Are you fucking with me?"

"No, I'm a high school student."

"YOU are a high school student?" He cracked. "Look at you!"

"I don't want to lie anymore," His screen shot back up, and there were the doughy features in Marq's face. I'm sure he's soft with a caramelized center.

"You know something? You haven't lied to me," he removed his locs from his hood and draped them over his shoulders like armor. "I wished you were older for my sake, but of course, I can't have a relationship with a sixteen-year-old."

"Would you be okay leaving the chat so I can continue promoting the film?" I asked, and he rubbed his face with his inked fingers—loosening his knuckles with a quick stretch. His mouth outlined a word, but I couldn't make it out.

"What?" I questioned.

"Is someone forcing you to do this?"

Elly popped his head up towards the screen and white pant strings simmered from his strands. My concerned eyes tracked him. "No."

"Is your friend still there with you?"

The manufactured lighting eclipsed and budded behind me. The growing warmth made my skin wash in and out of the camera's focus. It seized until Elly lugged the cord out.

"You know this isn't you," Marq went on. "I actually don't even think this was meant for you."

"What do you mean?"

"I think you're sitting in someone else's spot," he leaned out. "The *real* Tartula."

"You're a smartass," Crap. I didn't mean to *tell* him that.

"It's your friends, isn't it? The ones you came in with that night. The guy you were looking for—the same one who didn't come to find you."

"Shut. Up."

"Is he there with you? Are you looking at him while you're looking me? He knows the truth, that you can't be her."

I rattled my hair, forcing pieces of streamer to descend from the ceiling. "I'm ending this chat!"

"Basil, do you really want to be a Plaything?"

"THAT'S IT!" Elly lunged forward, sweeping the broadcasting set off the circular night table that praised it. The laptop catapulted from the closest's wall, creating an expensive dent that Wesley could afford. Elly and I watched the screen surge and sizzle, making the room flash in color. The computer said something to me until it decided it was better off to just die.

"Are you okay?" Elly questioned me. He stood to shake off the calamity around us, and that's when I knew the live was finally over.

My new favorite thing was walking around Wesley's house barefoot. Everything was so tall and cosmic when viewing it from 5'4, and the frost from the hardwood floors stimulated my freezing toes. Wesley's parents were figureheads, and maybe suppositious, but his house was so animate without them. Photos of the family captured stock depictions of health and blood. The rooms, halls, walls, and doors that could transport me to the sunny nights that made me reminisce on the first day Elly spoke to me.

Or the first and only time I told my mom I hated her. It was at an after-school event that she was too early to. She had on a khaki tracksuit and matching platform high-top trainers. Our car back then was an ashy navy blue Nissan, and I can replay the exact axis it took to roll into the parking garage. All the kids were there, and we all ogled in mid-play watching this woman demand our fun with her strut. I wanted no one to know she was my mom, but there was no one else's mom she could be, and I recognized that. So, I told her I hated her. I hated her for showing up, and letting everyone else know that I'm a part of her household.

My dad yelled at me for that because my mom was too bruised to rebuttal. I was eight and scared, but eight isn't stupid. Now I'm double that, and equally misguided.

"What caught your tongue, BB?" Lane shared a pan of sliced pita with Fen. I had fallen into Wesley's kitchen somehow —the mood-board rendition of the kitchen I've always fantasized.

"The live ended," I joined them at the wooden countertop, sitting beside Fen and directly in front of Lane. I took a piece of pita for myself. Bland. "I'm sorry you had to leave like that."

"Dude, I'm not gonna trip from some stoke ass sleep who claims they know you. It's all good, BB."

"I will head off to bed and let you two talk amongst yourselves," Fen skirted off her bar stool, and shielded herself with her silk robe. "I wish you both a goodnight."

"Goodnight!" Lane and I sang out.

Lane pushed down the rest of her pita, dousing club soda down her throat to help lube it up. "Sweet lady, can't cook for shiz."

"How long were you down here with her?"

Lane slapped the remaining crumbs from her face. "Thirty minutes—an hour, it's all the same! She only talks about Wesley and his sister. It's like yo, you have your own fets to worry about. She's like, 'Wesley needs to go to college and get good education!' As if it's my problem the kid's a trag."

Lane was usually cruel but tonight her cruelty came with a sheet of veracity that was unlike her. She usually goes on about Wesley's incompetence, but shortly after she'll make up for it by ending it with a backhanded compliment. I don't like it. I'll resort to bringing up someone Lane can't rag on. "I saw Declan today."

"I haven't seen Dec in a minute. How's she holding up?"

"She cut her hair."

Lane snickered. "Not well, I'm guessing. Good for her! You should tell her to come by. She's always down for a line, unlike the two upstairs."

"A line of what?" Lane rolled her eyes as soon as I asked.

"Shit you don't do. I really miss hanging with Dec. She's not a people person, but she's the person people prefer. Like me, I like-like people. I can be around people for hours—days!" Lane quivered pulling a cigarette from her bra strap; that girl can hide a cigarette from tobacco.

"I feel like Wesley is too," here's your chance to say something nice, Lane.

"So BB," she chose to change the subject. Smart. "What's it like kissing a brother and a sister?"

Not smart.

I took another grab at the stale pita, dipping it into some hummus to spare me some more time to react. Lane couldn't have seen what happened earlier today because she was here decorating the den. Then who? Did Declan tell Lane herself? No, Declan and Lane haven't spoken to each other in days. Then what gave it away? Has Lane spent so much time with Declan that she can now identify who's been lip-locking with her? Is that a real thing? I like Declan more than I'm admitting, but those feelings can't surface.

"It was only that one time," I fibbed.

"You were seen tonight," she lit the cigarette. "Someone bopped you two and tattled."

I could taste my palpitations. "You're not going to tell Elly, right?"

She began to laugh into a wheez. "I really like you BB, but I don't owe anything to you, or anyone. What's fair is right, and you're hurting my friend."

"I know I shouldn't do this to her, I'm so—"

"NO! Not Declan—Elly," she stumbled her tongue around her cracked blistered lips. "Elly has feelings, y'know."

How dare she. "I'm not trying to hurt him!"

"Lower your voice," she drew her shoulders in and slouched over the table closer to me. "I'll tell you one thing— Declan isn't the person you think she is. We're all keeping our distance because we know how warped she can be. She's doing this crap on purpose, trying to ruin our group. What we got is solid, y'know? Remember what I told you she did with Milo? Screwed MY guy."

"I thought that was before you two had dated."

"Milo always wanted Declan, and he uses me to be around her," the same way Declan uses her brother to be around me. "How sick is that?"

Lane didn't stop, but I drowned her out to peer into an empty cupboard. It was weathered with spices and stories, possibly all from Fen. A pink dash drawn for each year Wesley grew into a young adult, and a green dash that I assumed represented his younger sister. The cupboard emanated joy and daylight, and I remembered I had to get home soon, but home felt frozen in a time I don't think I could backtrack to. Wesley's home is so chilly because it's broad and underfed, but I can still see a presumptuous warmth that imprisons me here.

Chapter 23

:]

We met on a drug store line. I stood tall in my Lil Foun-Tain backstage pullover, rummaging through sulfate free conditioners. He drafted into the aisle, spying my hunchback and neck sweat. There was nothing for him in here, unless he loves a good texturizer. This Winston's crammed all their ethnic doodahs into an 11x11 baker's rack. The hair goods were in no way separate from the makeup. Names like *4 the Sista* and *Melalala* boxed me into a store-bought lifestyle, and this rando was effortlessly becoming a part of it.

The stubs on his chin looked more like blackheads. They made a better topic of conversation than whatever it was he was trying to pull. His dark hair was shaved into bashful curls with a sandy edge. I knew he was like, my age, but his raised chest behind his color-blocked polo aged him at least ten years. What sixteen-year-old stands like they own a cabin cruiser? Prolly one that does. Also, he had on a pair of bleach stained sweat-shorts, and that's what got me really befuddled.

"Do you have any recs?" I ignored him because there was no way he would be talking to me. He had Mallory Prep as a morning glaze, a private schooler would never give a Villetoner their regard.

"My mom's white, so I don't know about any of this stuff," I had now taken on the part-time of enlightening the mixed kid.

"I've tried this one before," I rose *GuuurlCuuurl* from the shelf. "It's okay."

"Your hair must be stupid long!" He doesn't have to talk like that to me. He moved in closer, hovering over my bobby pin collision.

"It's pretty long, yeah," I loosened a curl from the bunch and ran it down to my rib cage. His gape followed my shaky grip.

"Hells yeah! Yo, you're so dope! Can I get your addy?"

"My address?"

"No, sorry! Advice?"

I learned I was easy that day. That any guy could approach me and I'd give them a digit and an opportunity. He was also the first boy's number I saved to my phone, besides the tongue-tool who I kissed at my cousin Taz's Sweet Sixteen—my first kiss. We texted for a week and I learned that his name was Callum Belleville Dickson or *CBD*. The first night we hung out, I lied and told my parents I forgot some of my personal utensils in the school kitchen. CBD and I heavily canoodled for about an hour, as he clammed my breast with his palm and motioned it around like he was cleaning his BMW. I made up more excuses to see him, and the more I did, the further we'd get each time. I'm not sure if I enjoyed the intimacy or if I tolerated the company that always fell askew.

The night we agreed to go all the way I backed out last minute, and came up with a bigger fib that Purple was vomiting due to gas buildup. He replied by asking who Purple was.

16,387 unread messages on Playthings. 16,387 people want to get to know me. 16,387 people know that I am a star. 16,387 is a really long way from 50,000, but it's still 16,387. 16,387 people want my attention and mine alone. 16,387 is probably more people than my town's pop. 16,387 will get our film to win. 16,387 people know about *Sounds of the Noir Amulet*. 16,387 people's opinions I could consider, but I still only care about one.

User00324: Babe.
User00324: You're doing so good.
User00324: I'm going to give you a gift.
User00324: It's a surprise. :]

I don't need anything, Elly. Not when I have you.

I don't see color as well as I used to. I think it might be a result of looking at things too intensely. Before my mind used to skim over contrasting lines and dyes, now it only swallows things into an extremely bleak palette. My room especially doesn't shine like it did when I'd come home from middle school mush. My room used to be free with fuchsia and lilac letting go all around me, and purple was my favorite thing in the world. Now I look at my room, and I can only imagine what it thinks when it interrogates me.

Some of the fibers in my quilt were coming undone. I should've seen this approaching while spending 85% of my time at home under a blanket. It's so comfortable under here, I don't have to worry about who is looking at me or criticizing the way I waste. I have 16,387 better things to do than to worry about what is or isn't out there for me. If I come up from this cave, they'll be there—I know it! I can't confine myself to my parent's interpretation.

Besides all the unread messages in the Playthings portal, I had two real life texts in my phone. One was from Taz asking what I wanted to do for my birthday, and the other was from Declan. She forwarded me a video of a kid falling off his *Laser-Skater*, which I think is a contraption that should be banned altogether—still funny though. I watched the video about five times but never texted her back. I should've said *haha*, or let her know I'm thinking about her, and I haven't forgotten the way her mouth paints.

Playthings had a feature that allowed a user to view a message thread without alerting the sender. I previewed a few before noticing a common demand—the plea for nudes. The first and only nude I've ever sent was to CBD. He wasn't sure how to react to the zoomed in shot of my training bra strap, so he responded with a modest, *dayum that's hot!* I guess I succeeded in some retrospect. That was like a year ago, and now I'm stacking cash off of doing almost nothing. How much would they drop to see a bit of racy skin? I wouldn't know unless I tried.

Tartula: I want to take some photos

User00324: What for?
Tartula: for everyone

My phone was already in my hands, my blanket had encased me inside with all my defiant inquiries. I moved from the Playthings app to the camera, switching the direction of focus onto me. I expanded the neck of my tank top to stabilize my boob, and tried to get it to stay without having to take my entire shirt off—that was impossible; I could only accomplish my fraud flick if everything was off. OFF. The tank pulled on some sweat as it looped over my bun and out of the fortress. I lengthened my arm out to get all of me, including the dimples in my cheek as I grinned.

My tits are kind of boring.

I made my body do a 180 onto the mattress. I lifted my phone above my crown to capture my entire backside, or try to past my gargantuan bun. My underwear rode up my crack and as tempting as it was to pull out the wedgie, I think this was the kind of stuff Playthings users guzzled. The more uncomfortable, the better the picture. I tried to arch up more, and a small draft arose from under the blanket and past my dank armpits, giving me a full sample of my own reek.

"Oh my GAW—" I gagged into my phone screen, mistakingly holding down the capture button. It wasn't a bad photo, but it was way more suggestive than I intended. "Naw."

User00324: Is that you?
Tartula: yeah
Tartula: what do you think?
User00324: User00324 has left the chat!

CBD was a distraction from patches, and patches are used to replace hiccups. We were never together, we were incubating in our loneliness—freeing one another from the flummox of our names. We met each other to send the other off into the wisdom of what we inherited. We're cheated because we're cheap and we're easy. As effortless as I was for CBD to get, he was just as simple. But, without him who would I be? I shouldn't give a boy so much of my youth because he'll turn our time together into a game. He'll unbind these patches, and it'll hurt like shit when they do.

Tartula: Elly?

His internet must've gone out. He's going to sign back on and fawn over my curves. He's going to tell me how he doesn't only love the dimples in my face, but the ones at the end of my spine, the ones that only he had the attachment to. Elly? I can't delete this from the chat, it's going to resurrect whenever I decide to log on and talk to HIM. Each conversation will be burdened with the blurry sight of my ass, and I'll have to ignore his great escape that came right after. He should be signing back on now, Elly wouldn't leave me like that. My boyfriend wouldn't do that to me.

BUT HE DID.

He knew that I had BRB'd to take some snapshots for all of them. He became envious of Tartula exposing herself to everyone but hIm. The possibility of others writhing in Tartula's beauty butchered his soul because he knew that even he couldn't squander Tartula's storm without evaporating!

"You good in there?" My dad was in my room, and I was underneath a quilt naked and humid.

"Can you get out?" I blurted, trying to jimmy my hand across the bed to grab my tank.

"Let's try that question again," ugh.

I adjusted the pitch. "Can you please give me a second?"

He blew out some hot air. "Alright, I'll give you a minute to get yourself together."

I waited until I heard the *click* behind the door before I sent the cover flying. I threw myself into my dresser drawer, pulling out the first oversized t-shirt I could find. My mind lingered to the idea of my dad assuming I was buttering my biscuit, but I quickly decided not to sulk in that forever. My dad wanting to talk to me alone was either about two things, *what was the Wi-Fi password?* And, *what's the name of that one pirating website?* I'm not suggesting that my dad spends all of his off time online, but I wouldn't recognize him without a screen in his face.

Wait—

My dad spends all of his time online. Does he know what Playthings is? Of course he does. Has he seen Tartula? What if someone in his party was going on and on about some new chick on Playthings, and sent him the direct link to my channel.

"Basil!" He shouted. "I'm not trying to wait here forever!"

"Okay-okay! Come in!"

Staying up past 3am every night made my dad's eye bags prominent and spongey. He came in, lightly closing the door behind him, which meant it was def something he didn't want my mom to hear. "How's school?"

That's how we're starting? "Good, I'm not failing anything."

"That's good, keep doing that."

"Sure."

"Yeah," he was being awkward, more awkward than his usual aloofness. There was something on his mind, but he was dodging it. My dad and I share some quirky habits that advertise our relationship to those who aren't too sure. Like, we both furrow our brows—a lot. Not to imply anger, but to show we're thinking about something deeply. And tonight, my dad's eyebrows were to the tip of his eyelashes.

"I should probably get started on some homework now."

"We got a call today from that white teacher of yours," they're all white.

"Miss Lowe?"

"Yeah, that one. She was talkin' about a residency in Avignon next year, and how she'd be happy to sponsor you for it. Why didn't you tell me or your mom?"

Because I'm not going to do it. "That was so long ago, I think I forgot."

"If you want to do it, you can do it," I can? NO.

My dad is going to try to resell my dreams to me. Convince me that baking is my *modus operandi,* and I would be going against myself if I don't milk it for all that it's worth. My dad can't recall what it's like pursuing a hobby whilst in high school trying to maintain relevancy. Hobbies come second to boyfriends and social charades. I can't think about Avignon when I have 16,387 messages anticipating a response from Tartula. I'd prove myself to be egotistical if I left them out, and my dad raised me better than that.

He should know.

"I don't really want to."

His eyebrows held up. "You sure about that?"

"Yes, I want to stay here next summer."

"Do ya friends have anything to do with that decision?"

I took the thickest gulp ever. "Yeah," but why lie?

My dad walked over to my dresser with all the nail polish on it and found the stain Elly left. My dad scrapped at the dried lacquer, removing it chip by chip until residue drizzled along the floor. The red stood out against every silenced color around it. It was therapeutic watching it recolor the sweetness that was left.

"I'm not against you making friends, but ya mom and I are worried about you."

"What is there to be worried about? I'm doing good in school, I'm passing all my classes."

"I don't know if you remember the other night when ya threw a platter onto the table, and yelled at your mother for calling your boyfriend the wrong name."

"SHE DID!"

My dad rose his hands up as if he suddenly dropped something. "This shouldn't be the second time I'm asking ya to watch your tone."

"I'm not doing anything wrong! I'm sorry I'm not sipping your nips every two seconds."

"What does that even mean?"

"You and mommy want me to stay stagnant! You don't want me to grow up. No matter how many experiences you say I should have, you undermine me every second. You two were doing much worse at my age."

"Ya mom can argue with you, I won't. I came in here cause she won't talk to you after what you pulled."

She won't? It's not like I wasn't aware. I knew both of them were snubbing me from the minute I started coming home later than usual—specifically to set them off. They'd turn their cheek at my late night arrivals, and I continued to push them to see what else I can get away with.

HELP ME.

If they're going to punish me with their absence, they're doing me a maj-fav. I can be with Elly every night of the week, making our castles concrete, and they'll be stuck licking fables. They don't know what they just allotted me the freedom of. More time on Playthings means more votes, and more votes mean that we will win the Brunhart Festival, and if we win the festival, Elly will love me—like, FORREAL.

"If you came in here to convince me to go to France, I'm not. End of that."

He waltzed over, placing his palm at the back of my head, bringing my forehead to his hip. His belt buckle dug into my temple, but he smelled like Dad, and I love that smell.

"Basil, I know you've wanted to go to France for years, and baking was something ya wanted to do since you could use the stove. The decisions you make today can turn a wish into a sore. Please make the right choice."

DAD, PLEASE! "Can you get out now?"

He let go. He knew that he could throw a million sayings at my feet, and I'd step on all of them. "Basil?"

"Yes, dad?"

"I think you need to take a walk."

Independence is exhilarating. It lifts you with a nest that models itself after imperishables, but it's easy to forget how wind continues to move through large unused spaces. It's still burly and thick, and it stings more than a patched up loneliness. It will take anyone as a contender, and make them think they're worth charm and sympathy. But, no one sympathizes with true independence, they take advantage of it.

Tartula: Elly?
User00324: I'm already outside.

Chapter 24

:8

Some people have this impenetrable tie to nature; not me. There were too many skinned branches in my area that made standing out a grueling ambition and made every journey more isolating. The bare trees at night bunched up against every road, serving as a stanchion to an unwelcoming haven, and when they would ultimately fall, they'd impale the thing they stood tall for. It was a woeful experience to speed past them in Elly's quiet car, as much as they fought to be admired.

Elly dug into the gas, merging onto an underdeveloped forest terrain; the sticks and pebbles hollered underneath the jeep's wheels, catapulting me towards the car's hood. People live

here? No, no one can live here—we're not on a road. The sound
of mini critters flew and burrowed at the alarming signal light, as
a beam of terror tore through their desolate habitat. We drove
further until arriving at the tip of a cul-de-sac, where a proper
road was sewn right in the middle.

"A shortcut," he nodded, opening the car door.
"Welcome home, babe."

The close knit neighborhood held together with an
assortment of coordinating white townhouses. Each one had a
narrative that coincided with its occupants. One neighbor had a
vegetable garden growing in the front, the other had steps that
were half constructed, and one house held a grey Acura with a
bubblegum hula hoop leaning against it. I looked across the
street from that house, and directly ahead was a home that was
left behind.

The panels were layered with water stains, and the front
steps had no railing to hold onto. A large window with a busted
corner mirrored a cascade of wrinkled white drapes. I could hear
the wind travel through the troubled walls, cooling anyone that
hibernated there. The lid to the mailbox was hanging on by a
piece of duct tape, and with that same duct tape, pinned a torn-
out sheet of construction paper underlining the name, *Hayes*.

The front door wasn't locked, but the wood was swollen
and overused. Elly lifted the door and impaled it forward, leaving
distressed marks in the entryway. He walked ahead of me,
holding my backpack filled with athleisure wear, and one good
dress. My body tried to get a sense of the surroundings, but Elly
was swift to snatch my hand and haul me up the steps. My back
hit something on our way to the second floor, and the crash
caroled up the hallway and made an animal hiss—it could've
been a cat, but I really don't know.

The staircase was carpeted and made an *errrrrrrrg* sound the more we hobbled up. A cracked door to the left of the upstairs corridor sparked green and blue hues into the unforgiving hall.

"You don't know the answer. YOU DON'T KNOW THE ANSWER!" A throaty voice blasted over family game shows. "DEC! Is that you?"

SLAM.

Here it is. Elly's room was about half the size of mine, maybe smaller. Empty. A twin bed with a black duvet and orange pillowcases cornered the wall. A 1990s computer desktop rested against a hand-drawn map of the USA. The map wasn't drawn well whatsoever, but it's my nation.

Elly placed my bag into his task chair. "Do you want water or anything?"

"No," Don't act uncomfortable. I scrapped my sneakers off using the heels of my feet. "Do you have anything else to drink?"

"Beer. Do you want beer?"

Each time I get drunk with Elly, our solo time gets flushed and flawed. It was like I was giving it all away for nothing. "Sure," but one beer won't hurt.

Elly stared at me as if he were trying to translate my request. He pointed at the end of his bed where some orange cat fur infected the edge. "You can sit down."

I shook my head as he made his way out. This was my time to peruse where I'd be staying, to get closer to Elly before our sleeping bodies would this evening. I tip-toed to his closet at the back of the slim room—nothing but t-shirts and old jeans. I wandered by the window above his bed, removing the curtain panel from the sill. A haze of dust swarmed and retreated back to the frame, and outside was a clear view of his neighbor's Acura; the same way the girl from the bake sale bathroom described it.

Any sudden movements in Elly's space made the floor twitch and rumble, ratting out that there was an intruder. I resisted any additional snooping and listened out for his return. My silence only gave the room next door the permission to misbehave. I listened in more and heard the delicate voice rise from its confined quarters. I wanted to whisper to Declan and tell her that I'm here, and I haven't neglected our time by the bleachers. She must've had her headphones in the way she was belting out. She wasn't a second on tune, but she absorbed the house.

"I have an idea," he balanced two opened beers in his hand, pushing the door open with his back. "How about we do some roleplaying?"

"I've never done anything like that before," I positioned myself at the foot of his comforter.

"It could help you channel Tartula," he handed me my beer, seating himself close to his pillows. "I think people like seeing you, but no one is going to believe you if you're unable to become her."

I took a swig, beer always tasted like bad soda to me. "Isn't Tartula mainly a look anyway?"

"When I was talking to Phat Pheasant," he talks to her on a regular basis? "She was telling me how separated she feels from herself, and I think that is part of her success."

I laughed. "Okay then, I'll try my best, but you have to start!"

He watched me take a few extra sips of the can and finally took one from his. "Do you want to leave Wheatermite, Tartula?"

I guffawed, slinking my hand over my mouth to draw in the excess laughter. I belched, trying to put on my best old English accent. "Yes-yes, it's quite boring. Don't you think?"

"How can you make it more exciting?"

"Hm," I peered around the room and caught a pile of what I think were bells underneath the computer desk. "Music. We need sound and music!" I sprung up, thrusting the chair from the cardboard box.

"DON'T TOUCH THOSE!" His hand clutched my bicep, tugging me from the opening.

"It's okay, I won't," I caressed his fingers to release his hold. "Y'know, for someone who loves fish, I expected to see a full-on aquarium in here."

"Do you want to go see some fish?" He crushed his top lip under his teeth, and Declan's story came back to me.

"I'm cozy here," I looked out the window and caught the Acura again. "How many girls have seen this room?"

He crawled across the bed to where I was sitting and leaned against me. Elly and I were a couple, but we didn't get moments like this. He extended his arm out above my shoulder, closing the curtain and vandalizing the moon's character in the room. He didn't place his arm around me, which I figured would be an easy move, instead, he left it in his lap.

"Zero," he answered. "I don't sleep with girls, I sleep with women."

I sneezed. "Well, I'm not a woman at all."

"Why can't you be?"

"I think...I actually don't know."

"Tartula," he deeply inhaled. "Do you want to leave Wheatermite?"

In between sentences I could hear Declan still singing. Her song choice was emblematic—each one was cold, drab and hella thorny. Her voice would get louder when she'd reach the chorus and dwindle out during the bridge. She kept the tempo, but her shortcoming was the lyrics. She hummed in and out of verses, paraphrasing the rest with a *hmmm*. Her voice is eerily beautiful when it's noticeable. And when she came to the end, she'd giggle at her own self, then continue on to the next.

"There's nothing for me here," I answered, moving into the wall to press my ear against it.

"And what's out there?"

"Tenderness."

"And what?" Elly folded his arms around my lower half.

"Replenishment."

Elly removed the can from my grasp and placed it on the side of the bed. My palms traveled up the frigid walls and spread out towards the opposite ends of the room. On the other side of this wall was what I was hiding from, on the other end of the wall was ventilation behind cool lips.

The memory of Lane pierced my recollection. Her broad owl-like eyes peering into me across Wesley's counter—telling me that Declan isn't as she is, and that I'm hurting Elly the more time I spend with her. That night when I went home, I swore to Tartula that Declan wouldn't impose the way she has been, and that I'm going to give all my time to her—I'm going to give up all my time to Elly.

"Are you in love with her?" He whispered. I scratched the walls as her voice faded to black.

"No," I let go, rotating myself around to lean up against the barrier. Elly gaped into me.

"Can I show you something?" I heard what he said, but my neck had locked and hardened. I couldn't bob to let him know it was alright, and I wanted to see whatever it was he wanted to introduce. "Perfect."

He swiveled over the end of the bed and towed the box of bells out. They clanked together and the different finishes made their scratched surfaces squeal. He dumped them out and onto the cover, completely soiling his black bedding. The bells had many looks, a chaos of sizes and colors with materials to match. Some of them were clearly old, and there were a few that could've been purchased yesterday. There had to be at least a hundred different ones right in front of me, all with a colorful string attached to it.

"*Frumos*," he whistled into one, lifting it up. "Besides fish, I collect these."

"They're amazing. Why were you so afraid to let me touch them?"

"It's harder to explain yourself sometimes than to let someone in," he handed me a stringless bronze bell. "My dad used to work as an independent glazier, and many of his jobs came from local churches. When I was a kid he brought me with him to a job, and there I saw a bell—twice the size I was. While my dad was off taking measurements, I approached the bell and I rang it."

I gripped the bronze one in my hand, slicing my thumb open. "Then what?"

"I passed out," I snickered, and Elly matched me. His laugh widened, exposing his hugging front teeth and gums. "I've loved them since."

I lightly placed the bell next to my abandoned beer on the floor, kissing it before letting it go. I perched myself onto my knees in front of Elly, his smile had gone down and his lips were a gracious red. I was now the one with the tremors, inkling my arms to connect with his heartbeat. I dropped them down and under his shirt. His stomach was warm, a little hairy, and firm. I drew the shirt up like a parachute beginning to take movement. He helped me whisk it over his head, his hair crinkling down into his collar.

I avoided staring at him for too long because I could do it forever. I quickly pushed my lips into his, the crash startled him, but he soon began to accompany me. He unclasped my raisin colored sweater and the tank top that has left me for the second time tonight. He made an incision amongst the crowd of bells, and softly lowered me into the center. I was holding my breath to pause my trembles, but he ceased them for me. Both of our trousers came off and tarried to the side, collapsing and knocking over my drink that doused my new gift.

"We don't have to, Basil," the sockets around his stare were red and harsh, but the blue in his eyes settled the fire.

"Yes, we do," he fell into my grip, kissing me into calm.

The bells rang with the hindrance of Elias' name.

Chapter 25

;P

Is it supposed to feel like that afterward?

"Are you going to school today?" Elly brought a plate of steaming scrambled eggs into the room, with a side of toast and canned grape jelly.

"I guess I should, right?" It was BURNING. I needed to pee it out, but I was scared of who I might bump into during my bathroom conquest. Elly's home was way more brittle at daybreak, and his family allowed the silence to wither away with the previous night.

"You can stay here with me," he was so mousy after what happened, and I was exceedingly worse. Whenever he turned to look at me, I'd glance out the window to see if real people resided in the houses across the street. "My parents will be gone soon, so you don't have to hold it in for too long."

How does he know? "I don't want to shock them too bad."

"They know you're here," what? "Do you want to meet them?"

I was drenched in one of Elly's t-shirts that flaunted the Goblin's Guild logo; that's one way to tell his parents that I'm hooking up with their son. My hair was a wreck because I must've left all my responsibilities at home, and my morning breath was so bad it could lead a drug cartel.

"Maybe next time?"

"When they get home, or do you want to hide in my room for the rest of our lives?" I wasn't sure how long I'd be staying at Elly's. I pulled out my phone every so often to see if my parents had texted me, and they never did. They're just gonna give up that easily, huh?

The sounds in the house unexpectedly dulled out. I crept up, instantly commanding the opportunity to leak. I had no clue what direction the bathroom was in, or if there was a bathroom on the second floor at all. The banister was so small and rundown, that I knew if I placed a chunk of my body weight on it, I'd be on the bottom level by now. If there was one thing I occasionally assumed, was that every house had a bathroom on the first floor. I trotted down the L-shaped steps until I could see a revealed toilet across the parlor room.

"Heck yes," I skipped into the cramped area, barely locking the door. My bum hit the breezy seat and my pre-piss vertigo melted out of me.

I'm not a virgin anymore. It was my last thought after our kiss that resigned us from the day, and my very first thought when I shredded that absence. My mom was always going to be the first person I told, but I issued her place to Tartula. She didn't invoke the same reaction that my mom would have, but she shared the body.

"Can you accept me?" I murmured into the reflection of myself. I twisted the faucet on and gargled on some water. The bathroom held nothing but a sink and a toilet, no decor—no trinkets.

I opened the door into the parlor. A widescreen TV and a bookshelf with some trophies were the main staples of the room. A powdery Persian rug laid flat beneath a taupe couch that was well used and spotty. The house had a stench that never went away, no matter how used to it I got. The parlor seemed to be the main inhabiter of that smell, and I let it baste my skin. I walked up to the trophies to find Elly's name engraved into the gold plating, but instead, it read phrases like *Super Star* and *You're the Greatest!*

The kitchen was a short walk from the front room, and it was a wide open space with cracked tiled floors and furniture unevenly distributed. It was nothing out of a catalog, but it was quaint. A circular wooden table was positioned right by the window, and etched into the table were carved out names of everyone in the family.

Elly

Declan

Shawn

Misty

I should bake them something. The white cabinets were short and couldn't hold much but needless ingredients, half of which should've been thrown out. I found some flour next to a dead spider, and swooped the little thing up with some paper towel—I'm already proving myself to be an above mediocre housewife. The fridge was on a decline, and half of their dairy products were soaring past their best by dates. The butter was in stable condition, half covered and maybe with bite marks, but no one will know once it's melted.

"Excuse me," a pale arm reached above my head to grab an animated cereal bowl.

"Hey Declan," I wiggled my fingers and she slighted them, moving over to the fridge that held up generic cereal boxes. "I'm thinking about making some milk bread if you can hold your stomach."

She carried on pouring the cereal by the table, right where her name was carved in. If she was going to ignore me, I'd have to return the favor. I went into the fridge and dug out the milk before she had the chance to snag it for her bowl. I emptied a bit of it into a glass and remembered I also needed some heavy cream. I'd just have to double up on the milk and butter, but what about the yeast? I doubt they'd have that. What's a good substitute for yeast? I know this. I know this, right?

"Can you hand me the milk?" She barely spoke. I stomped over and dropped it onto the table above Elly's name. "Thanks?"

"I'm not mad at you as much as I'm mad that I can't remember a good replacement for yeast," I grinned at her because I knew I was being childish, and I wanted her to grin at me too.

"I don't care, Basil," she had her cheer uniform on and she never does, I know she hates wearing it because it's viciously tight.

"Why are you being this way?" I asked. I was the one who decided to extract her from my life, why was she trying so hard to beat me to it?

"You really have to ask? Are you stupid?" Wait—hold up.

"I must be since I have no idea!"

"You fucked my brother!"

Then the bells. They chimed in where I couldn't leave off, they infiltrated the silence and made angels exist. It was really beautiful for those soft seconds. I can still hear the dinging when the mattress would convulse and revive—Elly's skin. The ringing with the bells and pressure of the pulses in our wrists, gripping while they clang and outlasted our numb extremities.

Ding.

"He's my boyfriend."

"You kiss me one day, and a few days later hook up with my brother while I'm in the room next door. I couldn't sleep!"

"Get over it, Declan! I don't want you, I've always wanted Elly. If I wanted you, I would be with you already."

Next to the bells there was a whimper echoing from underneath a blanket. It plastered the wall beside us and reminded me that I'm not okay with where I am. I shut my eyes so tight that the bells became visions, and spurted in the form of tears. When I opened my eyes back up, Elly was looking down at me like he knew I wasn't alright, and it bothered me that he didn't ask why.

"You really mean that, Basil?" HELP ME.

"Yes, I do."

"She does!" Elly smiled leaning into the doorway. Declan couldn't stand to look at her brother, so she chose to put that hate on me. "Good morning, Declan. Did you sleep okay?"

Elly drifted over, slipping his arm around me. "I was making us some milk bread. You can share it with your parents too."

"I'm going to school," Declan announced.

"Do you need me to drive you?" Elly asked. Declan bent her knuckle onto the table, and threw the rest of her cereal into the trash.

"I'm taking the car."

"I need my car today. Maybe ask Wesley to drive you?" Wesley will make up an excuse because he knows that Lane doesn't want Declan around.

"What else do you want to take from me, Elly?"

"I don't understand."

"You do! And Basil is going to be the last thing," she ripped a pair of keys from a nailed in hook.

"Do you remember the film, Declan?"

Declan's eyes dilated, overtaking her entire face. Her fingertips shriveled around the keys until they fell from her palm and scattered across the tile. Her mouth hung open and a terror was left on her tongue, spiking her words and making them too drowsy to confute.

"I asked Basil to be in the film, and she said yes."

"Is that the only reason you're with her?" Declan tilted her head. "Do you even know about her residency in France?"

He flinched. "Yes," he's lying. I know he is.

"Stay out of it, Declan!"

"Why didn't you tell him, Basil?! You told me!"

Elly glanced at me. "Why didn't you?" He drank his breath. "You think I'm terrible."

"I think you're inferior to it," Declan interrupted, picking her keys from off the ground. She stopped at me. "Welcome, Tartula."

The milk bread came out a little dry, but Elly was my personal assistant. His hands wadding over mine while we turned and combined ingredients. The cookware in his house was worn and loose, but it got the job done. We didn't talk much, and when Elly did talk he'd give me a compliment, tell me how beautiful I looked with strokes of flour hiding in my dimples. He looked better with sprinkles of dough lining his hair, though I wasn't sure how it got there. It seemed intentional.

We ate the bread on his cold front step, watching the girl across the street swing her hula hoop around in the view of her planted phone. She had to be around my age, or maybe older. She performed acrobatics while simultaneously twirling the hoop on her shin, belly, and neck. Her final move was her crashing into a split, tossing the ring into the air, and letting it loop down and around her like a bad arcade game. Elly and I applauded from across the cul-de-sac, and she curtsied and waved—calling us out to come join her. She was beautiful and charismatic, and somehow I knew Elly had slept with her in the past.

"Maybe next time!" He opened the door and motioned for me to go back inside. "Do you want to help me write for the film, babe?"

"I don't know a thing about writing."

He chuckled. "Maybe we can have Lane and Wesley help once they get here."

"They're coming?"

"Yeah, we can't let this day go to waste," he closed and locked the door behind us. The small hint of overcast lighting stayed outside. "We should hurry before they arrive."

"Hurry?"

"Now that I have you, I can't go a second without you."

There was a bathroom on the second floor. The bathroom was next to a room, the biggest small room in the house. It was teal and wondrous, with built-in shelves on every corner—books that were so close to each other they could read one another. The drapes were a bright gold that gave the cloudy day remorse. The dresser top was spilling with trophies that held a name, and funny cereal box cutouts of all the sketch characters they promote to kids. Under some of the characters were signatures, including some from both Lane and Wesley, with pictures of them that took up the entire vanity.

A bed with no headboard or frame floated out in the open with a book by Lucien Michaud, French pastry chef, tossed in the center. Next to it was a mascara inscribed pillowcase, and next to that was a pair of knotted up broken headphones. I couldn't expect less from Declan, but what I didn't expect at all was to see a self constructed aquarium, dripping with discus, saulosi, peacock, and other types of cichlids.

Chapter 26

:\

"This tastes kinda villy, Black Beauty. Not as good as the little fruit things you made," Lane had just downed the last shard of milk bread.

"Sorry. I had to substitute the yeast, that's probably why the taste is a little off."

"Naw. It has to be something else. It doesn't even taste like you made it!"

Elly bullseye'd his pen to the center of the table. "I helped her a lot," don't take the blame, babe.

"You should never help anyone again."

The dining table was sectioned off from the rest of the kitchen, and a dim boob-light chucked its gleam around our small huddle. Each of us was labeled by one of the Hayes, Elly being the only vessel sitting in his designated station. I was lucky enough to be Misty, and I wondered what she'd say if she saw me taking up her seat. It would be a tremendous follow up question to her insight on mine and Elly's relationship—right after we discuss the film's seditious concept.

Our predicaments have been sitting for hours, and our ideas were still starstruck. Tartula was def in the room and she was patrolling harder than my parents could have. At one point, Wesley went outside to do cartwheels in the rain, and we all watched him as a cry of desperation. Lane did a line to boost her juices, and it only left us with a scatterbrained intellectual.

"I think it's going to snow next week!" Wesley hummed. "We should all go skiing!"

"Who do you think we are? Some 9 to 5 trags slerbing off their boss' dime?"

Elly joined in on Lane's sniff-fest. "Next week would be the perfect time to shoot. We have two weeks till the deadline."

Lane snuffed. "And who's in charge of the editing? You know I have colleges to impress."

"I'll do it," Elly responded. Lane smirked and misaligned her glasses.

"I'm sure you will," she tapped me with her pointy nail. "Now's your time to reese."

"I don't plan on backing down," I glanced at Elly and he sneered. "Tartula won't let me."

Lane's belly shook. "Oh yeah, BB?! Tell me what Tartula is saying."

I wouldn't be doing her a favor by bringing her into this —I don't think she wants to be. It isn't a choice to be this analytical, to Tartula it is her destiny. I try my very best to be respectful, but sometimes it leaves me more muddled than I ever was. Talking to Tartula as me is bringing a leaf to a Lion for food —it is demeaning and presumptuous. Tartula doesn't think of me as an extension, but an emblem, and sometimes less.

"You don't have to answer that, Basil," Elly kindly demanded.

Lane hocked a loogie into a zip tie bag. "You're always protecting her, dude."

Elly muffled. "She is my girlfriend."

"Yeah, she is! Just like Pavia was," Lane's laugh launched from the kitchen to the rest of the house. Wesley laughed with her, but Elly and I couldn't find them there. Why would she bring up Pavia?

"That's your last one for the night," he crumpled up Lane's sheet of aluminum.

What does Pavia have to do with this?

"You know that's against my working conditions!" Lane spat.

"You've written nothing."

Lane glanced down at her notes. "Shit! I think that's my first time noticing."

"Oh! Elly's going to get mad Laney-Lane!" Wesley brought his paws up and under his chin.

It wasn't like Elly *was* mad, but he wasn't looking at Lane as if she had sparked the most staggering idea there was. There were serious issues with the film, and one of the issues was that Tartula wasn't being heard. Tartula's story isn't something that can be easily engineered—particular steps were dire to a deity. I know that Tartula wanted me to stick up for her, and to be the one to collect her acclaim, but I'm not sure if I'm the person that could do that—I'm not sure if I'm meant to be here.

                                                                Basil.

"What?" I lifted my head up.

"What?" Lane wriggled her nose. "No one said anything."

"I got it," Elly croaked.

A tap came from upstairs and accelerated down the steps. A programmed *whoosh* rescued our baited breaths and drew them from their restricted aches. Elly's waves took off as a burst of lore climbed through the extent of his smile. It toured from the tip of his clipboard to the feeling in his nail beds. We all drew our seats in closer to make sure we could see him before he murmured, and that no words that fell from the page would cause the day to fall from us.

"What if we killed her off?"

"Tartula?" Wesley peeped.

Elly smirked. "Yeah." No.

"Killing off the protag is kinda drippy," Lane lit a cigarette.

"Why would we do that?" I stammered.

Elly fanned the fumes from his nostrils. "Lane, can you smoke outside?"

"Dude, the flavor is going to go out if I keep it lit for too long."

"I don't think that's a good idea," I insisted.

"I love it! How many movies have you seen where the main character dies? Besides the stoke screens they sell for ten bucks at Winston's."

"I like it too! I can work on a burial gown!"

Elly pinched the hood of his nose. "Lane, can you go outside to smoke? It's disgusting."

"It's like negative stupid outside! You want me to smoke in the rain?"

"The gown can be chartreuse!"

"I don't think we should do this. I really don't want to."

Wesley gasped. "Or maybe persimmon!"

Let her die.

"NO!"

It was unacceptable. Tartula was the force and the flight —if she were to die in the end, then it would be too uncultured. Tartula is the reason Wheatermite became the home she summoned from herself; the oddments that could never stick out, but found their way out of place. She can't die because she lives forever on a journey of trusting herself with her own grime ridden hands. Tartula is all that is in the end.

If she dies.

"Tartula is the main character. If we kill her off isn't that like, killing off the memory of her living on?"

Elly glistened. "Yeah."

"Then why? Why do that?"

"I think it could be beautiful! Imagine that dress!" Wesley tinkled.

"NO ONE ASKED YOU!" I shot up. They each peered at me in discomfort.

Elly closed his eyes, then opened them. Then he closed, closedclosedclosed, then opened them again. "What does Tartula really think, babe?"

"What happens to us if Tartula dies?" I questioned.

Elly peeked at Lane and Wesley. "Nothing," he included. "What happens to us when you go to France?"

I waited for him to bring it up all afternoon. We hadn't talked about it. After the fight with Declan this morning, we let it coast till it tripped. France was never going to be for me, even when it was foreseeable. I had to serve the film for Tartula, and the life that I've now committed to. I had no time for France, but I'd love to know if it thought of me.

"I'm not going."

Lane stretched her brow up. "And that's because you want to stay here with us?"

"Yes."

"Yaaaay! Summer with Basie!" Wesley galloped.

"BB, I have to admit your milk bread wasn't your best work, but I don't think it's worth you skipping Avignon."

"I've already decided, I don't need you to convince me otherwise. Aren't you busy worrying about Declan?" That could've stayed in my head.

Lane stubbed her cigarette into Declan's carved name. "Nope. Not at all."

"Getting back to the film," Elly crossed a line out from his clipboard. "I think I've decided where I want her ceremony to be."

"So, you're not going to listen to me?"

Elly bite the metal part of the clipboard, twisting it between his crossed teeth. "I'm sorry, babe."

"Can we do it at my house?" Wesley chanted.

A light flashed into the house's front window as a truck pulled in. It wasn't Elly's jeep, but a car I hadn't seen around the house before—towing in a secondhand once-beige armchair. It was too dark outside to understand who was coming in, but they made themselves known the minute they entered the skinny hall. It was evident there were two people; one had the weight of all of us combined, and the other person could only be traced by the luggage of their groceries.

"Help your mother," all I saw was an arm half the size of me fling a case of IPAs onto the counter. The grizzly man continued to move across the house, oiling the creases with his gristle.

"I'll be back," Elly stood up to jog to the front door, but was quickly interrupted by an elfish-like woman.

She had blonde brittle hair that fluttered with static, and the most subtle hunch in her back that made her shoulders sag. Her face was very plain and splintered by the cold—hardly moving at all. Everything about her was shrunken and beady. She had on a pair of loose jeans and a cable sweater immersed in cat hairs—the cat I'm still waiting to see. She had the same color eyes as Elly and Declan, but the blue in hers drifted the more she'd blink.

"Yooooo, Misty!"

Wesley shot up and curled himself around the compressed woman. "Mrs. Hayes! I missed you so much!"

"Mom," Elly lightly shoved her forward. "This is Basil. This is my girlfriend."

She trembled just looking at me, and I tried my best to not do the same. "It's so wonderful to meet you, Mrs. Hayes."

She smiled enough to let me know she was listening and nodded her head.

"We're talking about the film. We just got done with the ending, and I think I know where I want to film it."

The woman nodded through Wesley's embrace.

"A church."

It feels like, Tartula might be okay with that, but I don't know about Elly's mom. She looked up at Elly and nudged him towards the groceries. Elly began to restock everything into the cupboard and fridge with an enchantment I haven't seen. I think it was his mother's reassurance that brought it out of him—even if she hasn't said anything at all. She obviously knew about the film because he could talk to her without deterring. I can't even make myself admit to where I had been strayed. But, why isn't she saying anything? Can't she see her son is gliding on her unuttered words?

Why. Why is she just standing there?

Basil.

"That looks like a really good chair! Did you find it by the pit?" Elly asked and the woman nodded. "I'll bring it in before it gets soaked."

Elly trotted out the entrance, and I had to rob the moment before he could take it back. "Your son has been working really hard on this. I think you should know that."

She bowed, and started to remove the remaining items out of the bag.

"I think you can acknowledge his dreams a little more, y'know? Don't just stand there and nod at everything he says."

"BB," Lane intruded.

"This film is the only thing your son talks about. It might be the only thing in this world he actually loves," her back was to me. "He may even love it more than me."

"I doubt that!" Wesley giggled.

"No. I know he loves this film more than me. And, you know who I love more than anything else? Your son. So please, tell him how much you're in love with his work too."

The storm came in with the opened door before it slammed shut. Elly was out there for less than five minutes, but his hair had already been sewn together by the droplets. His mom gathered a toilette from the fridge's handle and patted his hair dry, draping it around his shoulders to keep the dribbles from his shirt.

The woman made a gesture at Elly, and he quickly returned the gesture back. "Um, I think so."

"Are you hungry?" She asked me. I didn't understand it the first time, or the second time she said it. It wasn't until she gestured to Elly that he was able to communicate on her behalf. And that was when I really hated myself.

Chapter 27

:[

The ingredients used to move on their own. Carouseling and ricocheting from one palate to the next—I could never be the one to mention it all tasted the same. *Good* has a particular zing from *great*, and cosmopolitan flavors are a fancy that seems to only come once a century. I thought that a peach was harmoniously different from an apple, but I learned that those features are only implied. A peach feels strange—tastes strange because that's the effect I want it to have, and an apple will do the exact same. Produce wants to work together rather than become nemesis, and that's why choosing favorites is so disastrous.

The oven emitted a strong forceful heat that made my arms fry. I loved baking, but I could never love knowing I'd have to sprint around in a long sleeve dress and silicone mittens. Being around the oven felt like a hug that never gave up, and it made me tread on commitment issues for a while. If I couldn't get used to the leash of a hobby, how could I make it my dream? It wasn't at all, not like it once was—but neither am I.

Pavia launched her face into Miss Lowe's peripheral, trying to re-sculpt a grade for an assignment that was way overdue. I'm pretty sure Pavia pegged Miss Lowe as a lesbian, and it all had to do with her never wearing makeup. It was totally selfish of her to interrupt our lesson, but who could stop Pavia? She was the goddamn Cheer Babe cap with the perfect roundabout. We respected her as that, or right before her bake sale meltdown. Villetoners pretended it didn't happen, all the Villetoners except for me and her.

I wanted to make it not so obvious, but there was a good chance Pavia had already caught on. I couldn't allow my eyes to strain for her polished demeanor, or the one she forces herself to have. It's helpful that she plays so into herself, but it is a setback when she won't give me anything to play off of. All the Villeton boys inspected her from their clafoutis, and she sought to make them jealous. But everyone knew no matter who tagged her and how long they did, she'd always be marked by Elly.

I loathed her for that.

"She knows," they murmured. "Go get her."

"What are you waiting for?" Their voice was both scratchy and arousing.

"I'm not sure," I answered.

Each of them cradled around me to pressure my movement. Their palms all redirected and made a sunflower outline around my post—bursting the more I scoped Pavia's conversation. A seed fell from one of my baby hairs, and I planted it at the base of my throat.

"Pavia," I called out. She heard me but instead decided to slight my call by deliberately hunching her back. "PAVIA!"

She twirled around, capering to reflect me. I excused myself from the budding row to approach her and analyze her away from the crowd. They all stood up to become my backing, holding their hands out to regain their morals. I lurked inside her auburn eyes, seeing how she lays out her faith. Pavia gave me no reason to trust her, but she also admits to being vapid. The simplicity of Tartula is a gradual feed on insecurities, and Pavia is already good at that. She's playful with her flaws so no one else could be.

During my freshman year, I assumed Pavia was a saint inside of a church. She was so dignified and stoic, but hella nice too. Not in like, an insincere way, but def in the way that would make someone feel filthy beside her. To top it off she was dating Elly Hayes, and he was some facet of corrupt creed. If I told her who I was, would she try and kill me?

"Hey girl!" Her pitch caromed off the steel tables. She dangled her fingers like a hidden meaning.

"Do it."

    "Do it."

        "Do it."

            "Do it."

                "Do it."

                    "Do it."

                        "Do it."

"I have to ask you a question," before I lose my ability.

"Sure thing! What's on your mind, lovely?"

"Have you heard about the film?"

Her eyes made a puzzle. "What film? For drama club?"

"No. Elly's film."

"Hmmm," she bounced, sticking her finger to her lip. "Elly talked to me about a film once, and said it was for his school thing."

Everything that has been touched by Elly now foams with his aroma. It wasn't only Pavia, but the strangers that took up the group behind me. They clipped their palms to my ankles and knees—they knew that I would be the only thing to save them from that encounter because they never wanted it for themselves.

"Did he ask you to be in it?" This was all I needed her to confirm, and I'll finally be able to move on the way Tartula needs me to.

Her arm became limp. "Maybe. Did he ask you?"

"She's telling lies," they said.

"Don't believe in everything everyone tells you," they hymned.

"You're the only one for Elly."

"Who is Pavia to Elly noW?"

"nO ONE."

The snow-like color in Pavia's hair wagered her sincerity. She knew that she couldn't escape from it because it wanted nothing to do with her.

"I-I don't think so."

She beamed. "And you're okay with that? You're his girlfriend, Basil. Why wouldn't he ask you?"

"I know."

She caressed my cheekbone. "You can tell me the truth. Tell me really, what is Tartula like?"

She's asking me to try and take her away, just like other people have tried to in the past. If it wasn't Pavia, then it would be the girl with the birthmark on her face; the one who is hella retired. If not that one, then vain Maude with the ponytail. No one wants Elly to be with me, and Tartula was the only map to him.

"Do you know what happens if I can't become Tartula, Pavia? Has it happened to you?"

"Who do you think is stopping you?" An incision spawned from the center of Pavia's head. A mulberry discharge played into her soggy split ends.

"Is there someone else he could possibly have in mind?" I asked.

The gook drowned out the character in her face. "There's always someone else."

"There can't be!"

Pavia fidgeted with the secrets she kept. "I want you to have this role, Basil. But, do you think Elly wants you to have it? Or maybe, Elly is happy to give it away to you."

I sauntered back. "Elly loves me."

"Elly loves who you can be. Elly doesn't even know who you are. Elly doesn't know himself!"

"SHE'S TELLING LIES," their voices coiled into a vortex, forcing me down the ambiance of their lesson.

The whirlpool distanced me from Pavia, and her reactions lowered through the center of the velocity. I hung onto her bark the more she sputtered into the abyss, and I could feel her nerves not believe in themselves. I yanked up using the torn disbursements of her ridicules. She didn't know that I held something over her that she could never have—something she was too afraid to admit.

"Elias knows me very well," I crawled myself back up to a standing position.

Pavia flounced from one end of the room to the other, marking it up with her contaminated euphoria. The rest of the class halted to make sure they weren't soiled by her antics. Her goo sprayed to my cooking gloves, and I wiped them against my dress to make sure it could never harden. She triple back handsprung from the counter stations to Miss Lowe's desk, and Miss Lowe sat there applauding the messy theatrics.

"Woohoo!" She whistled through her teeth.

"Pavia," I anchored out before her grand exit. "Have you never said Elly's name?"

She wrung the remains from her hair, telling me everything through her smile. "Why ask a question you already know the answer to?"

The sections of students broke off from me and regrouped at their tables. Pavia left the room before I could rake out the convo a little more. The walls returned to their mismatched whiteness, and the smell of fruit desserts welcomed itself right back in.

"Basil! What are you doing just standing in the middle of class?" Miss Lowe dug out her Tupperware salad that came prepackaged. She shook it until the dressing shaded in the see-through plastic and saturated the greens.

"I was waiting for you to say something."

"I always have a lot to say! Swing over by my desk so we can chitchat," she took a chomp as glaze held to the corners of her chew. She rose her hand in front of her mouth to block the unwanted spatter that got out anyway. "Let's talk about Avignon!"

Let's not. "Miss Lowe."

"The institute is going to need two teacher recommendations, a copy of your grades, and a character reference. That's the easy part. The hard part is the essay! Can you write a good essay? Your English teacher says your writing is so-so."

"Uhm," I thought Mr. T liked me.

"Doesn't your mom work as a writer?" No.

"She's a freelance HR consultant."

"Oh! Then she knows a thing or two about policies. Let me write that down, I could always use a connect."

"I'm not going," I almost whispered. "I'm not going to Avignon."

Miss Lowe laid her fork into her bowl and picked it right back up. "Excuse me?"

"I've decided not to go."

"That's not what your parents said," of course they did.

"I've already spoken to my parents about—"

"Nononnno! They put down a deposit. They said you'd be thrilled about it, they were sure you weren't going to turn it down."

"When was this?"

She swung her fork up and took another munch. "Earlier this week. I spoke to your mom and dad, we had a game plan going for you!"

It was before I moved into Elly's; before the talk with my dad. I knew he was being more fiddly than usual, but making payments without discussing them with me first? It was because they knew that I'd want to do it—they *assumed*. My parents wanted me to become them so bad, they were eager for my success to weld into theirs because they've always strived for that. I don't need that kind of success—I have it with me already. I have the notes, the track, and the goal. I just have to get to the answers.

I have to become Tartula.

It's all inside of me. The mechanisms of Tartula and her desire to be whole. The feeling she gets when she knows the story is written to compliment her soul. Even with Elly always being right there, he can't fully engage the way she needs to. That's why I'm the one; I've been the thing Elly has been looking for to help connect him with his greatest achievement. Pavia has solidified that she was never the first choice, and it's always been mine to declare.

"Basil, are you crying?"

I wiped my eyes with my silicone glove, and finally got rid of that God-awful stain. "Do you know a good substitute for yeast, Miss Lowe?"

Chapter 28

;"

A critical piece of the film was lodged in the crannies of my closet—the underwear. They were the furthest thing from light, and the last thing I wanted anyone to justsohappen to stumble upon; hidden in a bag that could deteriorate upon contact. I was sure we could record the film without them, but Elly refused. I get that they were a little more pricey than the regular cheek-sheet, but not sure if they were worth me breaking my silence with Olivia and Jerrell. I wasn't too certain on how my parents were feeling about me, and I think they weren't too confident themselves—hence why no one decided to flood my freedom.

"Do you want me to go in with you, Basie?" Wesley asked. It could be a good idea—my dad does love Wesley.

I shook my head. "I think I'll be good."

"Okay! I'm right here if you do. Just call my name and I'll be to the rescue!"

It's only been two days, and the smell of baking had completely evaporated. The oven was cold, and a black residue had built up and overtaken the bottom. The kitchen was dreary without spotlight and sound. There were no pans toppling over, no spoons spilling thunder. I had to rest in my sanctuary one last time before the film, the spots that were now too good for me felt sticky beneath my calluses.

A fried up skillet soaked in the sink, and beside the skillet were two wine glasses—one half empty. The top of the stove splashed pieces of burnt kale around the burner, and this proved my point; that I was the only person in the house who cleaned the stove. The countertop kept half-bitten store-bought snacks as decorations, and the cupboards were full of yeast and confectioners' sugar.

The worst thing I've ever made was snickerdoodles. Every time I look at confectioners' sugar, I think about how I could never measure the correct amount of cinnamon to balance the powder. It always came out too bitter, or a snag from a sweet tooth, and it made me revise my talent. Was I meant to bake because I was good at it, or was it so I could be recognized for doing something astonishing?

"I didn't know you were here," my mom had on her bonnet, she must've been sleeping all day or reading bad YA novels.

"I'm getting ready to leave again," I muttered. She nodded, passing me for the fridge. "And I might take some stuff with me."

She took out a can of seltzer and snapped it open. "That's fine."

I placed the jar of yeast into my bag, and my mom froze in my direction. She ambled in, examining my face from dimple to dimple.

"You had sex."

I'm not a virgin anymore. I wasn't scared to tell her, I was more afraid she'd find out some other unprecedented way. "I'm going to grab something from my room."

"I knew it would happen at some point, but I didn't think it would happen so soon."

I should tell her I didn't use protection, then she'll give me her genuine reaction. She'll launch the seltzer at the wall, and scream at me for being so damn hardheaded. She'll force me to forget the bag on the table, and head upstairs until I'm smart enough to start counting sense. She'll recite all the times she's had *the* talk with me, and how that was at the very top of the *don'ts*. She'll ignore me for an extra week, and cave in on the eighth day—hounding me for all the deets.

That's what she's supposed to do, so why isn't she?

MOM, HELP ME!

"What?" She adjusted her glasses.

"Huh?"

"I thought you said something," she removed an oatmeal cookie from its sealed container. "These are pretty good, but not as good as yours."

"They only list half of the real ingredients on those things."

JADE BROWN

She giggled just a bit. "That can't be true. They'd go to jail."

"Mom, who would go to jail? The entire manufacturing company?"

"The guys! Y'know, the guys who made 'em!" We both laughed until we remembered that we weren't on good terms.

Our encounter was almost as uncomfortable as the one I had with my dad. It dragged me back to him hugging me right before I stuffed a bag to leave. He's prolly upstairs now, taking a breather from Goblin's Guild because he and my mom finally have some time alone. I'm sure they're watching their favorite movie and talking about how they can't watch it in front of me because it's good writing, and I only binge melodramas and foreign soaps.

"Are you okay with me staying at Elly's until after Christmas?"

She shrugged. "I can't tell you what to do anymore."

She had her face on like she was about to cry, the exact face from when I told her I hated her years ago.

"And then, can I come home to spend my birthday with you and dad?" Her eyes opened up, and I could see the color in them—the blacks, the greens, the greys, and the browns that spilled to her skin.

Her lips pressed in, and a tear seeped beneath her lenses. "Of course you can."

I imagined a trail of petals following the car as we pulled off. Candles maybe, burning their scents so strong it would mask the gas. Our playlist would be alternative indie songs from underrated 80s bands. Wesley would be singing all the lyrics cause he knows them, and I would be throwing a peace sign out the window with my shades hanging low.

"Did you see that, Basie?! Did you see that dead deer?! Oh no! I hope nothing too bad happened to it," but instead, this was us.

"Yeah, me either."

"I should tell Elly and Lane not to drive down this road or it's going to make them sad," he pulled out his phone. "Oh! I think they might actually be at my house already! Elly texted me saying that they had some trouble getting through the gate."

"Does that happen a lot?"

Wesley released the wheel to scratch his nose. "My parents usually switch it when they come back home because they know I like to give it away."

"Wesley, you shouldn't just give your home's security code to anyone. What if someone tries to break in?"

He sighed. "I hope so."

"What?! No! That's a bad thing. Someone can rob you, or do something much worse. You have to try and protect your family and Fen-Fen!"

"I don't give it to *everyone*, but I like to give it to my friends and the people who I do like—I guess that does count as everyone!"

I laughed because it's hard not to laugh at Wesley. "If that's what you're comfortable with. You are a pretty lovable person. Remember how we almost dated? Well, we went on one date—a half a date."

He muttered. "I'm sorry."

"It's fine. I never expected us to go anywhere. I know you are pretty poly, and you like to keep it that way."

He placed his hands back on the wheel. "I want to make everyone happy, and I know when I'm with people I can do that. But, I don't know if what I'm doing is always okay."

"You can only be yourself."

"Sometimes I don't like that."

I turned to him. "Yourself?"

He grinned. "Yeah."

When we finally arrived at Wesley's house, Lane and Elly were standing outside, leaning against Elly's inactive jeep. Lane had on a floor length metallic blue trench coat, and Elly had on his usual muted attire. As soon as Wesley jumped out of his car, he immediately went into a texting frenzy with his parents to gauge the new lock code, but his parents quickly opted out for a phone convo. They went back and forth for a while, as Wesley grunted and *grrrr'd* into the receiver. It concluded with him still not receiving the code, but Fen limping her way out to the front gate to finally let us in—which should've been our tactic from the get-go.

A draft came in through Wesley's room, and shifted our guts the second we stepped inside. The side door to the balcony was left open, allowing a cleansing chill to flow in. I knew that I could use a drop of frigid oxygen, but Elly was opposed to the chase of winter. He continuously blew the warm air from his mouth between his fingers, and would resort to shaking them out when they got too dry from his breath. I could fully hear the crackle jut from his sanded down teeth, and I was beginning to think that it wasn't just the cold that was shaking Elly up—he was exonerating his anxiety.

"BB, this guy is asking you to gag in his mouth. That's a first! Must be some kind of vagus nerve stimulation thing," Lane was getting ready for the live by texting every guy on Playthings.

"Ohhh! Can we try?!" Wesley squealed.

"We don't have time, we need to get Basil ready. We also have to get this done before your parents come home," Elly's voice was hella shaky from the cold.

"Aw, I guess you're right! They do hate Laney."

Lane gargled her snot. "Geriatric sleebs."

"This will be our last live before we film next week," he turned to me. "We're going to end up shooting the day after your birthday, babe."

I'm petrified. "Exciting."

"Let's get her ready for nine," Elly shut the balcony door and lined the bottom of the entrances with Wesley's dirty laundry. "Is that enough time?"

"Uh oh!" Wesley skimmed his makeup pouch. "I don't think I have her color here! I must have lost it!"

Elly stomped over, emptying the pouch's contents onto the unmade bed. "What did you do with it?"

"I don't know! Sometimes Virginny likes to play with my stuff!"

Lane collapsed onto the desk chair. "Dude, that is not a good nickname for your little sister!"

Elly squinted. "What is she doing with that shade? She's white."

"Wesley, if your sister is blackfacing at five, then I don't know what to tell you," Lane showcased her Playthings screen to the rest of us. "Yo, bop this trag!"

"We don't have time for this," Elly exhaled.

"I want to see!" Wesley straddled Lane on the bed, and I plopped beside them to investigate the hype.

CornDog70: what time will u be there tartula
CornDog70: ive reserved dinner at 5

CornDog70: saturyda
Tartula: I'll be there at 4:59.
CornDog70: thank god
CornDog70: i cant wait to meet u
CornDog70: i told all my friends about u
CornDog70: they all voting
Tartula: Ilysm!
CornDog70: i love u
CornDog70: ill see u saturday
Tartula: Don't forget the installment! :)
CornDog70: ofc
CornDog70: CornDog70 tipped $70! ♡

Elly's shivers were now out of seismic zones. Tartula was Elly's prized possession, more so than me. There was something in Tartula that made everything around her cater to her reign. No one ever tried to defy her, or create instances that were so against her speed. Tartula was formed by Elly to be shiny and untarnished, not someone's obsession over a candlelit dinner. If that were her only purpose, she'd be lost in her own death.

I told them she shouldn't die.

"What are you doing?" Elly tackled the phone from Lane's hands.

"Dude! People on the internet are stoke as hell!" Lane humped the bed with her laughter, destroying the sheets more than they already were.

"Are you setting up dates for money?"

"Relax. It's not like anyone's gonna show up."

"Can I go?" Wesley tickled Lane beneath her pits.

"Oh my God! We should send Wesley, that would be hilz!"

"This isn't funny!" Elly. His voice was so different like this—so painful. "You're messing everything up!"

Lane flipped her short hair behind her ear, perching herself up on the bed. "It was a joke. It's not like these sleebs are throwing banx otherwise."

"We don't need their money, we need them to know about Tartula."

"*You* don't need their money. Now give me my phone back so I can tell Milo."

What. "Milo knows?"

milo knows everyone.

"Of course Milo knows BB, he's my boyfriend."

"Barely," Elly mumbled. Lane's shoulders twitched as she stood from the bed. The ends of her fingertips crackled from her lost device.

"Funny one. Now give me my phone."

Elly slipped the cell into his jean pocket. "Go get everything set up."

The rhinestones in Lane's sneakers trembled as she watched Elly. The bags and bottles that were hidden in her trench all rattled with her echoed irritation. Her cheekbones flared up, and the freckles underneath her makeup were no longer up for debate. Lane stood in the utmost stillness with her eyes trailing Elly through the room. Her glasses enhanced every isolation in her specks, and they frayed from dropping Elly—wielding daggers each way he spun.

"I'm not kidding, Elly. Give me back my phone."

"You're wasting time," Elly stopped to glare at her. "You're ruining the film right now."

"I don't care. GIVE ME MY PHONE!"

Elly turned away. "If you want an allowance, that's all you have to say. This film has never been for the money."

"If you haven't heard, Ivies are hella expensive. If I have to sell a date to every trag on the internet, I will."

Elly tugged the phone out, leaning it towards Lane. "You can leave. I got all I needed from you."

Elly went by the closet door to turn on the lights. The setup sparkled and called me in with him, but I didn't feel right leaving Lane yet. She had contributed to Tartula as much as we all have, and she deserved to continue being a part of the film. Was Lane the someone else that Pavia mentioned? Were we all fragments of Tartula's potential? Maybe that was the answer I was in search of. Tartula won't accept me as her own because she needs all four of us to succeed.

"Hey Basil," and I think Lane might know that. It was the first time I heard her say my name, and she completely butchered it. "Would you still do the film it was for nothing?"

"Yes, I would. If you want the money, then you can have it, but I still want to do this film with you too."

"Cute, but that's not what I'm getting at," she shot a look at Elly. "Would you do it if there was no way the film would be picked up by the Brunhart Festival?"

"Well," I accompanied her drawn attention. "It's not guaranteed we'll get in, but we can still try."

"We won't," she hissed. A vermillion ooze sprung in her glare. "We won't get in because we need to submit directly from a credible university."

"And that's what we're doing," I said. The strobes in the closet shut off.

Lane crowed. "BB, what school does Elly go to?"

He goes to.

He goes to.

It's somewhere around here because he's still able to travel from home. If it's not in our town, then it must be some online institution; I can imagine Elly attending something like that. He's so smart—he can do anything. That's what Elly does, and that's where he goes. I know that because he's my boyfriend.

I KNOW WHAT SCHOOL HE GOES TO.

"Are you having a hard time?"

"NO!" I was panicking. Why wasn't this something I knew? Why have I never thought to ask?

"You don't know because he doesn't go to school," she whistled. "He never has."

Chapter 29

:$

"Don't lie like that," I was laughing and begging at the same time.

"Like I've said before, BB—I don't owe anything to you, so I have no reason to lie," Lane tapped her foot to the beat of the stinted convo.

"I said I got all I needed from you," Elly muttered.

Lane stammered ahead, flinging her body towards Elly. "I'll leave as soon as you tell Basil everything. I want to hear it from your mouth!"

"I've told Basil everything."

Lane stabbed her finger into Elly's sternum, and I could feel it ding through my own chest.

"Everything isn't the truth!"

Wesley leaped forward, worming his way in-between Elly and Lane. The parallel walls in the room slummed in, toppling over our squandered ideas. Lane pushed against Wesley's embrace and swung at Elly's tee—attempting to catch hold of his slack. Elly swerved back until his shoulder blades collided with the closet's shelving. Lane promptly went in again, ramming against Wesley, and sending his rear into Elly's stomach.

"Lane, stop it!" Wesley was close to tears. Lane was already out of breath, but if she had to suffocate herself to be fully redeemed, she was going to.

"Tell her the truth!"

"I don't want to know," and I think I had forgotten how to ask questions. If I remembered what an inquiry looked like, I could've avoided this outcome. "I only want to do the film."

"Repot your dig, Black Beauty. You want to help someone who lied to you?"

"I want to feel good, and being Tartula makes me feel good."

"I never lied to you, babe. We can still make the film, and you can still be Tartula," Elly was motionless with a mutilated vision.

The freezing air leeched through the potted clothing, lurking across my arm hairs. "I believe you."

He smiled at me and mouthed *I love you*.

I want, just for a little bit, to be like everyone else. To not be so far apart from the truth, it sickens me to have it cleared. The world that has found me is a place that I can't claim, but I can overextend to make it mine. I have no qualms about being excruciatingly passive, if I can be that for him—if I can still be that, that'll be my only endeavor.

We were going to be the pharaohs of our town, all four of us. The film would be our announcement into a hiatus of splendor; our friendship would be an everlasting condition. I've fought hard for the places I knew I could never belong, and those incidences freed me. Tartula was the one who transported me to those nooks and abolished my grievances as Basil. The more Lane talks, the more I feel Tartula slipping, and then I'd have no filter from the hurt that was always coming. Love waits to be defiant, regardless of who it's for.

"Should I remind you, Elly?" Lane severed from Wesley's hold, brushing her metallic trench with her palms. "Should I remind you of your plan?"

Elly rolled his tongue over his bottom teeth. "I don't know what you're referring to."

"You don't?" She blushed. "You don't remember how we all met to discuss kidnapping Basil?"

Elly's hair swung above his forehead, shielding his eyes. "I would never kidnap Basil."

"That's because Wesley and I had to convince you that you can't just go around kidnapping people! Which is why *I* came up with the idea of inviting her to the bonfire."

"I'm really getting tired of these lies, Lane," I rose from the bed to meet them at the closet. Lane shook her head ferociously, sending her frays flying.

"I haven't told you one lie tonight, BB."

"You've told me several! How do I know you weren't lying about Declan too? You probably lied to get me to stop hanging out with her, and now you're lying to get me to break up with Elly!"

"I lied about Declan because Elly told me to!"

"Don't listen to her, Basil," Elly uttered. "She's a hophead."

Lane jolted around Wesley, throwing her balled fist up as a declaration. Her leg hit the display we created in Tartula's den, sending the already demolished laptop back to its demise. Elly stumbled into one of the streamers, blocking Lane's fist entirely. His hair wafted with the sudden thrust, causing the display lights to blaze and flash onto his bright beaten face. Lane pummeled through Wesley's grasp again, pelting at Elly's slim chest. Elly winced from the blow, raising his arms to protect his heart and the little that was left inside. The stinging sensation repelled from my aorta, and sent me across the room to where Elly was— right before Lane.

"If you don't want to get hit, I suggest you move Black Beauty."

"You're going to hit your friends?" I yelled out.

"You're not my friend!"

My confidence cracked. "Okay, but Elly is."

"Not anymore. He can't even be honest with himself about his illusions."

Wesley draped himself around Lane's back. "If it makes you feel better Basie, Lane isn't lying."

Tartula had officially exhausted herself. She no longer could hear the strums from the bells, the root of our dreams. I was internally renouncing her, and she passed up on any chance at being alive.

"I don't care about any of this," I have to get her back. "I still want to do the film."

"Elly wanted to use you as Tartula, and only that. So

Laney asked if I could bring you to the bonfire, and while we were away kissing, Elly would introduce himself to you."

"I'm not offended because I like being Tartula."

"That was the first step," Wesley dove his nose into Lane's collarbone. "Elly had to bring you to the water," Lane belched, cutting off Wesley's sentence.

"...he told us you're not his girlfriend, and it's all just for the film."

"Some of that is true," Elly's breathing was heavy behind my ear, but it delayed the more he continued. "The first time I saw you, I knew that I wanted you to be Tartula, and I told Lane and Wesley that. The more time I spent with you, the more I realized how much I've fallen."

"Don't twist it!" Lane interrupted. "You know there are layers to this that we can't discuss!"

"You are my girlfriend, and that would be hard to fake given all the time we've spent together. I know you will be an amazing Tartula, and I know how to get us into the festival. I can make it happen for you."

Don't cry, Basil. "Elly, are you in school?"

He brushed the tip of my spine with his finger. "I don't really like school."

"And what about everything else? They said you were planning on kidnapping me. What would you do with me if you did?"

"Bury you in Wesley's closet!" Lane snapped.

He shook his head. "You know me, babe."

He was so tender right now. It was like he was staring at me knowing exactly how this was going to go. He knew that we were going to make amends somewhere here because that was our written course. If everyone else were to leave, we would be dropped off alongside the things we couldn't reconcile. I'm still trying to dissect these parts of our relationship, and it's so foggy because they were never revealed in my favor.

"Let's go home," his lips grazed my jaw.

"Basil," Lane called out. "Open your eyes to what's going on around you. You can still get away."

I could feel Elly grinning against my back. I shivered. "If Elly is so bad, why did you let this go on for so long? You could've stopped it."

Lane took a couple of gulps. "BB, let's be real. I'm going to be back tomorrow veeping our assets, and Wesley is going to be here because he has nothing else to do. Sure—I outed Elly out of spite, but you can dodge being a trag. You come from a good family, and you've got skills. You don't need to be like us."

Elly ahem'd. "What is it to be *us*?" Lane shrugged her shoulders, stepping in.

"To put our crosses into myths."

I think it might've been too late. The reactions inside of me were dormant, and I haven't acquired the knowledge to reignite them. They weren't in a Playthings message, they weren't jammed down Pavia's shrewdness—they may not even be real. I've malfunctioned again, and this time it wasn't because of my withdrawals—it was because I was in the middle of one. I channeled the shavings that floated through my arteries. They were hella mingy, but they informed me that she was vital.

"I think you should say sorry to me, Lane," Elly ceased from our hug, taking Lane by the hand.

Lane tumbled to her knees and spiraled into a knot. Tears pranced from her eyes like they had been imprisoned there. "I'm so sorry, Elly! I'm so so sorry!"

Lane curled her back over Elly's sneakers. She intertwined her almond fingernails into his shoelaces and drew them out of their loops. The laces whirled around Lane's phalanges and twined with her collapsed hands. Elly crouched over Lane, pulling her hair apart from her drenched cheeks. Her sobs watered the beckoning of Elly's shoes and made them perk up.

"Why would you tell Basil all of these lies?"

Lane cowered the longer Elly observed. Her bones dilated and pulsed under his touch, and her skin took on a gnarled appearance. "I doN't kNOw!"

"It was my fault too!" Wesley fell to his ankles. "Elly! Laney wasn't the only one!"

"I thought we were friends," Elly whispered. The red in Wesley's hair hatched to his ends.

A thump sounded from the bottom floor. Christmas music from the neighborhood asserted itself through the victorian mansion. A heavy trudge shook the stairs, and we each quietly waited for the footsteps to wander off and take position somewhere—but they kept going. The weight took over the house's gravity, making the panels sway and be swooned.

A mellowed knock echoed from Wesley's door. We all became stationary to see if they'd go away, but the knock only multiplied through the encasing. Wesley removed his knitted beanie and used it as a handkerchief to wipe the snot from Lane's cheeks—raising them both back to their feet.

"WESLEY-WESLEY! WE'RE HOME! ARE YOU HOME? COME OUT! COME OUT!"

"It's Virginny," Wesley looked at Elly for approval. He hopped over to the door, as we all stayed inside the closet, hoping Virginia wouldn't seek us out.

"WESLEY! COME PLAY! COME DOWNSTAIRS AND PLAY WITH ME!" They had the same pentameter. It was like listening to a shrunken down pitchy version of Wesley.

I peeked at Lane, and her head was tipped to the ground. Elly smirked at me and mouthed *I love you* once again, taking hold of my loose fingers. The bulbs in the closet fizzled and burnt out at the inkling of Virginia's voice. The hanging chiffon pirouetted around our trifecta, and waned off the more it spun.

"I can't play right now, Virginny, but I will soon."

The tattered decor popped and fired around us, welcoming Wesley back with a flurry of shrills. Wesley took hold of both mine and Lane's hand, dipping his head down to the surface of our plights.

We just wanted to know where we were going—to impress each other, and lay in a bed of *ooohs* and *ahhhs*. We became inebriated from the shambles, and inside of them were the greatest stories we couldn't find. It started off as hotel stuff, and drastically fumbled into another. I wanted to go back to the core of where we were lost, and why it was never where we could return.

Chapter 30

:>

"You look different," she said to me with her now freshly shaven head. Taz had about fifty piercings in each ear, completely canceling her hearing.

"Maybe I should cut my hair, then we'll be twins. Triplets if I count my mom."

She giggled. Another piercing hung from underneath her lip skin. "Blame the girl I'm dorming with, she's a professional barber."

"She's eighteen."

"The perfect time to start a hustle!" It was good to see Taz, to see someone who could get me back. "What's new besides the nail polish?"

My brows shot up. "It's a new thing, okay? It's better than walking around with chipped butter under my nails."

"I prefer the buttered Basil, but so happy you can finally start using all the nail polish my mom bought you."

I simpered. "She's trying her best."

"But seriously! I haven't seen you in forever. What's new? I think your mom mentioned something about a boyfriend?!"

I had done an unsurpassable job at keeping Elly at bay. My birthday dinner had gone so well without the topic of my boyfriend, and no one brought up Uncle Paul—at least not his death. Besides the nail polish set Aunt Chrissy gifted me, she also painted a life-like portrait that took up half their living room space. My dad fussed at her because there was no way we would be able to fit it in our car, and he wasn't going to rupture his spleen trying.

Taz's present to me was a resin baked keychain her boyfriend Geoff made, but he's not really her boyfriend, and she asked me to stop calling him that. She keeps a picture of them on her TV console, and whenever we'd turn to watch lips move— there they are, sharing an umbrella. It was the newest addition to her room layout, and everything else was just as she left it before springing to pre-med; the massive collage of mementos falling over her computer desk—dating back to us pretending to be giant zombie cyborgs.

"I'm kinda pissed you never told me about him," she's so goddamn charming.

"He's hard to talk about," and where do I start? At the film, or the fight I managed to sidestep?

"If he's just some guy you're fucking, that's okay too!"

"We're not...doing that," I sipped my saliva. "Not a lot."

I'm not a virgin anymore.

"WHAAAAAT?! I was joking! Now you have to tell me about him. Wow. I can't believe you did *it*."

Deep breaths. "Why do you say that?"

"Idunno. I guess I thought you'd be asexual forever."

I cackled. "Here we go with this!"

Taz pulled her hood over her head and laced the toggles into a knot. "I've never heard you talk about anyone in a romantic way. Now you have a boyfriend, who you're fucking!"

"Can we keep it to '*it*'?"

"I'm sorry," She came in closer on her chair. "Who you're doing *it* with. Why haven't you brought him up?"

Because his friends made me think I didn't love him. They incited that deception and chose to ditch it in a dreary closet. I walked out of there not knowing if I'd sleep in the same bed as him again, whispering over each other about images we never really captured. I thought he'd make a bigger effort at acquitting his name, for the sake of Tartula. But he was Elias, and we couldn't redefine that.

I scrunched up over her braided jute rug. "I told you, he's really hard to talk about."

Taz looked down at me, straddling her rolly chair. "Do you want to talk about France?"

Not really. "What about it?"

"You promised me that in the future I'd be visiting you in France. Are you breaking that promise?"

I swore to Taz that someday she'll find me in France, looking over my villa while fresh quiche baked in the oven. That was years ago though, maybe not—it was like last year. I don't understand how Taz can remember these small conversations, even if they were drilled from big ideas. France was never going to be mine, it was something that I could talk to Taz about to distract her from my friendless tangents.

"France is so far," I grouched. "I'd be away from you and my parents."

She rolled her eyes. "Who else?"

Elly. "No one," and Declan.

"Are you sure?"

Wesley. "Yes," and Lane.

"When I first moved to DC, I was like crap—I'm still too close to New York! What if my mom sees me streaking?"

I snorted, and Taz began to laugh uncontrollably, flying across the room in her seat. "Are you spontaneously streaking, Taz?"

She caught her breath. "Not at all. A group of us actually plan to meet every night, there's a full itinerary—yes, it's spontaneous!"

"What does Geoff think about it?"

"Geoff is a good friend of mine who understands my needs as a voluntary nudist. I might even be able to find photos his friend took one night," she took out her phone and began skimming through images. "Look!"

She handed the album over to me, and I was greeted by a fully nude Taz censored by her friend's elaborate manicure. I went through a couple of photos, not so much analyzing Taz, but the group she surrounded herself with. They were all mesmerizingly edgy, pushing the boundaries of their solidarity to the extreme. I could hear the photos the more I stared at them, and they taunted me for being on the other side. I gaped until I came to one photo in particular, it was of Taz and a friend, holding hands while Taz attempted to lift her leg in the air. I didn't realize I had gone past all of the streaking pics, and was now roaming through her social life.

"Who is this guy?" I flashed the pic at Taz, and her head wilted in amusement.

"Oh man—that's my good friend Marq! I've known him for two-three years now. Him and Geoff are part of the same collective."

"Have you two ever dated?"

"Marques?! Hell no! He's more like a brother to me. He's really cute though."

The picture was before he locked his hair and bleached it. I wouldn't be able to forget his smile, and it came out hella detailed in a still shot. He was so handsome, and by the way he smiled it was evident he knew it too. It was the hexagon tattoos on his cheek that I recognized, the ones that boxed me into an awkward corner that night at Eight Ball; the same tattoo that propelled from Wesley's laptop during our Playthings private chat.

"Are you in an open relationship? If so, I can hook you two up. I heard he's more in the kink scene, but to each their own, y'know?"

The phone shook in my grasp. My hands couldn't hold what wasn't meant for me. "It's okay."

"Alright," she took the phone. "Just ding if you ever want his number."

DING.

"Do you know something?" I blurted, def not meaning to.

"Do I know what?"

"You know I know Marques, don't you?"

Her mouth puzzled up. "No, but I do now. How do you know him? I don't see why he would have any reason being upstate."

"Don't tell my mom, but I met him at Eight Ball a couple of months ago."

"Eight Ball? The nightclub slash bar in Brooklyn?" I guess she doesn't know.

"Yeah, with the bad sign."

Taz leaned back into her seat, holding the chair's shoulder pads for balance. Her combat boots lifted up as her torso delved to the cushion. She made a loud squeak under her closed lips, and shut her mouth with her fingertips.

"What?" Because I knew this was her way of telling me she found something out.

"Wait! No. Never mind," her lips became tighter.

"Tell me."

"It's nothing. WAIT. Naw."

"Taz!"

"Okay," she jingled her under-lip ring. "Geoff got a weird link one day from Marq. It was hella random, but it was a Playthings link. Y'know, the sex-positive site."

Shit. "I do."

"Marq was crying, not literally but figuratively, because he stumbled on some girl's live. He mentioned he met her at Eight Ball a few months back, but I was still stuck on Marq being on a website like Playthings. Like, does he have a subscription?"

Or who is he subscribed to. "Uhuh."

"Geoff showed me the chick, but I didn't take a good look at her. I didn't really want to. I knew she'd be some half naked vixen, and I didn't want to see that on my man's screen."

"He's not your boyfriend though."

"Right! Anyway, I remember for the second I did see her, she was beautiful. Like, wow! But, I also remember thinking... that can't be."

"Anyone can make a Playthings."

"It was you, Basil."

"Or some other girl Marq met at Eight Ball."

Her head rattled from side to side. "No—I knew it! I was going to text you, but I didn't want your mom to accidentally see," she leaped from her stool, darting over me. The chains in her noir fit drooped and chucked my cheek. "Why didn't you tell me about this?"

"I didn't tell anyone."

"Are you doing this because you need money for something you can't ask your parents for? I can give you some of my college refund if you really need it."

I bite my tongue. "I don't need money."

"Then why? Why are you doing this? You know how many creeps are on there doing God knows what!"

"I know."

"Your mom is gonna whoop your ass if she finds out, and I'm going to get an ass-whooping if I don't tell on you! You know it's only a matter of time before her daughter's mosquito bites pop up as an ad."

I covered Taz's mouth with my palm. "I've never been naked on there, and I never plan to be. I play a character."

Tartula had been idle since the fight, and I wasn't up to blurting that to Elly, Lane, and Wesley—especially not the day before the film. I had to come up with a plan to distract from the silent treatment she was giving me. Tartula isn't some kind of suit, I can't finish her up with a bowtie and prompt some paranormal agility. I thought the weekend would grant me enough time to figure her out, but she was more elusive than she's ever been before.

help me.

"Did anyone push you to do this? Hold up—did your boyfriend push you to do this? I need some answers!"

Why does everyone always go back to Elly? "No."

"Be honest with me. I care about you, Basil. Being on a website like this is dangerous, and you're underage."

Tartula would know what to say right now, but I'm the one who's left defending myself. It was soothing to be able to escape with them, to talk this over in the background of daily madness. Tartula, please give me enough to survive on. Who am I when you're gone? I'm still trying to rewrite my name to resemble yours. Basil isn't good enough, Basil doesn't know magnetism!

"Basil!" Taz went back to her chair. I unraveled from my ball of reservations, where I had kept the last speckles of Tartula conscious. "Basil, I need you to talk to me. Tell me what's on your mind, babe."

My torso propped up. "WHAT THE FUCK DID YOU JUST CALL ME?"

Taz veered back. "Babe? It's a nickname you call your pals."

"Don't you ever call me that! EvER!"

Her eyes wandered over me, searching for the particles that fell off. "Who are you?"

My cellphone began to glitz and vibrate. I turned it over to see who the caller was, and the name swooshed me down a dry well. I glared at it, waiting for the flashiness to take over my conversation with Taz. It shook my boldness out of its abodes and irked it to do a thing—do anything at all. Taz watched me, trying not to probe but there was no secrecy in anguish. I hadn't disclosed his name to Taz just yet, but even though she couldn't see me for who I was, she could recognize Elly's name.

When I didn't pick up, the ringing immediately resurrected. I could decipher every inch of our dialect even when the receiver was dead. I could sense him, the throbbing in his grip and the chafing of his teeth. I knew he was ready to tie me back in, and I knew I'd permit him to do just that.

"Are you going to pick up?"

"I have to."

Why didn't he call me sooner or send me a birthday text? This shouldn't be the first time I'm hearing from him after I exited our turmoil. If Tartula was all that he classified her as, then he should've been at my driveway the very next day with a script in his hands. And though I haven't decided who I wanted to be, I knew where I could invent myself—with him.

I walked home from Wesley's to mine after the fight. What could've been a twenty minute walk turned into an hour on a frosty December evening. I couldn't face anyone after what Lane admitted. I was still trying to process a lie, or what Lane and Wesley labeled as the truth. I used to really love my town in the winter because it brought all the elegance out of the trees, and they all made reefs around their lit houses. Residents always competed to get their front lawns to glint more than the others, and the competition domino'd from porch to porch. Inflatable Santas and menorahs sprawled like a fever and made everyone hot with jolly. It was the best distraction when I was a kid, and the greatest conversation I needed to throw everything away.

I shouldn't have gone home. If I didn't, Tartula might still be here.

"Basil, don't be afraid to tell someone no. You don't have to do anything you don't want to do. He doesn't have control over you."

I believed Elly was the person I woke up for, and everything that made me get carried away—that made me seen. I've brought in those emotions and made them practical beyond any means because that was a natural reaction to love. It bursts out and over, even in occasions it is too small to notice. I am so in love with Elly, but I am spoken for by Tartula. It is because of her that I was able to assist Elly in acquiring his fate. Tartula knows how to get me where I belong, and it's not here anymore.

"Hello?" I was wobbly, but somehow managed to hold onto Taz's presence for balance.

His voice was just like it was when we first met—galloping over a crackling fire just a few feet away, making sure that he was the only audio I could listen to.

"Come back home," he purred.

But I wasn't going back to him, I was going back for her.

Chapter 37

;'

"It's sticking out there!" My mom shoved the 25lb bag of salt into the small base cabinet. Tiny splinters of snow twinkled from her puffy down coat.

The snow blacked out the harshness of post-Christmas lights. The spastic sputter made the snow look as if it were moving in slow motion, and every flake would land on top of a sparked up cross. The blizzard favored my birthday and everything I received thereon after. Christmas at Elly's was helpless, and I couldn't tell if it was something I had grown attached to. The mistreatment of holidays was unusually pleasant and understood. His parents never knocked on our door as we rang our bells. We were calling on a savior, and she was missing in action.

Next to my parent's house was a family of toddlers, like, they were nothing *but* toddlers—frolicking past glaciers to climb onto each other's heads. Their thrill melted the snow, and I was hypnotized by their enthrallment. It was like watching myself at one point in time, counting every crystal with my bare frosted hands. My mom would yell at me from the tip of her tonsils to keep my gloves on, but they always got in the way of memorizing numbers.

The snow reminds me of my birthday. When the snow would come, that meant my birthday was approaching. This year to celebrate the occasion I received driving classes from my parents—ten in total before I could work towards getting my real license. It was the greatest insult to me they could've made, to gift me what I thought I was never allowed to have. This balance of power is really uncanny when it is outdone, and I have to be alright with it. I should've never given up the chance to leave my parents behind to get to know the new seasons of snow.

"It's time," it spelled out amidst the downpour.

"I'm going to get ready to go," I tilted myself from off the kitchen stool. "I'm heading to Elly's."

"In this weather?" She shook the excess icicles from her boots. Winter dust formed on her eyelashes. "How are you going to get there?"

"I'll ask him to drive me."

My mom wiggled out of her coat and folded it over the basement handrail. "Basil, I don't want you to go."

My phone held up the last text from Elly, as it trimmed the grip from my palm. The screen blistered through my fingers, making my sweat mimic the frosty residue from my mom's outerwear. *Come home* was instilled to my crossroads—fusing them into disorder.

"I need to go," I answered.

"It's been really nice having you back home with us, even though it was only for today. Dinner was good, well as good as it could get with Aunt Chrissy's cooking."

"It's usually worse. I kinda liked the barbecue broccoli rabe."

My mom inched over to my side of the table. "Can you stay? C'mon, I'll find a good game for us to play, or we can watch that one movie you hate to love."

"Mom, you know that I can't."

She parted the drops from her lashes. "I'm trying my best at being a mom. Am I doing good?"

MOOOOOOOOOOOOOOOOM!

"Yeah."

"I'm serious, Basilene," she stuttered. "Do you think I'm doing good enough? Good enough to be around?"

"I'm going to be late," I swung my keys from the island top, and my mom lifted my forgotten half-soiled plate.

"What's this?" She sniffed it before pulling it away.

"Can you throw it out for me? It's trash."

She spun the platter around the points of her finger. "You know how I am about wasting food, Basil. What is it?"

"Canelè."

"Why didn't you tell me you were making canelès? You know it's one of my favorites," my mom lodged a spoonful into her mouth. Her upper lip tonged up and under her nostrils, freezing until the full piece was swallowed.

"You don't like it," I muttered. She wanted to cry.

"No! It's great. It tastes a little different. What did you add that's new?"

"It's the same recipe I've always followed."

"Hm, maybe something went bad. It doesn't taste right."

My mom always had the best intentions, and she couldn't help that—she was groomed to be better than the standard edition of her siblings. I think I hate my parents for not giving me any because then I'd know how to turn things down. But, if I had a sibling they might be the person Elly would go after. I wouldn't be so special in this town that is fixed on being passable. I was raised in a fraudulent community, and Tartula can restore what was taken.

"I'm sorry, Basilene. That was kind of harsh," she emptied the battered canelè into the trash.

"It's okay. I should really leave now," I lifted the chat thread between me and Elly, highlighting his name with my vision.

"I'll drive you, Basil."

"It's a blizzard out there."

She snagged my phone from my hand and tossed her jacket from the banister. "I can't allow your boyfriend to drive in this weather. I'd be an even worse parent than I already think I am."

The snow brought us on a journey that murdered the passion from its cloudburst. The days we met were in the past like sandcastles being created for their occupants, we're made to be wonderful somewhere right here. It was beautiful to sit beside the snow and watch it fall, snow sketching the love of my life in my family's car. Fine-tuning the ugly that was picked up by the miseries we played to hide.

I know what Elly thinks of me when he sees me. He thinks of establishing a future where we can take away the deadened matter. I was spoiled waste up until the moments I've spent with Elly, and now I can forgive myself for being coarse and muddy. I could see their house before we swerved past the hula-hoops and tricycles that took up their street, and I could see Elly looking down at me from a window of triumph. We almost did it, and we're going to do it subsist.

"Which house is it?" My mom curved into the spherical road.

"It's that one," I pointed proudly. It's *my* house.

"Oh!" She removed her glasses, running them along her scarf. "I'll help you inside."

"It's okay mom, I got it," I tugged my bag out the back seat. "I'll see you soon."

"Basil," she took my wrist with her palm. "When are you coming back?"

"I'll see you soon, mom."

"Basil," The bitter wind halted my escape, but I managed to trickle through the small slit. "BASIL, WHEN ARE YOU—"

The front door was unlocked, and an abhorrent smell gathered in the tapered hall. I strolled into the kitchen, turning the burner down to let the concoction simmer. I'm prolly disrupting someone's timed nourishment, but maybe I'd be thanked later with acceptance. I checked the fridge to see if there was anything I could add or take out. My aged milk bread hung on the top shelf with chunks of its physique gouged out.

Elly.

The house sparked matches from my skin, tugging me into the other room. I felt that if I were to blow too hard, it would topple over and kill us all. An olive-tanned man with a charcoal beard slouched on a lazy-boy. His skin was moist with gravel and steel, and his belly hid behind a pair of dark beige overalls that were stained with dyes and paints. My body was the size of his calf, and I took a seat on the couch beside him—hoping he'd assume I were a mouse.

"What's this show about?" I asked.

He dislodged a tank from his throat. "Sword makers."

The house was taken over by the blade-smiths. Ruling and running with their sharp edges making slashes in the wallpaper and weathered walls. They spoke like they had something important to say, so I listened. Minutes flew by and I realized I had been transported into their mechanics. I'm sure that I would be pretty bad at forging because I'm not very good with balancing dangerous things. I'm sure Elly could wield a better life from the story he created out of Tartula, and I can't think of myself outside of it.

"I thought you left," I looked at the man, but it def wasn't his voice. "Why did you come back?"

Her hair was cut even shorter, trampling her cheekbones. "The front door was open."

"It's always open," her nighttime attire was an overgrown shirt and basketball shorts.

"Your mom is calling you," the man grunted, twisting the cap off a beer bottle.

"She's not home, she went out for wood with Elly."

"I can hear her, Dec," his voice elevated but cooled down the moment he took another sip.

"Basil, you can wait with me in my room for Elly to come back."

Declan's room was way better looking than it was before. The sheets on the frameless mattress were tucked into the floor's cavities, and the mascara marks that held onto her pillowcases had given up. The fishes that thrived in her homemade aquarium welcomed me into the space, and even after the weeks of blackballing, the photos of Lane and Wesley still stood tall on her dresser. I don't know if they were ever good friends to her, or who is a good friend anymore.

"I'm trying to be nice, that's all. I know sitting with my dad isn't the most entertaining."

"He's great. How are you?" I asked. It wasn't what I wanted to say, but it came out.

"I'm exhausted. Pavia is still forcing the Babes to practice during break."

"That's torture."

"It takes my mind off of things," she removed her rabbit slippers that resembled Purple. "How have you been?"

The worst feeling was to stand in front of a friend who you were no longer friends with. To look at them and know that in the past you've shared glorious moments of laughter, and they used to appear so beautiful when they would look at you with a smiling face that paved an eclipse. It's hard to know that I had friends who I've lost, not just Declan, but I'm sure I've lost Taz too after she found out.

"I think that I'm really starting to know who I am."

Declan smirked. She looks so much like Elly when she does that. "You do?"

"Yeah, I think this film is going to be good for me."

She went up to her tank, placing her fingers onto the plexi that held the school inside. The fish blinked at Declan as she admired them through her webbed fingers. You could tell that those fish were also Declan's friends, just as much as Lane and

Wesley, and they were friends that she knew would never leave. Always encased and always guarding.

"Do you see that pleco?" She pointed to a bristly black and yellow dotted fish. "She stays in there, and she keeps everything clean enough so that I can do less work."

"She's cute."

"Her name is Tartula," Declan looked back at me. "I got her the day after Elly asked me to be in his film."

Chapter 32

: †

A fissure spawned from the tank, and an everlasting stream erupted from the enclosing. The lake washed the room with the cool saltwater that fed both Declan and the fish. Declan and I treaded through the brook until it tipped the ceiling, and buried us into the torrent. The fish orbited around us, and the water life tripled to what it was before the clash. Every object that held color was now enhanced with its saturation, and the bright blue water reflected off the once plexi, and projected a photograph of myself drowning. Declan snorkeled with her lips crimped into a smile, appreciating what was happening. The fish brought me to an escape at the end of their grouping, and in front of me was a car sitting at the bank.

"A month before Elly pushed his car into the river, he told me he was making a film. This was right after he and Pavia broke up."

"While Elly was still a senior?" I asked.

She floated, tugging the sunroof with her fins to let herself inside. "Yes. He told me that the film was going to be fantastical, and the main character was this *thing* named Tartula. To be real, it didn't sound well put together—it sounded like an overthought idea, kinda dorky and lighthearted."

Not sure if we're talking about the same film. "What was it called?"

"He never told me the name, said he didn't have one yet. He went on about how it was going to be the greatest film possible, and once he was accepted into his university he would submit it to the Brunhart festival," she stopped. "Do you know about the Brunhart festival?"

"I know that they only accept applications from certain schools, and nothing is guaranteed."

"Colleges to be exact, but Elly never got into college. He actually never graduated."

Declan dove into the car's passenger seat, as her face revived through a gaggle of seaweed by the window. The turbulence in the car's motor made tornados with the water and carried me in and out of the riptides. The fish kept me floating on their backs and bopped me up the harsher the tidal flow became.

"When I first accepted to play Tartula it was only me and Elly shooting. It took us a while to get me into character, but after a week it started to overwhelm me. I wanted to do good as Tartula because I wanted my brother to believe he could do good —even if I knew it wasn't going to get us anywhere," Declan lowered the mirror down with her bare palms and escaped from the carving she made.

She hiccuped a row of bubbles and continued. "I soon felt myself succumbing to the role. I wasn't sure who was in control anymore, Elly or Tartula."

"Why didn't you just give up?"

"I stayed as long as I could for Elly.

The fish left me by myself to assist Declan from the car. "Why?" I asked. "You two aren't friends. Why go out of the way to make him happy?"

"It's always been like this. Elly hasn't been good enough, so I had to be. Elly couldn't make friends, so I had to make the friends. Elly couldn't pick up signing, so I had to learn for the both of us," she stroked over to where I was balancing.

"I know that's not true, Declan. I've seen Elly talk to your mom, and she understood everything he said."

"Our mom can read lips, but she can't understand everything. I remember when we were kids, Elly would yell so hard his throat would become raw. He would do this hoping that she would hear him someday," Declan made laps around me. "People on the street would stare, and whenever I'd try to get him to stop, he'd just yell at me too. My mom started carrying around bags full of chocolate bars to get him to stop talking—to get him to close his mouth!"

I pulled Declan in by her arms, her shorts rippled in the current and made her look ethereal. Her cropped hair galavanted from side to side, and the fish tickled the tresses that moved with her. She lost what it meant for us to touch, and her grin broke out again. The suds poured from her cracked mouth and floundered by our meeting hands.

"I miss being with you, Basil," her sentence was ruined by the lake's acid. "I don't want to talk about Elly anymore. I want to talk about you."

I released her. "I don't even know what that looks like anymore."

"If you give me a chance, I can show you."

"Declan, you know that I can't be with you."

"You can leave, Elly. You don't have to be Tartula. You don't have to claim her for yourself!"

The fish bounced off of our dialogue. Their attention swayed to the speaker, and their glinting eyes told me and Declan that they wanted this for us too.

"I made a promise to the film."

"You can still get out, I can help you get out."

The water vigorously whirled, and a group of fish retreated back to where the tank once was. A whirlpool appeared in every crevice in the room, and the water flushed past all the blues and blooms. Declan and I receded down to the floor until the height of the waves could no longer hold us. We stood around letting the drips and drizzles mess up the mood, though it wasn't like we started off the conversation happy. Declan stomped over to her dresser, her once airy trousers were now glued to her inner thigh. She pulled out a toilette to wipe her face, and once all the crying was gone, she flung it over to me.

"Thanks," I twisted my hair into a large bun. "I'm sorry."

She wiped her eyes and rediscovered her breath. "The night I refused to be Tartula, was the night Elly pushed the car into the river."

She's coming back. The eeriness inside of her life was now billowing out through my vessel. The room formed into a heavy smog and purple lightning, exhaling the idiosyncrasies of who she is.

"Declan," I stepped in. "I'll be Tartula for you."

She laughed and sunk in her sniffles. "I know you will be because Elly redesigned it for you."

"What?"

"Before I broke the news to Elly about not wanting to be Tartula, I told him about a crush I've had. A girl who I've loved since I saw her in our physics class last year, but was too scared to talk to her," with multicolored vroom-vroom skin. "A girl named Basil."

The blue coating that forced itself onto the walls was now a grungy ink. The liquid released the lapis, and shredded it to the corners of where Declan's room was left. The vines fished from behind the aquarium, and up above the ceiling that still dripped from our marine escape. The fireflies were groggy from their arrest, and they poked fun of the fish that were left to watch them soar.

"Elly took you away from me, Basil."

"You want to tell me more lies?"

Tartula.

"I'm not lying to you. Elly does not love you like you think he does. He is going to use you to complete the film, and once he no longer needs you, he's going to throw you away."

Come alive.

"DON'T LIE TO ME!" My nails grew into bayonets as the vines echoed around me.

Declan's skin transitioned to a slithery grey. "I'm not. Basil, please let me help you."

I bobbed forward as she winced. The remaining pieces of the lake fell from her eyes. "I think I finally know why Elly tried to get you into the car."

"Why?" She called out.

"Because he knew it couldn't be the both of us."

She stomped. "That's not it, Basil!"

"iT iS!"

"He's doing it because he thinks it will save him! He thinks that Tartula is the answer to his problems, that she's going to be the thing to get him out of this house—out of this town!"

"Don't talk to me as if you know me."

"And once he's able to do that, he's going to get rid of her. Elly is lying to you. He wants you to think that Tartula is the one who is calling the shots, but it's really him."

"SHUT UP!"

I propped my hands on top of her shoulders to get her to sink. The vines behind me raveled up her legs and across her arms, slivering down to her clammy colorless palms. She buckled at the weight of all three of us, tripping her further into the falsities that held her tall.

"Basil! Stop it!"

The ink boiled up and consumed the lower portion of her hobbled body. The deeper she went, the more she cried out, and the rest of her became simplified shrills that bombarded the decrepit house. The vines liberated her grasp as she clawed out and scuffed the raised wood that made up her floor.

"HELP ME!"

I interweaved my blades through her hair, being careful enough to not cut anymore strands. I boosted her chin with my shank and crouched in for one last kiss.

"I do love you, Declan."

"HELP ME!" She howled from her inner throat. She was nothing else but a head. The fish whimpered for their mother, their friend, and their only taste of a surface-based love.

"Thank you for bringing her back to me."

Where there is nothing left at all, there is vitality in the lines that we've crossed. I know that Tartula will now be with me forever, and Elly will be able to dislodge the voices that convinced him we were wavering. We were all strong in our endeavors, and Elly has seen us against the venom that we were trapped in. We were always ONE, and after speaking to Declan, I know what needs to be done to seal Tartula and Elly into prosperity. Elly is going to achieve the life he's always wanted, and I'm going to be by his side to enforce it.

"Happy birthday, babe."

He was thinner and paler than the last time I saw him, but he knew he had to fast to get to where he wanted to go. "Elly."

I sprung into his arms, forgetting what the ground felt like. "Please don't ever leave me again."

"I won't."

It felt like Elly had been turned down. In the beginning of our relationship I could feel him so close, and the more he spoke, the further he would embed himself into my outline. Something inside of him had dwindled since the last time I saw him. I'm not sure which part, but it made me hella dizzy. Everything else surged, specifically both Declan and Tartula. His heartbeat still pumped proudly, sounds just like bricks being thrown at a wall.

Over and Over.

"Are you alright?" I don't think I've ever asked him that before.

"Yeah. I just...I haven't been sleeping too good without you."

"I'm happy to be home," I whispered. His eyes bulged out, staring at the spot where Declan once was. His palpitations increased but smoothly settled down once they figured out I was listening.

"Can we go to sleep now? We have a big day tomorrow."

He spun me around to face the hall, and standing in the doorway with botched eyes, was the small woman with droughty hair.

His mom.

"Dinner?" She hummed.

"I don't think she's hungry," Elly insisted. "We're going to go to sleep."

"I'm," my voice discarded itself. A chocolate bar regurgitated from my gullet. I could savor the cocoa before it had the chance to reach my tongue.

"Dinner?"

"Mom, get out."

I think I was a baker before this.

"Dinner?"

Or something that really loved sweets.

"We're not hungry!"

A person who communicated through the art of dessert.

"DIN—"

I'm useless because I can't communicate with her.

"Mom."

Not in the way that she needs.

"DIN—"

"GET THE FUCK OUT!"

"I'm sorry," I muttered. "I'M SORRY!"

I'm sorry, I muttered.

JADE BROWN

I'm sorry.
I'm sorry, I muttered.

I'm sorry.

308

Chapter 33

;}

Milo Hunter's locker was empty. It was my first time seeing it without the mob that lacerated the flesh from his bones. Nothing was left inside but a sticky note from Lane that told him it was over. He had a better chance when he was clean, instead of snorting grounded up paper towels off the nurse's mayo stand.

Milo HUnter, you're a fucking sleep.

He used to snap the tops off of half used lipsticks he'd steal from glittery backpacks, and store them in a mason jar to later return to. I saw him refilling his stash every quarter period, and he'd adjust his locker door to obstruct the view I had of his perversion.

Lane is beginning to take ownership of herself, though she won't quit narcotics because it will only make her sexually impaired. If that happens, Milo won't want anything to do with her because he never has. She'll be a tall pretty blonde with nothing but a jean pocket full of unused condoms. Thank God Lane uses protection because I don't.

I'm not a virgin anymore.

I thought about who we'd screen this to someday, and my parents came to fruition. I'll make sure they can play it on a desktop, or someplace that isn't ruthlessly shameless. I want there to be love inside of it, and we can sprinkle it with a lullaby. Afterward, we can post it to a forum for people who have trouble sleeping. We'll make it into a day, and it will endure through the rigorous night.

People will describe us as affluent.

Villeton really stinks in the middle of the night, but there is still that chip-sized tension that forces me to remember that I'm in school. I don't know what my grades have done for me, but kill off the shadows of rebellion. I'm told to stay in line because it's for my wellbeing, I hate to sniff the ass of authority—that is what Villeton smells like. That is what Villeton smells like.

"BB!" A pair of trimmers nipped my arm.

"OW!" I bite off a piece of Lane's oxygen.

"Forgive me, but your strap keeps coming down. You have to reposition yourself to hold it up."

The rugged carpeting mopped my back with its whiskers. It wants me to get worse. It feels lovely to have it beside me, to pity the girl inside. "When are we starting? I've been laying here for so long."

"We've already started."

The lens capsule skewed down at my face, and I intimidated it. Lane slow walked in a circular motion, and Wesley sat at the end of my feet holding me still. The pink in his hair was fully gone, and the russet trim winked at the bedding that held me up. I don't think I know who that is. I know the boy with the lime beanie, and the birthday frosting tips that smiled so hard his wrinkles were in script.

"Where is Elias?"

"Probably taking a shit."

"Lane," Wesley groaned. "We're in a church, please don't swear."

Elly barfed in the car on the way here. The fragrance was like yesterday and week-old milk bread. The full in his cheeks were protesting against his weighted attitude, and he couldn't recall the path to Villeton. Halfway through the ride, Wesley had to take over as the designated driver. If there was ever a shot of me wanting to use my gifted driving lessons, it would've been now.

"I'm going to check up on him."

"BB, don't. You're going to ruin the blocking."

I need to see where he is. He may not be breathing for all that I know, and they could've gotten him. I'm the only thing that can reduce the trauma—he implored me for that! Elias. I can say your name like a song in a spasm. It hurts me like that, Elias! I thought I was the beautiful one, and you beat me to it the day you were born.

"When is he coming back?" I called.

"I don't know, neither of us knows. You have to stop talking."

"ELIAS!"

The brown undergarments took slices of my skin and stretched it out to become lace. They look like me, and they feel like fermented freedom. They keep me warm inside of the hole I was dragged into right beside Declan.

hey.

"Basie, please be quiet. It's going to shake the candles off."

What if Elly found the girl with the birthmark on her cheek? She stays in that bathroom, and I think she lives there. I know how she likes to watch over people from her closet of stalls and dates. She knows how to bring up things that stay in the mind until it gets too tired to deny she was there. Why haven't I asked her for her name? I need to start thinking better with something other than my heart.

"Basil, why don't you listen?" His elbows kept him up on the altar.

"I'm sorry! I thought you were gone, Elias."

"Where would I go without you?"

I teared. The makeup burned against my pupil. "I don't know."

Elly addressed Lane. "How is it coming along?"

"The light in here is kinda dark, but it works."

"What about Playthings?" Elly's hair sagged across his shoulders. "Are we live on Playthings?"

Lane took a look from Wesley. "Were we supposed to be?"

"If more people join, it will be merrier."

He thinks of other people more than he considers himself. That is one of the main reasons I love Elias Hayes. He never has someone's defeats in his Rolodex—he goes off of who the person is when he is with them. That is why Elly is the only one who knows me. I don't think my parents have figured me out to the extent of Elly's vision. He knows ME! I am not a virtual vista, I am Tartula on the better half. No one else could be, so I had to unsheathe her.

"How do you want to do the last part?" Lane turned the camera lens over.

"Should we pour the candle wax over her?" Elly loomed forward, flicking the flame with his index.

"She'll burn," Wesley freed my feet.

"She won't feel a thing," the aromas left my skin. "She looks so beautiful right now."

"POUR IT!" I cackled at the idea. He recognizes me. "DO IT NOW!"

He gleamed. "She wants it."

"I'm not sure if I—"

"DO IT!" Our voices molded.

If I become wax, who will carve me out? Who will turn me into a muse that has no place to wander? Who knows what Elly can do? Who knows what I can do now?

"It doesn't even hurt," my jaw quivered. "Don't be shy."

Elly rose from behind the altar railing. He scooped my head with his hands and kept me still in his lap. I had no recollection of whether or not I had been moving at all. His blue eyes bled from the ill caves that swarmed them. He leered over and wrenched my lips with his. Our connection is medicinal, and he knows how to lure me with his self-prescribed amount.

"Should we film this?" Lane crawled up to us. "Should I get my phone camera out?"

"If you film me kissing her, I might go to jail," his laugh was like a cough.

My parents will know what I've done for them. It was in light of an opportunity, and there was no one around to redirect my decisions. If I told them what I was up to, they would've met me with consequences. I'm not that anymore. I'm not a child that they can retain. I am the one who came out to show my family what I can realize by myself.

I told Taz that I was going to do the film. I confessed as she assisted me with twinning her mom's painting to the roof of my parent's car. When I told her that, she gave me an ultimatum and nothing else. She said that if I went through with the film, she was going to tell my parents everything she knows, and I'm confident she can barter more information from Marques. She wants to show me down, and I don't know why I ever appointed her my favorite cousin.

I hate her.

She thinks she's great cause she's in pre-med and received a scholarship because her dad died. That was the only reason she got a scholarship—cause her dad died.

She's not great.

I am.

"You don't know what you've done for me," Elly whispered into my ear. "Do you?"

Declan won't talk bad about you anymore, Elias. She'll stay where she belongs, and that is to be pasteurized until she can come back a human being. I always knew Declan was too good to be true. There is no one that stunning, that nice, or that naive. Only a trag would fall for the tricks she has, and she wasted her victories on allegations.

"I have a really good idea," I reached up. "Let's not forget what we've done for each other. We'll always be together."

He ran his tongue over his lips. His mouth parted open while his eyes stared at me. "Yeah. Everything was worth this last moment, huh?"

My eyesight hesitated. "It's not our last."

He scratched my lids open with his cold thumbs. "I told you what was going to happen at the end of the film."

"no."

"I announced it to everyone."

"elly, no."

"Aren't you happy to be here?"

"NO!" My legs writhed from their stunted position. Wesley had given up on strangling me down, but his clutch still pardoned what I was invested in.

"BB, we're trying to film."

"I can't feel my legs. I don't know why, I can't move at all!" My voice was being choked. I had renounced what had kept me buoyant.

"Get her to stop moving!" Elly pushed back and stood to his naked feet.

"She shouldn't be at all!" Lane hollered. The camera hovered back to me.

"Basie, please hold still."

My pelvis gave up the twitch. There were no longer the butterflies that split their wings to give me what I desired—a crush. I was the only one bold enough to fall in love with Elly Hayes, and I am still the only one bold enough to admire someone from the outside of their objective.

What an angel.

"no."

"I don't think I have to keep you inside anymore," he hopped onto one of the pews, his damp feet left marks where people should be.

The turned off chandelier above us harmonized with Elly's sermon. It sounds really good against the glass. It sounds like the bells dinging.

I was paralyzed beneath the shimmers. The chime from the chandelier whooshed with Elly's height. The theatre wardrobe that hung from coat racks all became solid headless figures. They each removed themselves from their hangers and waltzed around me—having no troubles following the camera's aim.

"I knew from when I saw you, Basil. That you were the ONE!"

My breast were no longer heavy bags of worriment.

"FACEEYESSKINHAIR!"

My fingernails that were now a shade of smut, dematerialized with the surrendered candlelight.

"I couldn't stop thinking of you, BASIL!"

He still calls me by the name he butchered. He should know that all things that have life need to be esteemed.

"I haven't spent one minute with you not on my mind!"

"elias."

"WE'RE SO REAL WHEN WE'RE TOGETHER!"

The worst part of being myself now is to not have any memory of who I was before. I think I prefer to have this amnesia with me, if it can take away the pain that comes after a break up.

"She's gone," I could hear Lane down the aisle. She was much further now.

"Did I make you happy," And Wesley. "Basie?"

My throat has gone out, and the veins in my neck were taken by the spirits of Villeton. I can't speak, but I can watch him be on top of the world. I have never seen him dazzle under stage light. He likes to be against the walls, commanding and reassuring people that they were his quest. I should've listened to the realms, but I had to witness it for myself.

"BABE!" He hopped from his pedestal. "Say something to me."

Before my eyes tell me what time it is, I want to plead for him. He breached when I fell, and I am endangered because of his escapades. I know things won't be anymore fruitful than they are right now. If it stings any more, then I want it to be agonizing as it goes.

"Basil."

I can't even hear the sound of my own voice.

"You did everything that you could."

And once it all ends, it will only be stuff that will burden someone else.

Chapter 34

HOTEL STUFF

JADE BROWN

HOTEL STUFF

Acknowledgements

My husband made these past few years less dark. This book wouldn't have been completed without him.
Thank you for always inspiring me to become the person you see me as.
Thank you, Chilli.

HOTEL STUFF

About the Author

Jade Brown never catches the bus on time. She's subpar at jump roping. She knows the fastest way to get out of the event. She can't read a text message and walk at the same time. Only one of her plants are dying. Her socks are never matching, and she'll never let you know that. Her right knee is crooked. She can name all the states in alphabetical order, and hates that.

HOTEL STUFF

JADE BROWN

Made in the USA
Middletown, DE
09 December 2022